Emma-Claire Sunday i[s] world's libraries with qu[...] has been a playwright, a [...] a competitive spoken wo[rd ...] different, but always a storyteller at heart. She lives in New Jersey with her partner, where they edit each other's writing, eat an abundance of butternut squash fries and collect as many library cards as is legally possible. *The Fortune Hunter's Guide to Love* is her second novel. She is the recipient of Harlequin's 2023 Romance Includes You Mentorship. Visit her website, emmaclairesunday.com, and find her on Instagram, @ec.sunday.author.

Also by Emma-Claire Sunday

The Duke's Sister and I

Look out for more books from Emma-Claire Sunday

coming soon!

Discover more at millsandboon.co.uk

THE
FORTUNE HUNTER'S
GUIDE TO LOVE

Emma-Claire Sunday

MILLS & BOON

First published in Great Britain 2025
by Mills & Boon, an imprint of HarperCollins*Publishers* Ltd,
1 London Bridge Street, London, SE1 9GF

www.harpercollins.co.uk

HarperCollins*Publishers*, Macken House, 39/40 Mayor Street Upper,
Dublin 1, D01 C9W8, Ireland

The Fortune Hunter's Guide to Love © 2025 Emma-Claire Sunday

ISBN: 978-0-263-34528-5

07/25

This book contains FSC™ certified paper
and other controlled sources to ensure responsible forest management.

For more information visit www.harpercollins.co.uk/green.

Printed and Bound in the UK using 100% Renewable Electricity
at CPI Group (UK) Ltd, Croydon, CR0 4YY

To the women who raised me, and to
the women who raised the women who raised me.
Linda, Donna, Lula, Lillian.
Alice, Marian, Elizabeth, Margaret.

Chapter One

June 1824

Sylvia Queensbury has it all.

Or, to be precise, Sylvia Queensbury *had* it all.

Standing in the doorway of her bedchamber for the last time, Sylvia Queensbury held on to the final three remnants of the only life she'd ever known: a pale blue dress, a small carpet bag of belongings, and a porcelain water pitcher that once belonged to her father's grandmother.

'Ah, there it is!' One of her uncle's hired moving men approached her with a long list in his hand. 'Porcelain…water pitcher…' He drew a line through the last item on his list, then offered a sympathetic smile to Sylvia from beneath his thick moustache. He took the pitcher out of her hands. 'Sorry about all this,' he said as he walked away.

Sylvia Queensbury held on to the final *two* remnants of the only life she'd ever known, tightly gripping the leather handle of her bag in case the next person she saw might try to take that away too.

She resisted the urge to turn around and take in the sight of her bedchamber one last time. She would not look backward. But she could not make herself move forward either.

This is where I belong, she thought to herself. There was no place else in the world where she fit so perfectly. The diamond chandeliers, the polished furniture, the grand marble staircase, and Sylvia herself… they all belonged together. So of course her feet could not find the strength to carry her onward. She might as well have been one of the many stone sculptures that lined the walls and garden paths of their London home.

'There you are,' Violet sighed as she reached the top of the stairs. 'The rest of us have packed up the carriage, and we're ready to go.'

Sylvia's heart broke all over again to see her sister in anything other than the debutante gown she should have worn at the start of the season. There were no jewels hanging from Violet's ears, no strands of pearls around her neck.

'You deserve so much more…' Sylvia shook her head. At least *she* had gotten a taste of the *ton* before it was all taken away. Violet had never even been to a ball.

'Enough with that.' Violet shook her head. 'Mother says there's no use dwelling on what could have been.'

'*Mother says,*' Sylvia mocked, then rolled her eyes. She was being harsh, as she had been for days. But she didn't care.

It didn't feel like there was anything left to care about.

'We're all hurting, Sylvia,' Violet said as softly as she could. But even Violet—sweet, gentle Violet—was becoming exasperated with Sylvia's miserable mood.

'We *are* all hurting,' Sylvia agreed. 'So why does it feel like I'm the *only one* who actually gives a damn?' She threw her bag to the ground and crossed her arms. Violet breathed in slowly, looked as though she might say something, then simply exhaled and walked back down the stairs.

Sylvia knew her behaviour wasn't helping. But she also knew that a grave injustice was happening to her family, and she didn't quite understand why no one wanted to pout with her anymore. They'd all been *dreadfully* cross at first, but now...now they just seemed sad. Resigned to their new fate.

If Sylvia had to be angry enough for the five of them, then so be it.

'*Sylvia!*' her mother shouted from the front door. Her stern voice echoed through the wide rooms and empty hallways, and Sylvia tried to remind herself that her mother had lost the most of all. Her mother, Sylvia had to believe, would come up with a plan to get them out of this mess.

She grabbed her carpet bag and descended the stairs, wearing the only nice dress she had been allowed to keep. Anything with lace, netting, or beadwork had been sold to pay for their meagre new lifestyle in... *Hane, was it? Hawne?* Sylvia couldn't be bothered to remember.

'I'm on my way,' she called half-heartedly. She held her head high and pushed down any tears that might try to escape. The elegant wallpaper, the velvet curtains, and the stately portraits all stood witness to Sylvia's final march through the Queensbury townhouse. She could feel the presence of every piece of art and furniture that her wicked uncle had decided to keep for himself, as if they were staring at her, *whispering* about her, behind her back.

She would never forgive that man for how he treated his brother's family—how he treated *her* family. She would never forgive him, and she *would not cry*.

She kept her eyes low as she passed her father's portrait. He had been such a jovial man, and he always hated how serious the painter had made him look. Here was the version of Charles Queensbury that his brother would choose to preserve, a version that had never truly existed.

When Sylvia finally approached the front door, she watched as her mother's face softened from impatience to compassion. She let her mother pull her into a warm hug, a new habit of her mother's that Sylvia was still getting used to. There had been more hugs, more hand-holding, more *I love you*s in the past few months than there had been in the last nineteen years combined.

This close to her mother, Sylvia could see the wispy strands of white that hid within her light blond hair. She had always felt a certain kinship with her mother, as the daughter who looked most like her. The same high cheekbones, the same angular face, the same wide, round eyes with pale green irises. It was per-haps because of this likeness that Sylvia had assumed her mother would be as righteously indignant as Sylvia was—but ever since the news that Charles's younger brother had no intention of sharing his new estate with the women whose lives depended on it, the Dowager Countess Ella Queensbury had been strangely peace-ful.

She had mourned the loss of her husband, of course, but she'd never cried for the loss of their property, their jewellery, or their financial security the way Sylvia and her sisters had.

'We'll be all right,' her mother said with confidence as she guided Sylvia out the door.

'We'll be all right *when* we find a way back to Lon-don,' Sylvia countered.

'We'll be all right *now*,' Ella said firmly, 'because we have each other.'

Sylvia didn't have the energy to argue further. She added her bag to their depressingly small pile of luggage atop the carriage, then took her seat next to Violet. Their horrid, cruel, monstrous uncle, whose name Sylvia refused to speak, had *graciously* allowed them one last ride in the Queensbury coach.

They didn't have the funds to rent a second carriage, so they'd have to take turns sitting on the floor.

'I was getting worried we'd have to carry you out of the house,' said Violet.

'I was starting to think you'd escaped out the back door,' said Rose with her eyebrows raised. From her seat on the floor, Rose could step on Sylvia's foot without anyone else noticing. This would, no doubt, be an ongoing bother for the duration of the trip.

'I'm not exactly *eager* to arrive in *Horn*,' Sylvia shot back.

'Heene,' Ella said calmly.

'Wherever and whatever it is, it's not for people like us.'

'*Mother* is people like us,' Violet said, 'and she's *from* Heene.'

Mary nodded, then leaned her head against her mother's shoulder. *I agree*, she signed with her hands.

'But then she *left*.' Sylvia had found the energy to argue after all.

'But if she could survive it for as long as she did,' Violet said, 'then so can we.'

'I will *not* live there as long as mother did,' Rose whined.

And then the four sisters all started speaking and signing at once.

'What do people even *do* in Heene?'

'Can we buy new jewellery once we're there?'

'They don't even *have* jewellery there!'

You're dramatic—of course they have jewellery!

'I'm sure the food is disgusting.'

'Enough.' Ella's eyes were tightly closed, a frustrated crease deep between her eyebrows. All five of them jumped as the carriage began to roll forward.

'Violet, you are leaving behind a library of books that you love *dearly*,' their mother continued with her eyes still closed. 'Rose and Mary, you have sold *all* your matching dresses. And Sylvia, you have lost your opportunity to find a husband and establish yourself in society. And I…' She took a long, slow breath. 'We've all lost so much. But we have not lost *each other.*'

She opened her eyes now and looked at each one of her daughters, one by one. 'We can tell stories around the hearth, we can find fabric for dresses, and we can make new friends in Heene. As long as we have each other, we are nowhere *near* as destitute as you claim.'

Nothing but the sound of wheels against road followed. They sat in silence for a long while. Sylvia felt naked without a string of jewels around her neck or a band of beads around her bodice. She was used to reaching for something fancy whenever she felt uncomfortable—she would buy a new dress, or have her room redecorated, or throw a ball to distract herself from whatever pain she was feeling.

But now, there was nothing left to reach for.

Eventually Violet and Mary fell asleep. Ella stared through the window. Sylvia braided Rose's hair without any ribbons to keep it in place. She wanted so much more than this cramped carriage ride to a strange new village, but not just for herself. She wanted more for her sisters. She wanted a proper season of courtship and dances and brand-new dresses for Violet. She wanted more time for the twins, time to make friends and grow into ladies. Rose would detest having to spend her days working, if it came to that. And would anyone in Heene understand Mary, who could hear but couldn't speak, who needed extra help getting dressed and making friends and moving through the world?

What kind of world, exactly, were they all about to be moving through?

Sylvia looked at her sisters and thought about their afternoon strolls in Kensington Gardens, when they would tease each other and share gossip with nothing at all to worry about. Everyone they passed would turn their heads—*Here come the Queensburys*, they would say. That unmistakable family of six, each one handsome and well-behaved. They strolled in unison with their butter-blond hair and colour-coordinated outfits. They were the envy of the *ton*.

What would the people of Heene think when the

Queensburys stepped out of their carriage? Would they marvel to see such well-bred ladies gracing their humble village? *Or will they see our faded dresses*, thought Sylvia, *our plain shoes, our lack of servants, and think we belong?*

No. Sylvia knew she would never belong in a place like Heene—and she would certainly carry herself in such a way that everyone who saw her agreed.

Hannah Wickersham had always felt like she belonged in Heene.

The town was filled with her kind of people—prudent and hardworking, there for each other no matter what. It was filled with all the smells she had come to associate with home: rich soil, salty seaside air, fresh bread wafting from the bakery. She had always known this was the place for her, but at today's meeting of the Heene Society of Artisans and Shopkeepers, that feeling was confirmed beyond a doubt.

'We're not going anywhere without a fight,' said Mrs Hayes, leaning forward in her hard wooden chair.

'No one is *fighting* us,' scoffed Mr Luxford.

'No one is fighting *you*,' grumbled the elder Mr Pyle. 'Those developers are circling the lodging house like vultures.'

'Are you calling my business a dead carcass?' the younger Mr Pyle joked, trying to defuse the tension in the room. No one else laughed.

Hannah listened intently to the discussion. She loved to witness the free exchange of ideas, concerns, and strategies that filled the society's weekly meetings. She rarely spoke up herself, but she was *thinking* the entire time.

'If we don't take this seriously *now*, we'll all be priced out of our buildings before we have time to do something about it.' Opal Hayes was the originator of the society, and her passion for protecting the good people of Heene had quickly caught on.

Hannah looked around the circle of chairs gathered in the middle of the old Quaker meeting house. Sitting under the rough wooden rafters were Edna and Ellis Pyle, who sold books and stationery supplies; Adam and Nancy Pyle, young parents whose lodging house appealed to any tourist who couldn't afford the new spa resorts; and Lewis Luxford, the clockmaker who'd lived here long before Ogle's wall was built to separate the *civilised* people of Worthing from the Heene neighbours they deemed *wild and lawless*. There was Alister Coyle, enterprising owner of the new oyster bar, and there was Opal and Francis Hayes, the dressmaker and her loyal fisherman.

Hannah's parents were sceptical when she had first urged them to attend—every new spa resort comes with a kitchen that needs stocking, and every new kitchen that needs stocking comes with new orders for the Wickersham dairy farm. But while the sudden boom in seaside tourism had bolstered Heene businesses at first, the long-term implications had become increasingly clear: higher rent, greater competition, and swaths of land razed to build holiday homes for the London elite.

Hannah's parents sat beside her now, the latest members of the society.

'We're already at risk of being forced out,' said Edna Pyle, shaking her head. 'All that press about Heene being a lawless den of thieves…it makes it easier for Worthing landlords to justify letting us go.'

'My grandfather really was a smuggler back in the day,' said Mr Hayes. He ran a seafood stall on Market Street with his sons. 'And with taxes the way they are, I've heard talk of some men resuming the practice.'

'Oh, that's *just* what we need.' Ellis Pyle shook his head.

'The smugglers aren't the ones pricing us out,' said Mrs Hayes. 'It's the landlords who *know* that Worthing is starting to attract the kind of people who can pay twice as much as we do for use of our shops.'

Hannah wondered what it would feel like to be the kind of person who spoke up in meetings, who asked people what they were thinking, who shared her own thoughts in return. Instead, she went on observing. She noticed how Alister Coyle fidgeted restlessly in his seat. She noticed how tired Adam and Nancy seemed.

And she noticed how Lewis Luxford very much looked like he was hiding something.

Mrs Hayes noticed too. 'You're awfully quiet today, Lewis.'

Mr Luxford raised his bushy eyebrows in surprise. 'I care just as much about the future of Heene as the rest of you, and you know that.'

Hannah's heartbeat quickened. If Mr Luxford had a secret, it could be—*no*, she didn't want to get her hopes up for nothing.

'We do know, Lewis.' Mr Pyle nodded. 'Is everything all right with your shop?'

Mr Luxford took a long breath in, then straightened his posture and exhaled. 'I've been making clocks for a long time.'

This could be it! Hannah sat on her hands to keep herself from fidgeting.

'I've owned my shop since before the wall, and… well, I've finished all I came here to do. I made a living, I raised a family, and that family's all in London now, so I think it's about time I retired.'

Hannah stifled a smile as the rest of the room erupted with *congratulations*es and *we'll miss you*s. She turned to her father with a hopeful expression on her face, but he only shook his head. She turned to her left, where her mother was already glaring. They knew what this meant to Hannah, how it opened the door to that foolish, impractical, waste-of-time daydream she never stopped telling them about.

'Do you have any offers on the building yet?' asked Mr Coyle.

'I'm keeping my options open,' was all Mr Luxford said.

'Now, you're not thinking of selling to one of those Worthing developers, are you?' Mrs Hayes was careful to keep her voice lighthearted, but everyone in the room knew that whatever happened to the Luxford shop could foreshadow the future of the rest of their town.

'You own your building, Lewis,' said Mr Pyle. 'This could be a chance to keep some Worthing property in the hands of Heene.'

'Aren't you taking in some boarders from London, Ellis?' Mr Luxford responded. 'Seems like you're trying to *develop* the area just as much as the landlords are!'

'Ella is just as much from Heene as the rest of us are.' Hannah was surprised to hear her mother speak up. 'She may have left, but she's back now. She's ours.'

'We've always been a hospitable town,' Mrs Hayes agreed. 'If we lose our character then we're damn sure going to lose our buildings too.'

Hannah had heard all sorts of stories about her mother's old childhood friend—depending on the source, Ella Queensbury had either *fallen in love with* or *strategically seduced* a wealthy earl, then left for London and never looked back. More than likely Hannah would only see this mysterious woman and her—*three daughters? Four?*—in passing, and then they would leave, and then Hannah would forget they were ever here.

She had more important things to think about now that the Luxford shop was up for sale. She had dreams to follow through on, promises she'd made to herself that she could finally try to keep.

But only if she was brave enough to speak up, of course.

'Her daughters have never even been here before,' said Nancy Pyle. 'How do we know they'll want anything to do with our hospitality?'

There were nods around the circle, murmurs of agreement.

'Those girls don't know it yet,' said Edna, 'but Heene has always been a part of them. This isn't the fall from grace they think it is. This is a homecoming.'

Sylvia was becoming more homesick with every passing day. Their first night in a ramshackle coaching inn had been even worse than she'd expected, and she'd woken the next morning on a thin mattress that had stiffened her limbs and puffed the skin beneath her eyes. One restless night followed another, and by their third day on the road the entire Queensbury clan was irritable, exhausted, and thoroughly uncomfortable.

Only Ella managed to keep her head high.

'You were once so *desperate* to escape this village,' Sylvia had said to her mother sometime on the second day, or the third—the whole trip had blurred together in her memory. 'Surely you can think up a way to escape again.'

'Heene might surprise you,' was all her mother had said. But that's exactly what Sylvia was afraid of—that Heene would find new ways to ruin her life, ways she couldn't even imagine on her own.

When their carriage finally rolled into town, Violet had everyone name what they were most looking forward to. 'Falling asleep without a stranger snoring through the cracks in the walls,' she started.

Living by the ocean, signed Mary.

'I *want* to say taking a bath,' whined Rose, 'but who *knows* if we'll even have a tub.'

'We'll have a tub,' Ella said. 'But we will have to fetch our own water.'

'What?' the four sisters exclaimed. Their mother only sighed.

'Leaving.' That was the answer Sylvia settled for. 'I am most looking forward to leaving.' The carriage slowed to a stop.

'And you, Mother?' asked Violet. They felt the carriage shake as the driver hopped off.

'Seeing old friends,' Ella replied. She smiled, but it didn't quite reach her eyes. She looked nervous.

Good, thought Sylvia as the driver opened the carriage door. *Let your nerves inspire you to get us out of here as quickly as possible.*

The first thing Sylvia noticed about Heene was the smell: musty soil, sour seaside air, stale bread wafting from nowhere in particular. She stepped out of the carriage and into a light rain, careful to avoid the puddles that were forming along the road.

'Ella Hogge!' The voice was old, affectionate, warm. It belonged to a short man with a bushel of grey hair beneath a grey hat. That's how Heene looked to Sylvia so far: grey, grey, and grey.

'Your name was *Hogge*?' Rose laughed.

Violet nudged her. 'You *knew* that already.'

'No, I didn't!'

'Mr Pyle,' their mother said with a curtsy.

He chuckled and bowed, as though the formality *amused* him. Sylvia didn't know what to do with herself.

'I fear my daughters need a nap before they are their best selves again. May we save introductions for later?'

'Of course, of course.' Mr Pyle nodded, still smiling. Sylvia stared now at the house behind him, a modest stone cottage—grey, of course—with dainty curtains in the windows and blooming peonies in the yard. It wasn't…*terrible*. It was actually much better than what Sylvia had been expecting.

Maybe it was the exhaustion, but for the first time since leaving London, Sylvia felt a glimmer of hope. She walked toward the cottage in a trance, pulled onward by the promise of a long nap. What she saw was certainly nicer than the inns of the last two nights. The beds probably were as well.

Things were already starting to look up.

Sylvia reached for the front door just as it opened from the inside.

'Oh!' An older woman with birdlike features stood in the doorway, holding a tray of freshly baked tarts. Hope swelled in Sylvia's chest—*Our very own housekeeper!*

'Thank you,' Sylvia said as she plucked a tart from the tray.

'Mrs Pyle!' Ella waved from where she stood. 'Meet my daughter, Sylvia Queensbury.'

Sylvia curtsied and mumbled: 'Terribly sorry, I'm so tired I forget my manners.'

'Please, eat.' In any other circumstance Sylvia might have appreciated the cheerful countenance of the person standing between her and sleep, but today she had no time for pleasantries.

'I was just looking for the bedchambers,' she said.

'Yes, of course! We'll give you a tour of the whole property after you've gotten some sleep. This is where

Ellis and I live—' she gestured toward the cottage behind her '—and *this…*' but Sylvia didn't hear the rest
of that sentence. Her eyes followed Mrs Pyle's point-
ing hand down the dirt path behind the house, which
led to a second house.

A much smaller house.

A much smaller house that was cracked and lop-
sided and falling apart.

Sylvia stuffed the tart into her mouth so she wouldn't
say her next thought out loud.

Shit.

Chapter Two

Hannah woke to the sound of the family rooster, just as she did every morning. She opened her eyes to the meagre light of dawn and stretched until her feet poked out from beneath her blanket.

'Can't you make him stop?' Esther groaned beside her.

'I find the rooster quite charming.' Hannah wrapped an arm around Esther, who kept her eyes closed and slowly smiled.

'Hannah, if a *cock* was what I wanted then I wouldn't be in *your* bed.'

'Esther!' gasped Hannah, laughing. She brushed long strands of brown hair from Esther's face and kissed her forehead. 'You'll be free of the rooster soon enough.'

Esther opened one eye and peered up at Hannah. She sighed. 'I suppose you're right.'

Neither was sentimental enough to say *I'll miss you* out loud, but they both knew it was true. They shifted their bodies to be completely entwined and watched the room brighten with the rising sun. Hannah had known from the start that they'd eventually run out of mornings like this. It came with the territory: Esther wasn't the first daughter of a travelling preacher Hannah had gotten into bed with, and she probably wouldn't be the last.

It was certainly better than getting attached to someone who *lived* here. Someone who would tire of hidden kisses and midnight trysts, someone who'd get married and break both their hearts in the process.

'I should get home before anyone notices I'm gone,' Esther said as she disentangled her limbs from Hannah's.

'And I should get to work,' Hannah replied. They helped each other dress, buttoning fabric and twisting hair in amiable silence. Esther slipped through the window, and Hannah walked downstairs in a practical beige dress, a white apron, and a braided crown of light orange hair.

She was greeted, as always, by the homey scent of oatmeal and warm tea. Her aunt tended the fire, her mother set the table, and her father stepped in from chopping wood. None of them had any idea that she hadn't spent her night alone.

That was the beauty of farm life: everyone was always too busy to notice each other's secrets.

Except for Amos, of course. At eighteen, he was

a year younger and a foot taller than Hannah, quiet and kind and unfailingly observant. He was also her dearest friend. He took his seat at one of the wooden benches that lined the table, and he gave Hannah that tiny smile of his, the one with the subtle eyebrow raise that said *I know what you've been up to.*

Isaiah Wickersham wrote out the list of tasks for the day as the oatmeal was served. Hannah watched as he wrote…and wrote…*and wrote.*

'Working on a novel over there?' joked Aunt Charity. Each month it seemed like the lists were getting longer and the family was getting smaller. Wickershams got married, moved away, died of illness, or—in the case of Amos's sister—ran off to join the circus. Now it was just the five of them left to tend the farm.

'No time for novels,' her father replied. 'At least, not until the cows are milked, the fence is mended, the butter is churned, the books are kept…'

'…the barn is swept,' continued Rachel, 'the orders are filled, the clothes are washed…'

'And the cheese is made,' finished Hannah. Her favourite part of the day.

'I think some herbs are ready for harvest,' said Aunt Charity as she joined them at the table. They could go on like this all morning if they tried, naming all the tasks and chores and errands that had to get done. Instead they joined hands, prayed in silence, then ate their oatmeal with haste.

Hannah wondered if Esther was already home, packing her bags for the next town over. The time they spent together had been easy and sensual, casual enough to keep Hannah from getting attached but enjoyable all the same. They might even meet again if Esther's father takes the same circuit next year.

But Hannah's mind only had a moment to wander. Soon came the clatter of bowls being stacked, then it was time for her parents to pack for market. Aunt Charity started the laundry and Amos left to mend the fence and Hannah gathered buckets to milk the cows. She greeted the calves and their mothers by name, stroked their heads and asked how they were doing. Sometimes she liked to imagine they spoke back: *And what will you do with our milk today?*

She'd bottle the milk to be sold in the market, to be delivered to resorts along the coast. Some she'd save for butter, some she'd save for cream, but her favourite milk was always the kind she could turn into cheese.

A few gallons later she was back on her feet, straining and skimming and churning and pressing. Then she was out in the garden, weeding and clipping and trimming and tilling. Then she was back inside for a midday dinner of chicken pie and baked beans before spending the afternoon managing finances and inventory.

Hannah's shoulders slumped with exhaustion by the time she sat on her wooden stool for the second milking of the day. Her mind felt like freshly shorn sheep's wool, fuzzy and tangled and falling apart.

'Finished with the cows?' She heard her cousin's voice as he entered the barn, but she was too tired to look up.

'Just about,' Hannah sighed. Amos brought a stool around and sat beside her just in time for her hand to slip, toppling a full bucket of milk on the ground. They sat in weary silence as the puddle of white pooled beneath their feet and seeped into the ground.

'I can't keep doing this,' Hannah grumbled. 'It's *too much.*'

'This is not a five-person farm,' Amos agreed.

'And I've done the math, by the way—I've gone over the books. I know we can afford to bring on another person and pay them well.'

Amos nodded back, and Hannah noticed the bags beneath his eyes. He was a quiet young man who lived a principled life, and he rarely uttered *anything* that might resemble a complaint. But even Amos—even strong Amos who could lift and carry more than everyone else in the family combined—was at the end of his rope.

They agreed to broach the topic with their parents at supper, then cleaned the barn and walked through the garden to the cheesemaking shed. The air changed as they walked across the Wickersham property; the warm musk of cows gave way to the sweet aroma of flowers and herbs, and then they opened an old wooden door and breathed in Hannah's favourite scent of all: cheese. Rows of it lined the shelves of the old shed, thick wheels of cheddar in various stages of development. Hannah breathed in the creamy, salty, earthy air, sweet and tangy and a little bit mouldy all at once.

'What do you have for me today?' Amos asked. He ducked his head beneath the door frame to enter the small space. Hannah unwrapped a palm-sized wheel that had been ageing on the bottom shelf for half a year, an experiment she tried after reading a book about Dutch cheesemaking. She blended what she read with her family's traditional Cheddar-style method, then sprinkled in some thyme to produce something that would be uniquely hers.

Hannah knew that cheesemaking was more than just a business: it was a craft, a calling, a kind of art. Where Michelangelo had used paint and stone, Hannah Wickersham used curds and whey.

Her heart jumped as she cut a slice for Amos. This was the moment of truth—if the cheese was too sour, too dry, too mouldy—or even mediocre—then she would have to admit that she'd wasted marketable milk and, worse, that her parents were right: meddling with a good recipe is no good at all. *But if the cheese was tasty...*

Amos took the sunny yellow wedge from Hannah's

hand. He chewed slowly, reverently, his teeth coming together like hands in prayer. He was the only person who took Hannah's dream seriously, the only person she ever brought into this room.

'Yes,' he finally said, and it wasn't until Hannah sighed in relief that she realised she'd been holding her breath. 'This is nice cheese.'

'Nice?' Hannah protested.

'Fantastic.' Amos smiled and cut another slice for himself. 'It tells the story of Heene.'

This was Hannah's favourite compliment. Her cows eat the native plants of the land, the grass and clover and flowers and hay that grew on its own or that Hannah planted herself. They breathe the seaside air and bathe in the blue-grey rain. All that flavour enriches the milk, and the result is a wheel of cheese that tastes like home.

'Someday,' she smiled, 'people will come from all over to get a bite of Wickersham cheese.'

'I don't doubt it,' Amos said. He leaned against the door frame and crossed his arms. 'And if the woman climbing from your window this morning is any indication, it seems people are already coming from all over for a bite of—'

'Amos!' Hannah widened her eyes and shook her head. She'd throw a piece of cheese at him—if doing so wouldn't ruin a perfectly good piece of cheese.

Amos blushed, slightly embarrassed by his own impropriety.

'*Esther* is leaving in a few days anyway,' Hannah finally said. 'And even if she wasn't leaving, her parents wouldn't approve of *us*. Her father worships a God who likes things *just so*.'

'Last I checked, Methodists don't worship a different God than we do.'

'I know, I know…' she sighed. 'But they don't talk about the *inward light*. Once you realise that the light of God already lives in each of us…'

Amos finished her thought: 'Then you realise that telling a woman she's wrong for loving another woman is like saying the inward light is wrong.'

'Exactly! But for some reason it seems that most Christians haven't figured that part out yet, so for now…' With gentle fingers, Hannah felt the texture of her ageing wheels to determine which would be ready soon. 'For now it's easier to be with the daughters of travelling preachers, or circus performers, or Londoners who stay for the summer so the sea can… revive their soul, or whatever it is they think is happening. Then they leave before we have time to worry about the theology of it all.'

Amos nodded. Some time passed before he asked, 'Will you miss her?'

Hannah took a slow breath and checked her body for answers. There was no deep, romantic yearning in her heart, no twist of nostalgia in her stomach. She respected Esther and cherished their time together, but she had never let herself get sentimental.

'Yes, for a time,' Hannah said truthfully. 'But not for a long time.'

'You may have a tough rind, Hannah Wickersham, but inside you've got a soft and gooey paste.' He knew a cheese metaphor would make her smile, and she resisted at first but eventually gave in.

'And don't you dare tell anyone.' She pushed at his shoulder playfully.

They gathered the cheddars her parents would sell at their market stall, the standard fare that residents and tourists alike purchased with their milk and butter. Hannah just couldn't help but dream of more—there were so many ways to make cheese, so many textures and flavours and colours to play with. Her parents were right that using up good milk on her *experiments* could be costly and risky, especially since there was no guarantee an unfamiliar cheese would sell. But they didn't have time in their day to check on the cheesemaking shed—her studio, her sanctuary.

As Hannah and Amos approached the main house, they breathed in the savoury scent of onions, carrots, and mushrooms that seeped from the windows. Hannah heard her stomach growl before she even reached the door. Everyone else was just as hungry and tired, so their silent prayer—punctuated by the crackling fire and an early owl—lasted only a moment before spoons clattered into bowls and root beer splashed into cups.

Hannah thought carefully about what to say next. She wanted to emphasise how busy she and Amos had been lately, but even more than that she wanted her parents to admit how busy they'd been too.

'Did you have time to see your friend today? The one who just moved back?' Hannah asked her mother, already knowing the answer.

Rachel shook her head. 'Between the market stall and a half-dozen deliveries…' she trailed off and continued eating.

Hannah nudged Amos underneath the table. *Your turn.*

'I'm wondering if anyone could help me move some equipment around in the barn tomorrow. It could use some reorganising.'

No one answered at first, and then Isaiah spoke up. 'The barn's fine as it is. Plenty of other work to do.'

Before Hannah or Amos could try again, their parents dove into a conversation about everything and everyone they had seen that day at the market. This time of year, their dairy stall was visited by both dependable locals and garishly dressed tourists, the latter of which often seemed like a different species entirely. Hannah had never understood the appeal of their elaborate outfits, their crisp white gloves, and their comically large hats. Their etiquette seemed so stifling, and their obsession with titles, wealth, and breeding…it made her happy to have grown up in Heene.

There won't be a Heene for much longer if we're all priced out of our shops, she thought. But in order to *buy* a shop in the first place—a shop that would be truly her own, with no landlord to raise the rent—she needed enough cheese to *fill* a shop. And in order to have *time* to make all that cheese…

'We need to hire someone,' Hannah said suddenly. Everyone at the table stared. 'I'm sorry for interrupting, but—it's important. We're all tired, we're all overworked, we're all used to having more help. I don't understand why we didn't hire someone when Naomi left last year, or in the spring when the hens escaped because we were all too busy birthing calves to notice anything else.'

There was a pause before her father spoke. 'This farm has been in our family for generations. It's always been a family farm.'

'Isn't that what you love about Heene, Hannah?' her mother said. 'The Pyles have been selling books here for as long as there have been books to sell. The Mercers have been taking their jam to market ever since markets were invented—they can trace some of their family recipes back hundreds of years!'

'And one farmhand isn't going to change the fact that this is the Wickersham farm,' Hannah countered.

'Who would we hire?' Aunt Charity asked. She was

rubbing the back of her neck, always sore. 'It's not a bad idea, but who's looking for work this time of year? Everyone's fishing, or working their own family's farm, or wheeling bathing machines into the sea.'

Hannah stepped on Amos's foot beneath the table and looked at him pointedly, hoping for some help. But Amos was always too shy in moments like this. He hunched over his soup.

'Ask around,' her father finally conceded. 'If you find someone who's looking for work and eager to learn, then perhaps—*perhaps*—we'll consider a trial period.'

It was more than Hannah had expected to hear. She smiled, then mentally put together a plan. 'I'll take deliveries tomorrow, if that's all right.'

'*That's* your plan?' Amos stared doubtfully at the sparse stack of papers Hannah held in her arms.

'And *now* you have something to say?' Hannah responded. It was just after breakfast, and Amos was helping her load the cart with dairy orders. 'If our parents aren't going to help get the word out, then maybe my flawless handwriting can.'

'Okay, now I *know* you're joking.' Amos took a sheet of paper from the pile and read it over. Hannah had tried her best to write slowly and steadily, but mastering the art of proper penmanship had never been a priority of hers.

'It gets the message across,' Hannah protested. 'Help wanted, dairy farm, all that… I'll come up with more ideas—and *you will too*—but for now this one's as good as any.' She yawned, tired from working on her posters late into the night.

'You could have had them printed.'

'And have no funds left over to actually hire some-one?'

Amos finished loading the cart and offered a soft smile. 'I'm giving you a hard time. It's a decent plan, and with any luck one of these will end up in the right person's hands.' He returned the flyer and left to drain some whey in Hannah's stead.

All morning she alternated her deliveries. She brought milk and cheese to the kitchens of luxury Worthing resorts, then posted flyers in Heene-owned businesses like Pyle Books & Stationery and Luxford Clocks. She brought butter to Alister Coyle's oyster bar, but he wouldn't accept a handmade help wanted ad in his *fine establishment.*

And then she was in the second-hand clothing shop asking the girl behind the counter if any of her brothers were looking for work when the bell on the front door rang and a very determined young woman marched to the counter and released a pile of clothes from her arms.

'How much for these?' the stranger asked. She stood confidently, her shoulders back and her chin tilted up.

But her eyes darted around the room and her nose wrinkled, betraying that—whoever this woman was— she saw second-hand shops as entirely beneath her.

Tourists didn't usually bother with this part of town, but Hannah couldn't think of what else this stranger could be. No one who had to work for their food would have time to curl their hair into those neat blond ringlets, and the fabric her dress was made of could buy Hannah enough food for a week.

Betty, the girl behind the counter, curtsied and said good morning.

'Yes, yes, good morning.' The visitor looked about Hannah's age. She began to pull apart the clothes and explain how expensive each dress had originally been, how exquisite the fabric is for *a place like this.*

Hannah bristled. *A place like this.* Just another tourist from London come to wade in the waters of Worthing.

Then what is she doing on this side of the wall?

'I can offer…two pounds for the lot.'

'*Two pounds?*' The tourist's voice was sharp. Hannah stood awkwardly in place. 'That's—that's a *fraction* of what I paid for these!' A stocking slipped from the pile and fell to the ground.

'These are last year's patterns,' Betty said calmly as she examined the dresses. 'Nowadays, wealthier clientele only want the latest. Very different from when my grandmother ran the shop, when a dress was simply a dress.'

The tourist huffed and crossed her arms. Hannah pretended to survey the bonnet rack, but her eyes couldn't stay away from the scene unfolding at the counter. She noticed bits of stray thread around the collar of the woman's dress, as though it used to be adorned with beads. And the more Hannah looked, the more she noticed how rumbled the fabric was— and how bare the woman's hands were.

No, this was not the usual tourist. There was something...*odd* about her. There was also something quite lovely about her too. Her bright hair was curled neatly around her smooth, angular face, and for all the bitterness this woman clearly carried she was indeed quite handsome.

Hannah could always appreciate beauty, even when the bearer of that beauty was decidedly unpleasant.

'I'll take my business elsewhere.' The stranger gathered her things and marched out the door as quickly as she had come.

'She'll be back,' Betty said, rolling her eyes.

'Does the peerage often bring their old clothes to sell on holiday?' Hannah had never taken a proper holiday before, and if she ever *did* get the chance, the last thing she would spend it on was running errands.

Betty leaned over the counter and whispered, as if

they weren't the only two people in the shop: *'That's one of the Queensbury girls.'*

Hannah paused. 'The family who lost all their money?'

'Terrible story. Their father died and his brother kept the whole estate for himself.'

'That shouldn't be allowed.' Hannah shook her head. 'Who gave men the right?'

'Some king a long time ago, probably.'

Hannah left a flyer with Betty and resumed her morning deliveries. She wondered briefly if her mother's friendship with the infamous Ella Hogge had survived whatever happened all those years ago, or if there were still unhealed wounds. She wondered if there was any trace at all of Heene left in Ella—but if Ella was anything like her daughter, the answer to that was a resounding *no*.

And as she wheeled her cart through Heene and Worthing, Hannah wondered if she would ever see that snobbish Queensbury girl again.

Ideally, their paths had just crossed for the first and final time.

Chapter Three

Sylvia Queensbury didn't mind a side of beans at dinner—when the table was otherwise crowded with venison, duck, gravy, cheese, and soups and puddings and sauces of all kinds, a dish of beans was quite tolerable.

But when a small bowl of barely buttered beans was the *only* meal present on their splintered wooden table, Sylvia Queensbury very quickly became the kind of person who hated beans.

'How was everyone's day?' Ella asked, as if that were a perfectly normal question for their family to discuss at dinner.

After a pause, Violet spoke up. 'I traded in the rest of the jewellery for a fair price, which should help with food for a while.'

Sylvia moved the beans around with her spoon.

'Mary and I walked along the shore,' said Rose. 'And we met some other children who were looking for seashells.'

'Were they kind?' Ella asked, and to everyone's relief the twins nodded. Mary was…*just a bit differ-ent*, is how their mother phrased it. She showed her emotions in ways that other people didn't always un-derstand—she liked to jump when she was happy, or wave her hands when she was bored, or crouch into a ball when there were too many sounds.

When she hadn't spoken a word by age five, there was no shortage of doctors encouraging her father to send her to an asylum—instead, he hired a tutor all the way from France who could teach her to sign words with her hands. Sylvia hated the way people would stare, or sneer, or offer to pray for healing, but usually Rose was the only one brave enough to do something about it; one time Rose pushed the daughter of a duke for laughing at Mary, which got the whole Queensbury clan uninvited from social events for an entire week.

We played in the ocean, Mary signed.

Sylvia was sceptical—if even the civilised ladies and gentlemen of London could be unkind when en-countering someone different from themselves, *surely* the uncivilised commoners of Heene would be twice as cruel.

'And you, Sylvia?' asked Violet. 'Did you have any luck with the clothes?'

'Not exactly…' Sylvia mumbled, then spooned in a mouthful of beans to buy herself some time.

They tasted just as bland as they smelled.

'Did you go to the second-hand shop?' her mother asked.

'Er…' Sylvia hesitated, then reminded herself she was in the right. 'She only offered two pounds for the whole pile! So I told her I'd take my business elsewhere. We deserve a better price.'

'Oh Sylvia…' her mother sighed and rubbed the bridge of her nose. 'That's not how our life works anymore.'

'But why not?' A bitter heat rose up her body. 'I understand we don't have money or jewels or a decent place to live anymore, but we are *still* the Queensburys. We are still deserving of respect.'

'She has a point,' Rose agreed.

'And how are you defining *respect*?' her mother asked. 'Did the shopgirl disrespect you by offering you less money than you think your dresses are worth? Do your new neighbours disrespect you by not treating you like royalty?'

No one at the table was used to seeing Ella Queensbury be this outspoken. She noticed their startled faces and settled into a gentler tone: 'Your whole life, *respect* hasn't required anything of *you*. It's something you expect from servants when you need your teacup refilled. It's something you passively adopt when you defer to a father or husband in matters of decision-making. But respect…works differently out here. It requires you to *do* something.'

'*Do* what?' asked Rose.

Ella started to speak, then closed her mouth. She searched for words. 'You'll just—you'll just have to learn.'

Sylvia shifted uncomfortably in her seat. It was hard to remember that her own mother—who just a few days ago had been elegant, quiet, and refined—had spent the first twenty years of her life here. Ella Queensbury could have been the girl behind the counter at the second-hand shop, the girl whose name Sylvia had never even bothered to learn.

She would not concede defeat—she would not let Heene change her—but she could admit that being more *polite* was perhaps in order.

'It's my fault for never teaching you differently,' Ella continued. 'Sylvia, tomorrow you will go back to the shop and apologise, and if we're lucky they will offer you the same price. We are not in a position to turn down two pounds.'

Sylvia wanted to protest, but instead she just kept eating beans. *Maybe two pounds can buy us something tastier to eat*, she thought.

'How else can we help?' Violet asked. 'I think we've otherwise sold everything we can.'

Ella avoided her daughter's eyes when she answered. 'You could seek employment.'

Rose dropped her spoon. Everyone was quiet now, even Violet.

'You mean…we could *work*?' Sylvia asked, incredulous.

'Money has to come from somewhere,' Ella responded.

'Money *comes from* somewhere?' Rose wrinkled her nose. 'I always thought it just…existed.'

Ella laughed. 'I really should have taught you more about the world early on. Work will be good for all of you, I think.'

'What kind of work?' asked Violet.

'We can talk about it more tomorrow. For now, I need some help with the dishes.'

The girls gathered their bowls and spoons and awkwardly washed them in a bucket of soapy water. Sylvia knew there was more she could do to adjust to their living situation—however temporary it may be—but *employment* was a step too far. She was the daughter of an earl.

Of all the ways to obtain money, *earning* it was by far the most dreadful.

'You can visit the modiste on your own, Violet, if you'd like.'

Sylvia and Violet had technically heard the words that came from their mother's mouth, but they struggled to understand.

'On my own…as in, without a chaperone?' Violet said slowly.

Ella nodded. And then Ella *smiled*.

'But our reputations,' Sylvia said. *What would people think?*

'The good folks of Heene love to gossip just as much as the *ton*, but down here an unaccompanied woman hardly counts as a scandal.' Their mother was sitting in front of a small mirror curling her hair with a papillote iron, one of the few beauty tools they'd agreed not to sell. 'Women walk to and from work all the time, and they can't just wait around for someone to accompany them.'

Violet and Sylvia looked at each other apprehensively.

'You *can* go together,' Ella continued. 'I'm only saying you don't *have* to. There's somewhat of a freedom living out here.'

'Finding employment just so we can eat doesn't sound like freedom,' Sylvia countered.

Ella clamped the hot iron shut over a papered ringlet of hair. 'No, it certainly doesn't.'

Sylvia thought her mother might elaborate, but instead she started to hum to herself as she continued curling her hair. *What a confusing conversation*, Sylvia thought. She linked her arm with Violet's, and together they left for the modiste.

'If we see anyone we know,' Sylvia said as they approached the bridge between Heene and Worthing, 'we tell them we're staying in Worthing for a spell until we can purchase a new townhouse in London.'

'No one will believe that,' Violet responded.

'We still look the part. Our clothes are decent and our hair is styled. Now, if we could just purchase a ribbon or two…'

'I should be able to manage that,' Violet said, her voice wavering ever so slightly with nerves.

'There must be another way.' Sylvia shook her head. She looked down at their dresses, the same ones they'd worn for three days now. If the hems tattered, or if something spilled on the fabric…some weekly wages would certainly come in handy. Violet's resolve to find employment wasn't a bad idea—but still, Sylvia just didn't like the idea of her sister working. 'You should be dancing with gentlemen instead of stitching patterns in the back room of a dress shop. You should be greeting suitors by the dozen.'

'Did you meet anyone you wanted to marry, your season?'

'Oh…no, Father used to say the first season was a lark, a time to enjoy the dances and make connections before seriously entering the marriage market. But plenty of girls do marry their first season.'

'I think plenty of them have to. Not everyone has the funds to wait for a love match.'

And there they were: the two words that had haunted

Sylvia since she was old enough to recognise what her parents shared between them. *Love match.*

Sylvia knew her parents had found something special, and surely she was destined to find the same. In her first season, she had friends whose parents couldn't stand each other, who had married for need of an heir, or a fortune, or a titled husband who could believably be the father of a baby that was conceived with a footman. She knew she was lucky to wait for a gentleman who touched her heart, only…that gentleman never came.

She had danced with every eligible bachelor of her season at least once, and even now she could remember their handsome faces, their broad shoulders, their strong jawlines. They called upon her in the parlour and brought flowers. They regaled her with stories from their time abroad. Through all of this, she felt nothing.

She could easily dismiss the worry that something was wrong with her, that some essential piece was missing from her heart—she'd been out in society for just one year, which means the swoon-worthy man of her dreams was just…somewhere else that year, probably. He was more than likely on his Grand Tour of the Continent. Or maybe he was in mourning, like she had been during what was meant to be her second season. Wherever he was, Sylvia knew one thing:

her Prince Charming absolutely, definitely, without a doubt *existed.*

She just hadn't met him yet. But she would—as soon as she found a way out of Heene.

Unless Prince Charming is *the way out of Heene.* The thought struck Sylvia like lightning. People often talked about marrying for love and marrying for money as if they were entirely separate things, but... what if Sylvia could find both?

She was pulled from her thoughts by the sight of the modiste. She made a promise to return to this idea later—a wealthy husband to rescue her from Heene was ideal, but a job for Violet would have to do for now.

They entered the shop and asked for Opal Hayes, who was fitting a mint green gown onto a customer, complete with a floral bodice and ruffled hem. Sylvia tried not to stare, but she could feel envy burning behind her eyes.

When Mrs Hayes was finished, she found Violet and Sylvia admiring her wares on mannequins and smiled brightly. 'Now, you must be Ella's daughters.'

'Yes!' Violet said overenthusiastically. She curtsied, gripping the basket that held her embroidery samples. Sylvia curtsied too, admiring the crimson brocade of the modiste's gown. Her mother had told her that Mrs Hayes was one of the most successful Heene business owners in Worthing, that this dress shop had been in

the Hayes family since before the wall, before the resorts and bathing machines.

And, as their mother had also told them, it is a truth
universally acknowledged that a successful modiste
without a daughter of her own must be in want of an
apprentice.

'I'm terribly sorry about your father,' Mrs Hayes
said earnestly, 'and about all that happened after, with
your uncle. Such a dreadful way to treat family.'

'Our uncle never considered us family,' Sylvia said.
'He never forgave his brother for marrying—' she almost said *beneath their family*, but thought better of
it. 'For marrying outside the peerage.'

Mrs Hayes shook her head. 'Many of my customers
come from your world. I used to envy your mother,
when she first left, but…well, let's just say Heene isn't
as bad as it looks.'

Violet widened her eyes. 'Oh no, we didn't mean
to imply—'

'It's fine, it's fine.' Mrs Hayes laughed. 'These last
few days have probably been…quite *grim* compared to
what you're used to. I'm guessing you've never fetched
your own water before?'

Violet and Sylvia looked at each other and relaxed,
their shoulders lower now.

'My fingers ache from carrying buckets,' Sylvia
admitted.

'And from washing dishes,' Violet said.

Sylvia shuddered in agreement.

'You'll get used to it eventually,' Mrs Hayes said with a sympathetic smile. 'But for now—what can I do for you?' She eyed them both up and down. 'New dresses?'

Sylvia closed her eyes. 'I wish.'

'Actually,' said Violet, 'I was hoping to show you some samples of my work. I know embroidering napkins and pillowcases isn't the same as making dresses, but I'm a quick study.'

'Let's see then.' Mrs Hayes nodded toward the counter, and Violet laid out her finest work. Both sisters watched as the modiste trailed her fingers over delicate threaded flowers, leaves, and butterflies. Some of the patterns were impressively complex, and Sylvia felt at once proud of her sister and embarrassed for herself. She had nothing like this to offer to anyone in town.

Sylvia's particular set of skills were suited for high society parlours, so unless someone was looking to hire a talented charades player who knew two Christmas songs on the pianoforte, she had no idea where she would even begin to look for a job.

'Quite good…' Mrs Hayes mumbled to herself. 'Quite good indeed.' Then, she turned to Violet. 'You're a bit old to learn a new trade. You're up for the task?'

Violet rushed to answer. 'Absolutely. I mean, I think so—yes. Definitely yes.' Sylvia noticed that her sister was beginning to blush.

'And you?'

It took Sylvia a moment to realise that Mrs Hayes was talking to her.

'Me?'

'Do you have anything to show me?'

'Oh…' Sylvia shook her head. 'No, I never took to embroidery.'

Violet nudged Sylvia. When Sylvia didn't pick up on what the nudge was for, Violet said: 'But she would be ever so grateful if you could suggest some places that are hiring.'

Sylvia clenched her jaw and stepped on Violet's foot. They were here to find employment for *her sister*, and for her sister only.

And what kind of sister does that make me?

Mrs Hayes ran her fingers through her slightly greying brunette hair. 'I don't have time to train from scratch, but the girls at the second-hand shop might. I used to get a great deal of fabric from them, but these days my customers want the latest designs from London, Paris, Rome…'

'So I've heard,' Sylvia muttered. *What I wouldn't do for a Parisian gown right about now…well, other than work.*

She felt her stomach twist. *So I just sit back and watch Violet work instead?*

'The hat shop may be looking for help,' Mrs Hayes continued. 'Otherwise you could try the resorts. They always need extra hands in the kitchen. *Oh!* And the Wickersham farm is hiring. I just heard about it this morning.'

'I don't think I'd be a good fit for—' But Sylvia stopped short when she saw the way Violet was looking at her. Those round, pleading eyes melted Sylvia's heart. 'Thank you,' she said to Mrs Hayes. 'I mean, sure, I don't know how to farm, or cook, or make hats, but it can't be that hard, right?'

All three of them stood uncomfortably in the silence that followed.

Eventually Mrs Hayes spoke. 'It's amazing what a person can learn when they don't have servants doing it for them.' Her tone wasn't rude, but it was…cynical. She looked at Violet with discerning eyes, then finally said: 'All right, I'll take you on for two weeks. If you can prove you're a hard worker and a quick learner, we can talk about something more long-term.'

'Thank you,' Violet said again, this time with real emphasis.

When they were out of the shop and walking back home—or, more accurately, to their temporary dwelling that was most certainly *not* their home—Violet asked Sylvia if they wanted to stop at any of the places Mrs Hayes had suggested.

'I suppose…' Sylvia hesitated. From where they walked, they could see the shore between buildings, and they could see the bathing machines rolling out into the sea. *That's where I should be*, Sylvia thought. *Relaxing in the ocean before an evening at the theatre, or a ball, or...*

But that's not where Sylvia was. 'I suppose the hat shop is worth a visit.'

Violet smiled, and a few minutes later they stepped into a quaint yellow building. Inside, the shop was a garden of silk and velvet and straw and lace. Hats of every colour and bonnets of every size lined the shelves and stands. There were vases of fragrant flowers, illustrations of fashionable women, and half a dozen shiny oval mirrors.

The sight made Sylvia want to tear her own simple white bonnet from her head and throw it into the nearest fireplace.

'Good morning!' A tall woman with dark brown hair and an Irish accent emerged from the back room. She was followed by an orange cat, who proceeded to sniff the Queensbury girls with suspicion.

The woman introduced herself as Katherine O'Toole, co-owner of the business and proud resident of Heene. She was friendly and cheerful, but ultimately not in the market for a worker with no prior experience.

'You could try the farm,' suggested Violet. 'The name sounds familiar... I think they knew Mother, when she lived here?'

'Everyone knew Mother,' Sylvia grumbled. 'And

no, I don't think I shall spend my days among cows and pigs.'

They visited a carpenter next at the suggestion of Mrs O'Toole, but he took one look at Sylvia's uncalloused hands and turned her away. They tried the resorts, but none had a need for someone who didn't know how to cook. They almost tried the lending library, but it was too close to the docks and smelled potently of raw fish.

By the time the sisters arrived at the uneven cobblestone path to their house, Sylvia was in high spirits. She had tried to find a job—*no one* could say she had not tried. But there just…wasn't anything suitable. It really wasn't her fault.

Inside, Rose and Mary were arranging a bouquet of freshly picked wildflowers in a tin pitcher. They both smiled when their sisters entered the room.

'Are you a *modiste* now?' asked Rose in a playfully fancy tone of voice.

Violet nodded bashfully. 'Soon I'll be able to make all of us new dresses.'

Ella stepped away from the meal she was cooking to place her hands on Violet's shoulders. 'I'm proud of you,' she said. 'I'll be helping at the second-hand shop, mostly mending that I can do from home. We'll have to teach each other new stitches as we learn them.' She returned to her pot and wooden spoon, then winked at the twins.

Rose sighed dramatically, her chin falling into her hands. 'And *we'll* be in the kitchen of some fancy resort on the shore.'

'The *kitchen?*' Sylvia asked a little louder than she intended. 'How—what—why?'

We know how to bake, Mary signed, as if it were the most obvious thing in the world.

'Back before all this—' Rose gestured at their surroundings, 'Mary and I used to sneak down to the kitchen to steal treats. We got caught so many times that eventually the kitchen staff taught us how to make our own biscuits.'

And cakes, added Mary.

'And puddings.'

'Am I the only one here who doesn't have a single marketable skill?' Sylvia crossed her arms.

'It appears so,' Rose said with a smirk, earning a stern glance from their mother.

Sylvia and Violet washed their hands and changed into the simple grey dresses they had purchased upon their arrival in Heene. *These are practical*, their mother had said, as if *practical* was a good thing.

The Queensburys settled into their chairs for *dinner*, a word that Sylvia had always used for an evening meal but here took place in the afternoon. Heene seemed designed to confuse and discomfort her at every turn.

And then, Ella placed a large bowl of beans in the centre of the table. The same bland, mushy, yellowish beans they had eaten at every meal for the past three days.

Heene seemed designed to *destroy* Sylvia at every turn.

Her family's wages might soon be enough to get something tastier on the table, but they wouldn't be enough to earn back the favour of their peers. They needed a windfall, the kind of cash that only comes from the death of a distant relative who was secretly rich, or from the generosity of an uncle who isn't an absolute reprobate.

Or, thought Sylvia, remembering her promise from earlier, *from the pockets of a well-to-do husband.*

She sat still even as the thought buzzed inside her. She couldn't let her family in on her plan—which wasn't even a real plan yet, just the faintest wisp of an idea—not now, not when they were all celebrating their new jobs. And there were still so many details to work out. Which resorts are most frequented by wealthy bachelors? How would she secure an invitation to social gatherings? And how would she persuade someone to marry her without a dowry?

Sylvia may not know how to sew, how to bake, or how to carve wood, but she did know how to scheme. She'd spent long enough learning the nuances of etiquette and hierarchy to work her way back to the top— she just needed some time to plan. To think.

And, she realised, she needed money. Not just for

food—for dresses, and ribbons, and sweet-smelling perfumes. She was no longer a member of the *ton*, but she would have to convincingly play the part.

Despite her dread, tomorrow Sylvia would seek employment at the Wickersham farm. *And perhaps*, she thought, *spending time with cows and pigs will be good practice for spending time with men.*

Chapter Four

'Do you ever think of spending more time with humans?' Rachel Wickersham called from the far side of the fence. Hannah was out in the fields again, saying hello to their many cows and monitoring for signs of disease and injury. Like most days, she was met with a happy and healthy herd.

'Now when would I have time for that?' Hannah shouted to her mother with a chuckle. She was sitting in the grass, stroking the ears of a playful three-month-old calf.

'Well, now that we've hired a new farmhand…'

'We *what?*' Hannah stood quickly. The calf nudged her legs for more attention. 'Whoever it is, Buttercup,' she said to the baby cow, 'they won't be more important than you.'

'I love Buttercup and the rest just as much as you do,' said Rachel, 'but maybe you could get some more…*people* friends. Maybe you could even *court* some of those people friends.'

'Right,' Hannah groaned. She crossed the field to join her mother. 'Can we go back to the part where you *hired a new farmhand*?'

Her mother sighed and muttered to herself, 'I did try...' And then, louder, she said, 'She's in the kitchen. I'm off to buy some new cheesecloths—*you're welcome*—and some gardening tools. I told her you'd be inside momentarily to start her training.'

Hannah breathed in—slowly, deeply—to savour the rich and peaceful scent of their quiet pasture. She watched the grass sway in the wind, the gauzy clouds drift across the sky, the shuffle of cow hooves moving through a hot summer's day.

With a contented sigh, she turned her attention to the house and began to walk.

She could already see it—the excellent, unprecedented, award-winning cheese she would be able to invent with her afternoons free. And when she wasn't in the cheese shed, maybe she could walk along the shore, feel the bubbly edge of the ocean lap at her toes.

She climbed over the old wooden fence and picked some wildflowers on her way inside. If she was lucky, the new hire would already have some experience— maybe even plenty of experience—and the training would take a day or two at most. And even if this person had never worked on a farm before...*well, milking a cow isn't all that difficult.*

Hannah opened the back door of the house and

stepped into the kitchen full of hope. Things were finally looking up for the Wickersham household, and for her in particular.

And then she saw the Queensbury girl. The one from the second-hand shop.

Hannah stopped. She blinked and shook her head—maybe this was simply a different blond woman with perfect posture and delicately curled hair.

But no, Hannah's eyes had not been mistaken.

Before Miss Queensbury had a chance to speak, Hannah turned on her heel and marched stormily from the house.

'*Mother,*' Hannah called as she rounded the corner, face red with indignation. Hannah—calm, steady, practical Hannah—was not used to being this *vexed.* Especially not by a stranger.

And *especially* not by such a rude, pretentious, frustratingly beautiful stranger.

'Out shopping,' her father said as she entered the barn. *Right.* In her frenzy of emotions she had already forgotten.

'Did you have a hand in this?' Hannah asked, her voice sharper than intended. Embarrassed, she paused to slow her breathing and steady herself.

Isaiah Wickersham set down the tools he was organising and raised an eyebrow. 'Did I have a hand in… hiring the extra help that *you* asked for?'

Hannah knew she should be grateful. And she *was*

grateful, really. But…*couldn't they have found any-one else?*

Her father continued: 'She came to us this morning. Says her family funds are nearly out. They need help, and we… Well, like you said, so do we.'

'I'm not confident she'll be able to help us at all.' Hannah looked around the barn and tried to imagine Miss Queensbury shovelling manure, milking cows, or guiding a sticky calf through its mother's birth canal. She almost laughed at the thought, until she remembered the joke was at her expense: *she* would be the one teaching this new farmhand, wasting her own time until Miss Queensbury inevitably quit.

Isaiah paused for a long while. He let the silence bloom between them, and Hannah let herself be calmed.

'Give instruction to a wise man, and he will be yet wiser,' her father finally said.

Hannah finished the verse: 'Teach a just man, and he will increase in learning.' *Proverbs*, she remembered, *chapter nine*. 'But I don't think… I know this sounds harsh, but I don't think she is particularly wise. And she is definitely not *just*. No one with that kind of money is.'

'She doesn't have *that kind of money* anymore.' Isaiah turned back to his work but kept talking. 'But she does have the inward light, just like everyone else.'

Hannah could sense this was the end of the conversation. She left the barn and returned to what was hopefully by now an empty kitchen.

'The first thing you need to understand,' she said upon finding that the kitchen was *not* empty, 'is that your behaviour in the second-hand shop will not work here.' She crossed her arms. 'Oh, and I'm Hannah, by the way.'

Miss Queensbury nodded. 'I'm Sylvia,' she said, curtsying.

Hannah grimaced.

Sylvia rose from her curtsy and looked confused. 'I know the clothing and the food and…well, *everything else* is different here. But surely there's not some special type of curtsying too.'

'I can't speak for the rest of the town,' Hannah said, 'but we're a Quaker family. We don't curtsy.'

Sylvia stood slowly, an inch or two taller than Hannah. Her eyes were wide, inquiring. They were pale green like the underside of a leaf.

'We believe in equality,' Hannah continued, making no attempt to hide the frustration in her voice. 'We're not interested in the *etiquette* of hierarchy.' She extended her hand, which Sylvia took hesitantly. Hannah noticed the bewildered look on Sylvia's face when she received what was probably the first handshake of her life.

'I've never seen women shake hands,' Sylvia said, narrowing her eyes.

'And I've never seen someone act like you did yesterday.'

'Right, yes, about that...' She tugged uncomfortably at her her plain grey skirts, clearly stalling. Hannah noticed for the first time how out-of-place Sylvia looked wearing the type of dress that...well, the type of dress that Hannah would wear. It was a lovely dress, in Hannah's opinion: clean, simple, and practical.

The fabric looked soft, too, but Sylvia wore the dress as though it pricked her every time she moved.

'I did go back to the store this morning,' Sylvia admitted. 'To apologise. I'm just not...' She gestured vaguely around herself. 'Not used to any of this. And I don't like it. I don't like it at all. I *am* sorry for how I behaved, but I still—' And then she bit her lip.

'But I still...?'

Sylvia tilted her chin higher. 'I suppose I shouldn't speak this freely to one from whom I seek employment.'

'That's another thing you'll have to get used to. People tend to speak freely around here.' Hannah sighed, then gestured for Sylvia to follow her through the back door. *'A lying tongue hateth those that are afflicted by it; and a flattering mouth worketh ruin.'*

Sylvia said nothing for a moment as they stepped into the sunlight of high noon. 'Er...what?'

'It's from the Bible.'

'Oh—well, I know *that*. Of course.'

Hannah rolled her eyes. 'Do you know the passage?'

'No…but I know plenty of people who sit in church every Sunday and still go about their lives with *lying tongues* and *flattering mouths.*'

Hannah started to laugh but stopped herself. She was grateful Sylvia was behind her and couldn't see the half-smile that was forming on her face. She didn't want Sylvia to get the wrong impression—that any wit, or charm, or beauty would change how Hannah felt about Sylvia.

They walked along a path of large stone slabs until they reached the milking parlour attached to the barn. She turned to see Sylvia's face: irritated, fussy, already exhausted. And then Hannah realised—*I don't actually have to work with this person. I can just tell her all the worst parts of farm life…and she'll see herself out!*

'Now, when was the last time you milked a cow?' Hannah said as she opened the old wooden door. 'Or helped a new mother give birth to a calf? Or looked after a sick and dying animal?'

'Such tasks have always been beneath me,' Sylvia shot back.

'Which tasks *aren't* beneath you?'

Sylvia raised a hand to her scrunched-up nose as the full scent of the barn bombarded her senses.

'Ah, yes,' Hannah said. 'That's how it smells, every day. You might get used to it…after a few months.' She kept her voice nonchalant, pausing so Sylvia could really imagine the *horrors* of having to smell a barn for months on end. 'Anyway, your tasks? What did you do with your days, before you committed yourself to a life of shovelling cow dung?'

'I—' Sylvia started. She lowered her hand. 'Well, I...promenade in the park. Or at least I used to. And I danced at balls. I was quite talented at charades—'

'Oh! Well that will come in handy.'

'Really?'

'No! When would charades *ever* be useful *on a farm*?'

Sylvia blinked, and, for a moment, it looked like her eyes were beginning to water.

'I didn't mean—' Hannah started, suddenly aware of the ugliness of her own words. *You're supposed to scare her off, not make her cry*, thought Hannah with a pang of guilt. 'I'm just surprised you would want to work *here*, so I—'

'Oh, to be clear, I do *not* want to work here.'

'But you're out of options, right?' Hannah softened her voice. She could feel her heart softening too. 'You're just trying to make the best of the situation you're stuck in. That's all any of us are trying to do.'

Sylvia dabbed her eyes discreetly. 'Isn't this supposed to be a tour?'

Hannah sighed. She had always been the first one to scoop up a baby bird fallen from the nest, to flip a flailing beetle stuck on his back, to leave out a bowl of milk for the neighbourhood strays. This quality was admirable when it came to helpless critters, but it was downright dangerous when it came to human beings.

And utterly useless when it came to hiring a farm-hand.

'This is the milking parlour,' Hannah said and gestured at the room behind her. 'Milkings happen once or twice a day depending on the season. In a few days time you'll know the underside of a cow better than you know yourself. And today...' She glanced out the window to see where the sun had landed. 'You're right on time to learn.'

'Now?'

'Yes, now.' Hannah left the barn and walked toward the pasture, where the herd was grazing, lounging, and swatting flies with their tails. The rolling fields swayed in the gentle wind, a dozen shades of dazzling green beneath the early evening sunlight. Birds flew over the trees that lined the edge of the farm, and butterflies looped around the wildflowers that helped give Wickersham cheese its distinctive Heene taste.

'But we don't—' Sylvia said, catching up with Hannah. 'We don't have any milking gloves.'

Hannah stopped walking. 'Sylvia...' she said gently. 'You don't need gloves to milk a cow. You just... do it with your bare hands.'

Sylvia looked horrified, and it made Hannah squirm—she barely knew this person, and she had ever reason not to like her, but she just didn't want to keep hurting her. So she walked forward and put her hands on Sylvia's shoulders.

'Close your eyes,' Hannah said.

Sylvia hesitated, but closed her eyes. This close, Hannah could see the slope of Sylvia's nose, the curve of her jaw, the gentle bend of her lashes. She couldn't deny what a small part of her had already known: that Sylvia Queensbury was strikingly beautiful. *Enough of that*, she chided herself. *Plenty of women are beautiful.*

'You've never been on a farm before,' Hannah said, 'so all you see when you look around you is mud, and flies, and cow shit.'

Sylvia's eyes flew open in surprise, but she closed them again.

'But Sylvia—think about your favourite cheese. Or the best butter you've ever tasted. It all starts here, *right here*, with you and me in the milking parlour. Your time in Heene might be short, and it might be messy and hard and...what I'm trying to say is, *something good can still come from it*. I truly believe that. Do you trust me?'

Sylvia chewed on her bottom lip.

'You can open your eyes,' Hannah said, and when Sylvia did, she looked at Hannah with new vulnerability.

Sylvia nodded slowly, not entirely convinced.

'Good enough,' said Hannah. 'Now it's time for you to make friends.'

'I don't have many of those left,' Sylvia mumbled as Hannah reached out for Alice, a honey-brown Jersey with large, affectionate eyes. Alice strolled over to Hannah, who rubbed her hand under the cow's chin and down her neck.

'Alice can be your friend,' Hannah offered. Sylvia laughed, but her face froze when she realised Hannah was serious.

'You don't actually want me to...*pet her*, do you?'

'Oh, it's all right,' said Hannah. Gently, she guided Sylvia's hand—soft, delicate, not a callous in sight—onto a patch of white fur between the cow's ears. Together they brushed their fingers through Alice's hair and felt the warmth of her body against their palms. Hannah looked over at Sylvia and saw the faintest of smiles upon her face.

And then, as if colluding with Hannah on her plan to chase Sylvia away, Alice unfurled her thick grey tongue and licked Sylvia's cheek.

'*Oh!* No no no no *no*!' Sylvia jumped back in disgust. She grabbed her skirts and scrubbed furiously at her cheek. Hannah bit her lip to stifle her laughter.

Sylvia continued to mop her face and stumble backward until she tripped over a divot in the soft ground and fell flat into a fresh pile of cow dung.

Now Hannah couldn't stop the laugh that rose

through her body. She tried to cover it with a cough—unconvincingly—then walked over to help Sylvia off the ground.

But when she reached out her hand, Sylvia didn't reach back. She only lay on the ground, staring up at the sky in defeat.

This is it, thought Hannah. *She's had enough. She'll refuse the job, she'll find a better fit somewhere else in town, and I'll never have to see her gorgeous face again.*

'This is,' said Sylvia faintly, 'quite literally, the lowest I have ever been in my entire life.'

Hannah knelt down on the grass beside her and said nothing. Sylvia had to come to this conclusion on her own, without being pushed. *Go on.*

'I was *good* at what I did, what I used to do,' she continued, her voice gaining steam. 'I was *the best*. I had friends, and admirers, and I had a full dance card every night, and I was at the top of every guest list… I was at the top of *everything*. And now I'm *here*.'

Hannah nodded, but when Sylvia didn't continue, she tried to nudge her onward ever so gently. 'I'm sure there are jobs in town better suited to a person of your…rank. Farm work really is as low as it gets.' Hannah had to force these last words out of her mouth. *I'm doing it again*, she thought, embarrassed, *saying things I don't really mean.* Farm work was hard, but she wouldn't trade her life for any of the jobs in town.

She loved her cows, and she loved the mysterious art of cheesemaking. And she certainly didn't think a person's societal *rank* should determine what kind of job they should take.

She felt a stone drop in her stomach—getting Sylvia out of her life was turning her into a liar.

'I've already sought employment elsewhere,' Sylvia whispered. 'No one wants me.'

A bitter silence hung heavily between the two women, neither of whom were feeling like their best selves. Hannah stretched and lay down beside Sylvia. Alice joined them, resting a head on Hannah's lap. Clouds drifted from one side of their field of vision to the other before either of them felt like speaking.

'I would have had the most wonderful birthday party last month,' Sylvia said eventually. 'I've been thinking about that all day…here I am getting my hands dirty, staining my dress with sweat and mud, not a friend in the world…and I would have—I was *supposed to have*—a marvellously expensive ball thrown in my honour. Everyone would have danced with me. Everyone would have been there. Not a single cow in sight.'

Hannah didn't know what to say to this. Her birthday had also been a month ago, and the small celebration her family had held had, in fact, had cows in sight—but that'd made it no less wonderful. Maybe Sylvia just needed to see things differently.

Maybe working here could help her do exactly that.

'I truly am sorry, by the way,' Sylvia continued when Hannah said nothing, 'for how I acted in the shop. I was…*so rude.* I wouldn't blame you if you didn't want to hire me.'

'No, it's not that, it's…' But Hannah was done lying. 'Okay, you're right, I don't want to hire you. But that's not fair. And it's certainly not kind. I'm sorry too.' She tilted her head until her cheek rested on soft grass. She watched Sylvia watch the sky. 'I'm sorry for being so hard on you. I really meant it when I said that something good can still come from your time in Heene, and maybe…*just maybe*, it's possible that *something good* could be here at the farm.'

When Sylvia turned to face Hannah, all the tears she had held in earlier were sliding down her cheeks. 'It wouldn't be for long, you know.' She sniffed. 'I have a plan to get out of here. To get back on top. I just need some money to get it started.'

'All right, let's hear it then. Tell me your plan.'

'You'll think it's daft.'

'Probably.'

They both laughed, together, for the first time all day. Sylvia wiped the tears away from her face, then propped herself up on her elbows. 'I'm going to find a rich gentleman on holiday in one of the Worthing resorts, and I'm going to marry him.'

'Well, that sounds easy enough,' said Hannah. 'Isn't

that the kind of thing women of the peerage have to do all the time?'

'*Sometimes.*' Sylvia rolled her eyes. 'But most of us want a love match these days. And anyway, it's not hard to find a wealthy suitor when you're already decently wealthy yourself…or at least look the part. But I have nothing. No fancy gowns, no exclusive invites… I'm starting from scratch.'

'Hence the need for employment.' Hannah understood now just how desperate Sylvia was for a job. 'So you can buy yourself a dress.'

'But once I have *the dress*, I don't even know how I'd go about finding *the man*,' Sylvia confessed.

'Your mother grew up here. Can't you just do… whatever she did?'

'I wish, but her story is entirely different. Her's was an honest love match. She wasn't even trying to escape, it just kind of…*happened.*'

'So…no strategy to copy.'

They were silent again, until Sylvia sat straight up and spoke with renewed hope. 'You could help me.'

'I could what?'

'You could help me. You know Heene, and you know Worthing. You have connections, probably, with the kind of people who could help me scheme my way into a ball.'

'I—'

'And I could work for you, and save up money, and

we could find some fabric for a dress that would *look* more expensive than it really is—'

'Why would I help you?' Hannah was sitting up now too.

Sylvia widened her eyes innocently. 'Out of a sense of Christian charity, of course. Helping the less fortunate, and…and all that.'

'Try again.'

'Fine,' Sylvia huffed. She turned her face back to the sky. 'Because the sooner I'm out of Heene, the sooner you can hire a real farmhand who knows what they're doing.'

'Fair point…keep going.'

'And…well, surely there's something you want too. Something I could help you with.'

Hannah shrugged. 'I like my life.' And she meant it, truly. But Sylvia was right—there *was* something she wanted.

And Sylvia was smart—and persistent—enough to figure that out. 'There must be something else you want to spend your time on, if you're willing to delegate tasks to *me*. You need someone to work for you so you can do…well, whatever that *something else* is. So what is it?'

'You'll think it's daft.'

'Probably.' Sylvia smiled.

'I want to make cheese.'

'I thought you already *do* make cheese.'

'Yes, but…only one kind. The kind that sells easily. I want to *create*, to *experiment*. I want to make cheese with bold flavours, and fascinating textures, and I want to sell them all in my own shop.'

'It sounds like you could benefit from marrying rich too,' Sylvia muttered.

And then they looked right at each other, the idea hitting them both at the same time.

'I could marry rich for the both of us,' Sylvia said slowly. 'I could buy you a shop.'

Hannah searched for reasons to say no. 'I already have enough money for a shop,' she said. It was technically true, but she knew how easily she could be outbid, and she knew the expenses wouldn't end once she had purchased a building.

'But…' Hannah continued. 'But this isn't my world. The glamour, the opulence, the—the *scheming.*'

'And *this* isn't my world.' Sylvia gestured at her surroundings. 'But if we step into each other's worlds for just a moment—a few weeks, no more than that—we can *both* return to our own worlds, and we will *both* be better off for the experience. And then we'll have no need to ever meet again.'

'You'll be a wealthy wife of some viscount or duke…'

'…and you'll be a ground-breaking cheesemaker with your own shop.'

Hannah had to admit—it wasn't a bad idea, not at all.

'All right,' she said before she had time to change her mind. 'Let's do it.'

Sylvia extended her hand. 'This is how you do things here, yes?'

Hannah laughed and shook Sylvia's hand. 'Welcome to Heene, Sylvia Queensbury. You're one of us for now.'

'I guess I am,' Sylvia agreed. 'But not for long.'

'Not for long.' Hannah patted Alice's head and stood. 'We should get you cleaned off—you can borrow a dress until you have time for laundry—and then it's back to the milking parlour.'

'Right...' Sylvia's face fell. *Oh dear*, Hannah thought to herself, *she's remembering that this plan of hers requires actual work.*

Except it wasn't just Sylvia's plan anymore. It was theirs, together.

What have I gotten myself into?

Chapter Five

'I fear we've greatly underestimated whatever we've gotten ourselves into,' Rose whined as she examined her flour-crusted cuticles.

'I fear the same,' Sylvia agreed. She laced up the old leather half-boots the Pyles had loaned them, shoes that had already seen a lifetime of work.

I miss sleeping in late, Mary signed while Rose helped with her laces. The twins had biscuits to bake before the resort guests were ready for breakfast, and Sylvia had a morning milking to attend. Yesterday she had convinced Hannah to just let her watch, but she knew she'd get no such luck today.

Violet, meanwhile, had nothing to stitch in the back room of the modiste until a far more reasonable hour.

The three sisters yawned on their way out of the house.

'Is that a new dress?' asked Rose when they had stepped into the faintest light of early dawn.

'Oh, this...' Sylvia looked down at the almond-coloured cotton dress she was borrowing from Hannah. It didn't quite reach her ankles. 'It's not mine, I'm just wearing it until I can get the grey one cleaned.'

'Is that why the laundry bin smelled dreadful this morning?' Rose asked.

'Don't worry about it.' Sylvia walked a few paces ahead.

But when they reached the edge of the property, where she would turn right and the twins would turn left, she stopped. 'I do have a plan, you know. To get us out.'

Rose and Mary stopped too, then looked at their sister expectedly.

'Don't tell Mother or Violet yet... I want the plan to be more...*sophisticated*, before I bring them in. But I will tell the two of you, so that you may have some morsel of hope in your hearts as you sweat about the kitchen day in and day out.' She leaned in, and beckoned them to lean in too. 'I'm going to find a wealthy gentleman, and we shall be wed, and his fortune shall restore our family name.'

'You're going *fortune-hunting*!' Rose exclaimed.

'Well I don't appreciate such a crude characterisation—'

'But it's what you're doing, right?'

Sylvia sighed. 'Yes. I'm *fortune-hunting*. So fear not, for though your days may be grim now, I promise you there are better days ahead.'

The twins seemed more *amused* with the plan than buoyed by the prospect of its success, but at least Sylvia had given them something to smile about.

She watched her sisters walk toward Worthing, then leaned against a nearby fence post and drifted into a drowsy daydream, the kind with champagne towers and crisp white dance cards and glittering diamond chandeliers. An imaginary prince was just asking her to join him for a waltz when a rather rude dragonfly flew into Sylvia's face.

I'll be late, she thought as she hurried down the winding road to the Wickersham farm.

Hannah was already milking a cow in the parlour when Sylvia arrived.

Oh how my fortunes have changed...from the parlours of royalty to the parlours of cows.

'You could have waited for me,' Sylvia said between laboured breaths. 'I mean, I know I'm late, but I wasn't trying to get out of milking—'

'It's not up to me,' Hannah said calmly.

'Well then your parents—'

'It's not up to them either.' Hannah let go of the udders, rolled up her sleeves, and wiped her hands on her apron. 'We milk when the cows are ready to be milked. We churn the butter only after the cream rises, and we press the cheese only after hours of heating.'

Sylvia didn't entirely understand the references, but she got the point: *don't be late*. She sat, chastened somewhat, and grumbled, '*You* could have waited for me too, Alice.'

Hannah laughed and ran her fingers affectionately across the cow's flank. 'Alice is with her calf today. This is Henry.'

'How can you tell the difference? They all...look the same,' said Sylvia. Light brown fur, large ears, musty smell.

'I bet we all look the same to them, at first. But then they get to know us.' Hannah lifted the full bucket of milk effortlessly from under the cow, her forearms rippling with muscle.

Sylvia had never seen a woman so *strong*. It made her feel...well, she wasn't entirely sure what it made her feel. She tugged at the collar of her borrowed dress.

'Wait...' said Sylvia, her gaze caught on the bucket. 'Henry? I thought only girl cows produced milk.'

'After my grandfather died, we decided the next calf born would be named in his honour. The next calf happened to be female, and cows...well, they don't really care what you call them, a girl's name or a boy's name.'

Sylvia's eyes drifted back to Hannah, with her rolled-up sleeves and her pulled-back hair, and she realised with a start that Hannah was...well, beautiful. *If she ever put on a ballgown and curled that wavy orange hair of hers*, Sylvia thought, *she would have a line of suitors out the door.*

'Anyway,' Hannah said slowly, noticing that Sylvia

had been staring at her. 'You have to pet Henry before she lets you anywhere near her teats. She really makes you work for it.'

'I think Henry and I will get along then,' Sylvia said, rubbing her hand across Henry's soft underbelly. 'I like a woman with high standards.'

Hannah smiled and placed a fresh bucket under Henry's fuzzy, round udder. 'Position your hands like this.' She closed her fingers around two pink teats.

Sylvia leaned forward, but her hands wouldn't move.

'Sylvia…?'

'Right, yes, of course.' But her hands stayed firmly in her lap. 'But…well, remember our plan?'

'The plan to find you a wealthy husband?' Hannah asked.

'Yes, that plan,' Sylvia confirmed. 'What if I…oh, I don't know, what if I extend my hand for a gentleman suitor to kiss, and he notices…'

'Notices what?'

'Notices…whatever it is that udders do to one's hands.'

Hannah didn't say anything at first, and then she laughed. Sylvia wanted to feel embarrassed, but instead she found herself laughing too.

'First of all,' Hannah eventually said. 'I may be wrong, but don't you lot wear gloves when you're around *gentlemen suitors*?'

'Yes, but—'

'And *secondly*, you don't get hands like mine from a few weeks of milking. If our plan works as swiftly as we hope it will, you'll be back in London soon without a scratch.'

'Excellent...' Sylvia nodded. But she still couldn't get her hands to move. 'What does it feel like?'

'The best way to find out is to just—' But Hannah stopped herself, thinking. Then she placed her own hand over Sylvia's. 'Let me show you. Yes?'

'Yes,' Sylvia said, her whole body suddenly focused on the warmth and strength of Hannah's hand. She let Hannah guide her toward the udder and wrap her fingers around one of the squishy pink teats. At first she wanted to flinch away, but letting go of the cow would mean letting go of Hannah—and for reasons Sylvia didn't understand, that was the last thing she wanted to do.

'Now the other one, like this...' Hannah shifted behind Sylvia and guided her right hand into the same position as the left, so that Sylvia was surrounded by Hannah's steady embrace.

'And then we tug,' Hannah said, tightening her grip and moving Sylvia's hands down each teat in a quick rhythm as streams of white milk poured into the bucket. Sylvia was trying to pay attention to the task in front of her so she could replicate it on her own later, but every time she noticed Hannah's closeness— every time she noticed Hannah's arms pressed against her own, or Hannah's body leaning against her back, or Hannah's breath on her neck—her attention was pulled suddenly and blissfully away.

This is a very strange thing to enjoy, Sylvia thought, then told herself she must be so starved for genuine entertainment in this town that milking a cow was enough to excite her. And as for Hannah's closeness? Sylvia was simply longing for the familiar feeling of dancing with gentlemen.

She sat uneasily with these explanations, but they had to be true.

'My arms are getting sore,' Sylvia said, choosing to focus on the one bodily sensation that actually made sense. 'How do you manage this every day?'

'I think you mean *all* day,' Hannah said. 'We've only just begun. We come back in the evening for more milk, and in between we do everything else.'

The milk stopped flowing from Henry's udders, so Hannah let go of Sylvia. She leaned back and rinsed her hands in a nearby bucket of water. Sylvia's whole body was suddenly cold.

'Does *everything else* include a post-milking nap?' Sylvia asked, stretching her increasingly sore arms.

'No, but it does include a post-milking breakfast.'

They washed up together then left the barn for the main house, where they joined Hannah's parents, aunt, and cousin at a long wooden table in the kitchen.

The room was cosy: shelves of copper pots and cast-iron pans lined the cream-coloured walls, bundles of dried herbs hung from the ceiling rafters, and a bright fire crackled in the large stone hearth. On the mantel sat cooking utensils of all shapes and sizes, and Sylvia could only guess what they were used for.

'Welcome to your first meal at the Wickersham farm,' said Hannah's aunt as she placed a steaming bowl of porridge and peaches in front of her.

'Thank you,' Sylvia said, enchanted by the rich aroma of cinnamon, nutmeg, and brown sugar mixed with the sweet scent of cooked peaches and fresh milk. Her stomach rumbled and she reached for her spoon, dragged it through the creamy porridge and tasted the best thing she'd had all week.

Sylvia closed her eyes to relish the flavour, but when she opened them, she noticed no one else was eating. Everyone sat around her in unsettling silence, eyes closed and heads bowed. It took her a moment to realise what was happening. When she finally did, she dropped her spoon awkwardly on the table and assumed a posture of prayer.

The silence continued. Sylvia squirmed. She could never stand silence—the tension, the boredom, the forced proximity to her own lonely thoughts. When Mr Wickersham finally said *amen*, Sylvia breathed an uncomfortably loud sigh of relief.

'How's your first day on the job?' The question came from a remarkably tall and muscular young man with soft orange hair and wide, protruding ears. 'I'm Amos, by the way.'

Sylvia jumped at the opportunity to fill the silence with talk about herself. 'Exhausting,' she said between spoonfuls. 'I know what it feels like to be tired and aching after a long night of dancing, but *this* is something else entirely.'

The family exchanged glances, the kind that only those in the know could interpret. Sylvia pretended not to notice. 'Of course,' she continued, 'I am excited to learn more.'

'What does Hannah have you doing next?' asked Mrs Wickersham.

Sylvia glanced at Hannah, unsure.

'There's butter to churn,' Hannah replied. 'And cheese to pack for market. Who's on delivery today?'

'That'll be me,' said Amos.

'Ask around about how people are doing, will you? The Mercers especially, and the Hayes family.'

Sylvia's ears perked up at this. It had been a long time since she'd participated in any good gossip, and though she had no idea what Hannah was talking about, any conversation about people who weren't in the room felt like a scrap of home.

'Alister Coyle is doing all right,' said Amos with a tinge of bitterness in his voice. 'I can tell you that.'

'Hush now,' said Mr Wickersham. 'We don't have to like the man, but nothing good comes from gossip.'

There goes my scrap of home, thought Sylvia. It was then that she noticed Mrs Wickersham staring at her with wide amber eyes, the same ones that Sylvia had gotten used to seeing on Hannah's face. Her hair was pulled back beneath a white kerchief.

'I'm sorry,' said Mrs Wickersham as she lowered her eyes. But they flicked back up again, and she continued. 'You just…look *so much* like your mother did at your age. I see you there across the table and I have to remind myself it's 1824.'

'Did you know her well?' Sylvia asked. Her bowl was almost empty.

'A long time ago, yes.'

Sylvia had hardly spoken to her mother since their arrival in Heene, busy as they were. And before now—before their terrible fall from the peak of society—Sylvia had never wondered about her mother's life in Heene. All she knew was that Ella Queensbury had risen from some terrible, destitute past and transformed into one of London's most sophisticated, refined, and cultured ladies. That was all she ever needed to know.

'What was she like, back then?' Sylvia asked.

Mrs Wickersham didn't respond right away. She looked into the distance, lost in nostalgia.

'I didn't know her well,' Hannah's aunt chimed in. 'But I've heard she was a free spirit. Always climbing trees, or walking barefoot along the shore.'

'She collected shells.' Mrs Wickersham let her face soften into a smile. 'Bits of sea glass, colourful pebbles, whatever she could find. It might not sound strange *now*—plenty of women fancy themselves conchologists these days—but the Ella I knew did it just for the beauty of nature. Just for the fun of having something to find.'

Sylvia tried to imagine her mother scraping her knees against the bark of a tree, or strolling down the beach with shells in her hand and sand in her toes. The thought was incompatible with the Lady Queensbury she knew, the woman who stood in elegant gold gowns in front of spacious ballrooms welcoming nobles and royals into her home. Even now, after everything they've been through, Ella kept her hair curled and braided in the latest styles.

'But that's enough about the past.' Mrs Wickersham shook her head. 'We have plenty to do in the present.' She rose from the table, and she and her husband collected the dishes.

Amos and Hannah walked ahead of Sylvia on their way out of the house.

'I'm guessing you have…*plans* this evening?' Amos asked his cousin.

'Yes,' sighed Hannah. 'But it seems this will be the last evening I'll have *plans* for a while.'

'What plans?' Sylvia picked up her pace to catch

up with Hannah and Amos. 'I didn't think Heene had much of a night life.'

'It doesn't,' answered Amos.

Hannah glared at her cousin and said, rather tersely, 'I'm just saying goodbye to a friend.'

'So you'll be looking for a *new* friend, I assume?' Amos asked with a mischievous grin. He seemed to find this conversation much more amusing than Hannah did.

'I have plenty of friends. I have you, and…the cows…'

Amos looked over his shoulder at Sylvia. 'How long are you planning to stay in Heene?'

'A fortnight, at most.' It was an ambitious answer, Sylvia knew, but there was no harm in hoping.

'*A fortnight*,' Amos said to Hannah, then winked. 'Seems like the perfect amount of time for a *friendship*.'

'Don't you have cheese to deliver?' grumbled Hannah. She marched ahead to the barn, stepping on Amos's foot as she passed.

Though Sylvia wasn't exactly sure what to make of their conversation, she was starting to suspect that there might be more to Hannah than butter-making and Bible verses. She was also starting to suspect that continuing to learn more about Hannah wouldn't be the worst way to spend her time in Heene.

But first, of course, the butter-making.

'These are settling pans. They've been sitting out for two days,' Hannah said when they entered a small kitchen attached to the barn. She peered into the wide bowls on the counter, each one filled with milk. She explained to Sylvia how the cream rose to the top, and how they could use a flat brass disc with holes across its surface to skim the cream right off.

'Is that where the phrase *skim off the top* comes from?' Sylvia asked as she watched Hannah glide the skimmer across the surface. The cream folded in on itself like a swatch of pale yellow silk. Sylvia found the whole process more fascinating than she would ever admit out loud.

'It is indeed,' Hannah said. 'We have folks like that here, believe it or not. Folks across the wall who take more than they need, that don't leave enough for the rest of us.'

'Is that why you were asking about your neighbours, at breakfast?'

'I don't want to gossip...' Hannah started. She let the remaining milk drop from the skimmer before she continued. Sylvia was not getting used to the moments of silence that came so frequently at the Wickersham farm.

'But, yes.' Hannah placed the dollop of cream into a smaller bowl, then handed the skimmer to Sylvia. 'Worthing has been developing as a resort town for a few decades now, and it's beginning to grow into Heene.'

'But isn't that a good thing?' Sylvia's turn at skimming the cream wasn't nearly as smooth and graceful as Hannah's. 'I mean, if the people on holiday spend their money in Heene, or even move here—wouldn't that make life better for everyone?'

Sylvia imagined the hovel her family currently lived in. It was the type of residence that wouldn't have to exist if someone with money came and reimagined the village.

'It would make life better for some people. But most of us would get priced out of our shops, or even our homes. Land is needed to build resorts, and that land would be coming from the people who live here now.'

'But...' Sylvia wanted to keep arguing. Money *solves* problems. It doesn't *create* them. 'But you'd have all sorts of new customers for your cheese shop, someday.'

'I won't have a cheese shop if someone swoops in to buy all the buildings. And with wealthier residents and tourists come rising rents...you've never had to think about this kind of stuff, Sylvia. But trust me. There are better ways of lifting families out of poverty than placing them at the mercy of the rich.'

The comment stung. Sylvia was part of the group Hannah was criticising—but she also wasn't, not anymore. She was in between, unsettled, unsure of where she fit in.

'Well you won't have to worry about rising rents if we get you that shop first,' she offered. 'Shall we talk strategy?'

Sylvia hoped, for a moment, that Hannah would interrupt her clumsy cream-skimming to show her how it was done, just as she had when milking Henry. Part of her craved the touch of Hannah's hand over her own, moving in tandem across the settling pan.

But Hannah seemed determined to let Sylvia figure this one out on her own.

'We know you'll need a dress,' Hannah said. 'And a necklace, and a fan...'

'And a lady's maid!' Sylvia said excitedly. 'That's how we'll get you to join me.'

'Join you?'

'In Worthing, and at balls, and for luncheons and... Hannah, it wouldn't be proper for me to be seen without a chaperone.'

'Why not one of your sisters?' Hannah started to scoop their bowls of cream into a large wooden barrel, then handed Sylvia a small ceramic jug that she could use to church her own single batch of butter.

'Rose and Mary are too young, and Violet...she doesn't know yet. She has too much going on right now.'

'And your mother?'

'Oh, she's—it's complicated!' Sylvia was becoming frustrated. Need she explain her entire family dynamic to Hannah?

Then again, she had asked Hannah far more personal questions today than Hannah had asked her.

'We're still in this together, right?' Sylvia quickened the pace of her handheld churn.

'Yes, but I assumed I'd be playing a more…advisory role.'

'But courting is…it's a whole production! Usually there's a *team* of people preparing a young lady to catch a husband. I'll need you for promenades, and dates, and hair and makeup of course—'

'I didn't realise your courtship rituals were so complicated.' Hannah finished filling her barrel, then gripped its handle and spun.

'Well, what about you?' Sylvia asked. 'What are your courtship rituals? If you don't care about appearances, how do you attract suitors?'

'Who says I don't care about appearances?' Hannah's face was serious.

'Oh—' Sylvia stopped churning, her hands now over her face. 'I'm so sorry, I didn't mean to imply— You just don't, you don't curl your hair or anything, but— but you are quite comely. Really beautiful, I think.'

Hannah held her expression for just a moment longer, then broke into a wide grin. 'Of course I don't care about *appearances*, Sylvia. But now I know the best way to get a compliment out of you is to just let you talk.'

Sylvia gasped, embarrassed but glad that she hadn't actually insulted Hannah. Still, she decided it was best to stop talking for now. She listened to the scrape of damp wood against the butter-making jug, the squish of cream going solid. Flecks of white splashed across her hands. Her armpits dampened with the sweat of hard work. She sighed.

'Do you actually like them?' Hannah eventually asked.

'Who?'

'The suitors. The men. Do they make you feel... *smitten*?'

'Of course they do,' Sylvia said, but her words were more automatic than genuine. She was becoming too exhausted to be anything other than honest. 'Or, they *will*. They'll make me feel smitten, enamoured, enchanted, all that...but no, not yet.'

'Why not?'

'I had no suitors while in mourning, and the year before I was too young to take the whole thing seriously. This year—this was supposed to be my year.'

Hannah nodded. 'The year of falling in love?'

'Exactly. The year of falling in love. But now...now it's the year of fortune-hunting.'

The churning ended and they transitioned to straining the buttermilk from the cream—which was now, astonishingly, real butter. Sylvia smiled. 'Like magic!'

'Like hard work,' Hannah said.

They rinsed the butter with water several times. Sylvia was so tired she couldn't imagine doing anything else but falling into her bed and staying there for days. Then she remembered that Hannah, somehow, had the energy to entertain a guest tonight.

'Who are you seeing, after this? The friend you're saying goodbye to.'

'You really are a terrible gossip,' Hannah said.

'It's not gossip if I'm talking *to* you *about* you!' Sylvia crossed her arms. 'That's just a *conversation*.'

Hannah didn't say anything for a while. Sylvia grew nervous that she was annoying Hannah—which shouldn't matter, really, because Hannah's opinion of her had no bearing on their fortune-hunting scheme. They didn't need to like each other. They were partners in husband-hunting, nothing more.

But Sylvia couldn't stop herself from feeling relieved when Hannah eventually spoke. 'You're right,' she said. 'It *is* just conversation. I'm not…very good at talking about myself. But I'm seeing a friend who… was special to me. *Is* special to me, for now. But this friend is leaving, so, our friendship isn't going any further.'

'Oh…' Sylvia didn't know what to say. Hannah had given her practically no details, but Sylvia got the sense that even this was more than Hannah was used to sharing. She eventually settled on: 'That's terribly sad.'

'I'm all right, really. We knew it was going to end from the start.'

'It sounds like... Correct me if I'm wrong, but it sounds like you fancy him? This friend of yours.' Sylvia was curious now. She'd never felt any real desire to be with a man—not in *that* way, at least. She wanted to know what it was like, so she could recognise when it happened to her. Which it definitely would, as she kept telling herself.

She had been telling herself that for a long time.

Hannah hadn't spoken yet, but had a complicated look on her face. She was smiling, but it was...a protective smile. A secret smile.

Sylvia kept coaxing. 'How can you tell when you fancy someone? This definitely isn't gossip, it's just me asking for advice.'

'Have you ever swam in the ocean, Sylvia?'

'Of course...?' Sylvia was thrown by the sudden change in conversation.

'I don't mean have you ever *been* in the ocean, with a bathing machine to carry you across the sand and a dipper to hold you in the water. I mean have you ever *swam* in the ocean, all on your own?'

'Do people really do that?' Sylvia raised her eyebrows. Hannah stopped talking for a moment to show

Sylvia how to shape their butter into rectangular wooden moulds, then press them onto plates and prepare them for sale. Sylvia fidgeted through the entire process, eager to hear how Hannah was about to connect swimming in the ocean to falling in love.

'Go for a swim someday,' Hannah said, 'then you'll know how it feels when you fancy someone.'

Before Sylvia could ask further, Hannah continued.

'On second thought, don't go for a swim on your own. That wouldn't be safe. I'll take you someday, maybe. If you'd like.'

'I think I would,' Sylvia said without really thinking about it. The idea of being thrown about by cold, salty waves was absurd…but as she settled into the rhythm of shaping butter into bricks, her mind drifted to that giant blue-grey expanse, and what it would feel like to be held by Hannah, to be pulled into the sea by Hannah's strong, steady, muscular arms…

Sylvia dropped the wooden mould. Butter splattered across her torso and up her neck, which made Hannah giggle.

'You are quite a mess,' she said.

Sylvia laughed too, but she felt her cheeks turning pink.

'Here, let me help,' Hannah said. She turned Sylvia to face her, and her eyes travelled the length of Sylvia's body. Slowly, she reached out her hand, then gently swiped a spot of butter from just below Sylvia's lips. Hannah placed her buttered finger into her own mouth, and hummed with satisfaction.

Sylvia felt a twist in her stomach that she'd never felt before, a tumultuous twist that spread to her chest and her knees and the tips of her toes.

Like spinning too quickly on the ballroom floor. Like riding a carriage through bumpy roads. Like both of these things, but not quite.

Maybe, Sylvia wondered, it was like swimming in the sea.

Chapter Six

'Do you ever wonder about the moon?' Esther asked.

She and Hannah had been lying next to each other for a while before either of them spoke, stretched out on a thick blanket over the damp grass of the Worthing Common. They were listening to the waves crash over the sand and rush back to the sea. They were watching the clouds, dark and thin, drift across a bright crescent moon.

'Wonder in what way?' Hannah asked.

'In Genesis, the moon was made on the fourth day. So were the sun and the stars. But *light* was made on the first day…before the sun, before the stars, before the moon. Kind of strange, don't you think?'

Hannah rolled to face Esther. 'Very strange. What do you think it means?' She liked to watch Esther's thinking face: her dark eyebrows knit together, her lips folded inward.

'I guess it means the light comes from somewhere else,' she eventually said.

'And the moon is just taking care of it for a while,' Hannah added. 'Sharing it with the sun.'

And then they were quiet again. It was far easier to talk about the sun and the moon than what they were really there to say.

Hannah moved her fingers slowly around Esther's open palm, like an ice skater on a frozen lake. She dragged her fingers up Esther's arm, lightly touching her warm skin for one more night. She let her mind wander across time: skipping stones with Esther when they had just met, setting out to own a shop sometime in the future, cleaning butter from Sylvia's face earlier that day.

'I'm so terrible at goodbyes,' Esther blurted out.

'I think everyone is,' whispered Hannah.

'I want to say I'll be back next year but…who knows? Maybe by then I'll have settled down somewhere, or found myself a husband.' She sighed. 'Maybe you will have too.'

Hannah thought back to what Sylvia had asked her earlier: *How can you tell when you fancy someone?*

Hannah had felt great affection for three young women in her life—maybe even love, but they never stayed long enough for her to decide if that's what she was feeling. She'd felt that way for a young man once, a fisherman's son who had sailed to other ports soon after they'd met. She enjoyed kissing him just as much as the others, but…somehow she just knew she didn't want a husband.

But she'd never met another woman who truly wanted a wife.

'We don't have husbands yet,' Hannah said, and leaned in to kiss Esther's neck, her cheeks, her lips. Esther kissed back, slowly at first. And then they were a passionate mess of roving hands and shifting legs, both of them terrible at goodbyes and not wanting to be any better than this.

'I've missed butter,' Violet pined. 'I've missed butter *so much*.'

It was the first morning all week that none of the five Queensburys had to work, and so they had by popular decision resolved to throw a picnic. Ella set a blanket in the meadow beside their cottage, Violet unloaded a gift basket of food sent by their neighbours, Rose and Mary arranged the leftover scones they'd smuggled from the resort—and Sylvia presented to all of them a small disc of butter she'd made herself at the Wickersham farm.

You made this? signed Mary.

'It's like magic,' said Sylvia. 'Like…like a witch's brew. One moment you have a jar of milk, and then you wave a wand around for a while until you remove the lid and you've got butter!'

Her sisters giggled, but their mother was unconvinced. 'It's a great deal of hard work though, isn't it, Sylvia?'

'Oh, *yes*,' Sylvia said with an exaggerated sigh. 'I fear I may never move my arms again.'

'You're moving them *right now*,' said Rose.

'I may never move them again for something other than eating.' Sylvia reached for the basket and added some blackberries to her plate.

'I hope that's not true,' said Violet, who had finished her scone and moved onto a juicy plum. 'You're quite the talented butter-maker. Delicious, really.'

'Does it feel good?' asked Ella. 'To make something with your own hands.'

Sylvia thought about her question for a moment. The ever-present ache in her forearms certainly didn't feel *good*, and neither did the stiffness in her shoulders. But when she looked at the butter dish, nearly empty now, her heart swelled with…something.

Something like *pride*, perhaps?

And then she remembered where else her butter had been. She thought of Hannah standing in front of her, swiping butter from Sylvia's face and tasting it on her own finger. Sylvia felt a rush of heat through her entire body.

But even though the memory was decidedly pleasant every time it bubbled up in Sylvia's consciousness, it was an *unfamiliar* kind of pleasant, and Sylvia had already met her quota for unfamiliar experiences by the first day of her temporary life in Heene.

She had no desire to get used to this place—and she *especially* had no desire to grow attached to Hannah Wickersham.

'Not really,' Sylvia said, returning to her mother's question. 'It's nice to have something to share with you all, of course, but we cannot lose sight of where we belong. *We* purchase butter that *other people* make. We don't make it ourselves.'

No one argued—*quite right*, Sylvia thought to herself. And then they each had a barley sugar drop, and Mary and Rose left for their afternoon shift at the resort, and their morning together was over.

As they folded the blanket and gathered the dishes, Sylvia offered to style her mother's hair. 'I think you've forgotten to put it up today,' she said. Ella's thick blond locks were wrapped in a bun beneath a white kerchief, like the one Hannah's mother had worn the other day.

Ella didn't answer at first, but as they reached the house she said: 'I think I'll keep it this way.'

'But—' Sylvia tried to protest.

'Not expecting any visitors, are we?'

'Well no, but—'

'Then it doesn't seem to matter either way.' Ella's voice was cheerful. 'The two of you have work today, yes?' She turned her attention to the pile of gowns and pants and stockings that sat on their kitchen table. Sylvia and Violet eyed each other nervously, but left the house without a fight.

'She *is* right,' Violet said when they reached the road. 'We're not expecting any visitors…so it's not like anyone is going to see her…'

'Right, right.' Sylvia nodded. 'Completely harmless. But…it is strange, yes?'

'So strange!' Violet exclaimed. She and Sylvia had both gotten out of bed before the picnic to curl and style their hair.

'That will never be me,' Sylvia said. 'We've got to remember who we are—and we've got to remember that we don't belong in Heene.'

'Well…' Violet said hesitantly. 'I mean, I do agree with you, of course. But I also want to know people while I'm here. To make friends. In fact, I've already met…' She bit her lip.

'You've met whom?'

'I've met a friend.'

'All right…tell me about her.'

'He's—'

'He's?' Sylvia's heart began to pound. *Great, now my chest is just as sore as the rest of my body.*

'Yes, *he's* a kind young man who lives in Heene. I met him at the market.'

'And what are his *intentions*?'

'It's not like that, Sylvia…he's just sweet.'

Sylvia didn't like the wistful look in Violet's eyes, the tiny smile that was forming at the edge of her lips.

'And anyway,' Violet hurried to continue, 'I don't have enough time in the day to really *spend* it with anyone. You don't have to worry.'

'I'm going to worry.'

'Well don't.'

They were standing in the middle of the road now, staring at each other defiantly. Sylvia studied her sister, a year younger and an inch shorter. She had the angular jaw of their mother and the vibrant hazel eyes of their father. Neither sister blinked.

Tension filled the space between them, until Sylvia reminded herself that *this was nothing*. Sylvia was going to save her sister from this place before any serious attachments could be formed.

'All right,' Sylvia conceded. 'I will try not to worry. I am happy you're…' She forced a smile. 'Making friends.'

'I hope you are too,' Violet said, as she set off in the direction of the modiste.

On Sylvia's way to the farm, she turned her thoughts to finding a husband. She needed to secure an invitation to…something. Anything, really. An event with dancing would be ideal, but a dinner or even a luncheon would do. And to secure an invitation, she needed to know who was spending their summer holiday in Worthing; then she would need *them* to find out *she* was in Worthing—

But not like this! Sylvia panicked as two young ladies exited the hat shop—two young ladies from two of the most esteemed families in England.

Sylvia dashed off the road and crouched behind a tall potted bush. She placed a hand on her chest and tried to slow her breathing, then peeked through the branches to watch the pair stroll by.

Tall and dainty with chestnut hair and an eye-catching sea-green grown, Miss Augusta Beaumont was everything a woman of nineteen wanted to be. Her sister had made a decent match earlier that season—nothing too impressive of course, not even the heir to a title—but still more than what Sylvia had. Augusta walked past the bush where Sylvia was hiding, too busy admiring her new wide-brimmed hat to notice someone peering at her through the shrubbery.

'Do you think it's too much lace?' she asked Miss Catherine Fitzroy.

'There's no such thing as too much lace.'

Their lady's maids walked several paces behind them, carrying shopping bags. Sylvia heard them whispering about how there *was indeed such a thing as too much lace.*

And then came an entirely different voice.

'Do you often hide behind bushes?'

Sylvia turned with a sharp inhale to see a man standing behind her. No, not just a man—a *gentleman.*

She looked to make sure the street was clear of anyone who would recognize her, then she stood and curtsied. 'I did not wish to be seen by…' By *whom*? Sylvia didn't have time to come up with a story, so she simply said: '…people.'

'People?'

'Yes. For personal reasons.' She crossed her arms.

'Well, far be it from me to get in the way of a lady and her covert machinations.'

A lady.

Sylvia really looked at the gentleman standing before her, whom she was *sure* she did not recognize. And he must not recognize her, either, though he did recognize something vital *about* her—despite the modest dress, despite the naked ears and gloveless hands, he could sense that *she was a lady.*

This gentleman, of course, had no trouble communicating that he was of noble rank: his clothes were well-tailored, his cravat crisp and white, his top hat of the latest fashion. *And*, realised Sylvia excitedly, *he is handsome.* His dark curly hair perfectly framed his straight nose and strong jawline.

'It appears,' Sylvia said as she glanced behind herself once more, 'that the people I was hiding from are no longer nearby.'

'Then you're safe,' he said with a chuckle. His eyes flicked down to her feet and back, so quickly Sylvia almost didn't notice. 'And are you…all right?'

Sylvia paused. 'Yes,' she said slowly, constructing her answer as she spoke. 'I decided to spend my morning walking along the shore collecting seashells.

I didn't want to sully any of my dresses…the laundress has enough work to do without me mucking about in my Sunday best.'

He smiled and nodded. Sylvia couldn't tell if he believed her, but he seemed amused nonetheless. And then, he raised his eyebrows as if remembering something important.

'If you fancy yourself an amateur conchologist…' He searched his pockets for a moment, then produced a small, swirling seashell. 'Allow me to add to your collection.'

He placed the shell in her open palm, carefully, so his fingers wouldn't graze her gloveless skin.

'You are too kind,' Sylvia said as she admired the golden spire. She ran her thumb along the bumpy ridges, from the round opening to the pointy top. 'I take it you're a collector as well?'

'Not me,' he said. 'My aunt. But she has plenty of these already. Shelves and shelves of everything, really—fossils, plant life, jars of sand from faraway places.'

'Is she travelling with you?'

'No, no, she mostly stays at her home in France. I just came from her house, actually, the last stop on my Grand Tour.'

Sylvia could hardly believe her luck. This whole time, while her life had been falling to pieces, Prince Charming over here had been travelling the Continent unaware of anything happening to the Queensburys.

It was almost *too* perfect.

Sylvia opened her mouth to respond—but a nearby voice interrupted their moment.

The gentleman spun around and called something back—*in French.* She cursed her past self. She really should know what was being said, but she had never paid enough attention in her French lessons.

He turned back to Sylvia and shared another smile, this one wide and charming and just the slightest bit mischievous. 'Perhaps our paths shall cross again.'

And then he was gone.

Sylvia stood still. Then she slowly closed her hand around the shell, checked the road for old acquaintances, and hurried to the farm.

'I found him,' she said when she finally reached Hannah, who was out in the herb garden pulling weeds. 'At least, I *think* I found him. A potential *him.* For fortune-hunting.'

'Excellent,' Hannah said without looking up from her work. 'What's his name?'

'His name is—' Sylvia stopped. She didn't know. One day into fortune-hunting and she had already messed up. '*Shit.*'

Hannah wiped her hands on her apron, then looked up at Sylvia. 'Interesting. I've never met anyone named *shit.*'

Down in the dirt, the sweet and savoury scents of rosemary, basil, and thyme enveloped Hannah's senses and filled her with peace—a peace that had just been interrupted by hurried footsteps, panting breaths, and now this announcement about a potential suitor for Sylvia.

'I'm joking, of course,' Hannah said as Sylvia glared down at her. 'His name obviously isn't… Oh, just come sit with me. You can tell me all about this mystery man while you learn how to weed a garden.'

'I thought this was a dairy farm,' Sylvia said as she settled into place next to Hannah. 'Last time I checked, milk doesn't grow on trees.'

'A very keen observation, Sylvia. Now lean in and smell the plants, then tell me if you'd rather be in the barn right now.'

She watched Sylvia close her eyes, then breathe in deeply. A small white butterfly floated around Sylvia's shiny curls, then dipped along the slope of her neck and out into the pasture. Sylvia was trying to stop herself from smiling, from letting on how *delicious* this experience was. But Hannah could see the joy in her face nonetheless, a warm and contagious joy.

'It's okay to let yourself like it here,' Hannah chided. But Sylvia's smile was already fading.

'I won't be here long enough to like it. Especially now that I have a suitor.'

'You don't *have* a suitor.' Hannah rolled her eyes.

'Not *yet*. But I do have—'

'Work while you talk,' Hannah said, even though

she had pulled most of the weeds by now. 'You've got to earn that dress, remember?'

'Right, yes.' Sylvia nodded. She yanked out a small, dark green sprout, leaving the roots embedded in the soil. 'I do have a *potential* suitor. He's been on the Continent for a few years, so he doesn't know me— and more important, he doesn't know I'm penniless.'

'That's promising,' Hannah agreed. 'But first— you've got to pull the whole weed, Sylvia. If you leave the roots in the soil, it'll just grow back. Here, let me show you…'

She reached for Sylvia's soft, slender hand. Fingers entwined, they pressed into the warm, damp soil, twisting gently in search of the buried root. Hannah tried to ignore her quickening heartbeat, her shallow breaths, the warmth of Sylvia's body against her own…

And then, with a quiet *pop*, they loosed the root from the ground. Hannah pulled her hand away a bit too quickly. 'Just like that,' she said weakly.

Sylvia flashed a triumphant smile. 'I suppose there's no use in being good at something I'll never do again, but it seems I just can't help myself.'

Hannah ran her fingers through her hair, and any lingering tenderness evaporated. *That's the Sylvia I know*, she thought. *Vain as ever*. 'So…tell me more about this *potential* suitor.' Hannah monitored the growth of the herbs while Sylvia took care of the remaining weeds. She pulled about half of them correctly.

'He's very dignified. He speaks *French*. And I didn't get his name, but surely it won't be hard to find out who he is. My usual channels of gossip are cut off, of course, but I'll think of something.'

'I'm sure you will,' Hannah said and offered a hand. She helped Sylvia off the ground. 'But before that you'll need a dress. I don't know anything about fashion, and frankly I don't care to, but I *do* know a thing or two about resourcefulness. Frugality. How to take something ordinary and stretch it into whatever you need it to be. So let's just get you enough money to buy an old dress in a nice colour and we'll spruce it up from there.'

Sylvia nodded. 'Surely all those weeds get me part of the way there.'

'Maybe the ones that aren't still rooted in the dirt…'

Hannah was equal parts exasperated and amused with Sylvia. There was something charming about seeing farm life through new eyes—tasks that were second nature to Hannah were remarkably strange and difficult for Sylvia. She had to admire the tenacity of this pale, delicate woman who would not give up, day after day, even though she so clearly wanted to.

But tenacity alone was not enough to get the weeds out properly.

'Let's get you going on butter,' Hannah said. 'We

have some big orders coming up.' And then, though she usually didn't bother to think of where her orders came from and why, Hannah had an idea. 'I suppose that might mean some dinner parties are happening this week. Something to look into, maybe.'

'You're brilliant!' Sylvia said excitedly.

'Just observant,' Hannah countered. She got Sylvia started with the butter—this time with the heavy barrel churn—then left to spend some quality time with her cheese.

Hannah had only rotated three shelves of cheddar when Sylvia was back, knocking on her door.

'Is something the matter?' asked Hannah.

'The butter is all wrong.'

Hannah paused, then rotated one more wheel. She whispered to the rest of the cheese, 'I'll be back for you in just a moment.'

'Yes?' Hannah said when she had stepped outside. Sylvia peered into the cheese shed as the door swung open then closed. She widened her eyes.

'Those look heavy.'

'I'm strong. What's happening with the butter?'

'Oh, come and see,' Sylvia said dramatically, as if the whole barn had burned down.

They walked to the barn kitchen and Sylvia opened the barrel churn. 'It's just…not butter.'

'Not yet,' Hannah said. She found a spoon and tasted the lumpy cream. 'You're…halfway done.'

'*Halfway?*' Sylvia began to massage her arms.

'Dairy takes time,' said Hannah, trying with little success to sound patient. All she wanted was to get back to her cheese. *You think butter takes time?*

'I *hate* this,' Sylvia whined. 'I hate making butter, I hate that my arms are burning, I hate that I'm so *bad* at everything here!' She buried her face in her hands.

'What if… I let you teach *me* something,' said Hannah slowly. As irritating as Sylvia could be, Hannah couldn't stand to see her like this. 'Once you finish with the butter.'

'Teach *you* something?'

'Something you're good at and I'm not. Something like…oh, I don't know, how to curtsy.'

'Surely you know how to curtsy.'

'Never learned.' Hannah shrugged. 'Do we have a deal?'

Sylvia bit her lip, clearly trying to cover a smile. And then: 'I don't mind that deal.'

'Very well.' Hannah was already regretting the offer.

Back in the cheese shed, Hannah paused as she often did to marvel at the small cathedral she had built for herself, the columns of yellow and orange and gold that lined the walls like fiery stained glass windows. She approached her wheels with reverence—tending them was hard work, of course, and often frustrating, but Hannah never needed something to be easy for it to be holy.

She managed to rotate the rest of the wheels, to wrap portions of various sizes for market, and to tinker around with her own secret recipes before Sylvia returned.

'Are you ready to become a lady?' she heard Sylvia call.

'Let's see that butter first.' Hannah stepped outside, hoping the final product was decent enough to sell. And, much to her surprise and delight, it was.

She nodded approvingly. 'You'll need to clean up some of those edges for the next batch, but this…this is certainly butter.'

She looked across the table to see Sylvia's proud smile, but also the exhausted slump in her shoulders, the stray bits of hair flying from otherwise orderly curls.

Now it was Hannah's turn to be thrown out of her element.

'You begin with heels together…' Sylvia said when they had reached the far edge of the pasture. Hannah didn't want to risk being seen by anyone as she made a fool of herself. '…and with your toes pointed out, you have something of a *V* shape. Like so.'

Hannah mimicked Sylvia's steps.

'Very good,' Sylvia continued. The confidence in her voice was unmistakable, and Hannah realised that this was likely the first time in weeks Sylvia had felt like herself. 'Next, bring your right foot behind you in a circle, then gracefully shift your weight to the back leg...' Sylvia dipped back until her legs had swapped poses: now the right knee was bent and the left toes were pointed forward, her waist elegantly tilted and her eyes lowered to the grass. '...then pinch your gown with your fingers and lift your skirts so that the fabric fans out but doesn't lift too high.'

Hannah exhaled loudly through her nose, a habit of hers whenever she was annoyed. But she shifted her weight anyway, dipping low until her left leg was extended and her dress was stretched open. She held the pose as Sylvia walked around her, examining, and tried to remember a Bible verse about the virtue of patience.

'A good start,' said Sylvia. 'You'll need to clean up those edges, but this...this is certainly a curtsy.'

'Tell me what to do differently.' Hannah held the pose.

'Well first—' said Sylvia. 'You're gripping the fabric. There's never a reason for a lady to make a fist like this. Just use your fingers... And now you rise as slowly as you dipped...'

Hannah did as she was told, wobbling, her eyes moving up from the hem of Sylvia's dress to the soft pink of her face.

Sylvia's skin wasn't used to getting this much sun, but Hannah thought the colour suited her quite well.

Buttercup pranced over to Hannah's side and interrupted her thoughts before they had time to develop into anything other than a passing appreciation of Sylvia's beauty.

'Are you here for curtsy lessons too?' Hannah asked as she knelt down to pet her sweet friend.

'There's such love in your eyes,' Sylvia said as she knelt gingerly in the grass. 'Every time you look at her. Or any of the cows, really.' She delicately placed her hand on Buttercup's lower back. 'And the plants too.'

'I guess that's because I do.' Hannah shrugged. Sylvia joined her on the ground. 'I do love them. Some people see cattle just as objects, as products, as a source of income…especially on the larger farms. One time I met a farmer who didn't even know all his animals by name. My dad says that was unheard of a generation ago. They're living beings, just like you and me. They're worthy of respect and love.'

'And so are the plants?'

'So are the plants.'

'Except the weeds?'

Hannah laughed. 'They're added back to the soil, where they decay and nurture the herbs. Even that is a kind of love.'

Grass swayed in the quiet wind and brushed against their bare legs, stretched out from under their skirts. The sweet scent of wildflowers wafted their way, and hints of sunlight drifted down from an otherwise cloudy sky.

'Isn't there more work to do?' Sylvia asked.

'Oh, plenty.' But Hannah didn't want to get up just yet. Sylvia would be gone from Heene, from the farm, and from Hannah's life soon enough—she supposed there was no use spending the rest of her day exasperated with so temporary a guest.

And there is no use getting close to her, either, Hannah reminded herself. The fact that Sylvia fit the description of Hannah's usual type was not lost on her—a transient young woman with plenty of free time and no current marriage prospects—but Sylvia was also too…shallow. Too talkative. Too attached to the very society that had abandoned her in her time of need.

But even as Hannah's thoughts spun in circles—*Sylvia is annoying, and beautiful, and clever, and rude*—she sat still and listened to the wind-rustled trees. She listened to the bellowing cows and she breathed in the floral air and she watched the silver rain clouds in the distance drift over the sea. She let herself be held, embraced, by Heene.

'Shall we get started, then?' Sylvia asked. But when Hannah looked over, Sylvia was lying in the tall green grass, her eyes closed, a satisfied smile on her face.

'What's all this work for,' Hannah asked in return, 'if not for moments like this?'

Chapter Seven

'I still don't know what business you have opening a cheese shop outside of Cheshire,' Mr Luxford grumbled as Hannah entered his store just as it was closing. She hadn't even said anything—he could tell by the look of her face she was there to bargain.

'Cheshire makes fine cheese,' Hannah said. 'But I'm trying to make the best.'

Hannah had forgotten the eerie *tick, tick, tick* of the shop's display clocks that filled the silence between sentences. Their wide, round faces glared down at Hannah, reminding her that Heene was running out of time.

Hannah pulled a thick slice of cheese wrapped in cloth from her apron pocket. She held it out to him. 'I don't just want people to come to Heene for a cheese named Heene,' she said. 'I want them to come to Heene for a cheese they've never tasted before, a cheese they'll never taste again.' She was projecting a kind of confidence she rarely showed other people, and she hoped it was convincing enough.

'I've known your family a long time, Hannah.' His voice softened, but his face was still firm. 'I respect what you're trying to do here, and I'm not entirely opposed, but can't you see the way the world is headed?'

She lowered her hand, clutching the cheese. 'Where do you think the world is headed, Luxford?'

He sighed, then looked around his shop. He pointed at a towering longcase clock with flowers and leaves and bundles of grapes carved into its reddish-brown wood. Hannah admired its beauty in the dim evening light that fell from the windows.

'Took me two weeks to make,' he said. 'Someday a machine will be able to make ten of them in an hour.'

'That's ridiculous,' Hannah said quickly, but she knew there was some truth to what he was saying. Every day the newspaper ran some new story about some new invention that was going to revolutionise all of England, and then England would revolutionise all the world.

That's the language people were using, but Hannah didn't think a world of mechanised labour and factory wages was any sort of revolution at all.

'Just try it,' she said. 'And I'll leave.'

He eyed the bundle in her hand suspiciously, but

eventually took it. 'Mark my words,' he said as he un-folded the cloth. 'As go the clocks, so go the cheese.'

Hannah didn't argue further. *Let the cheese speak for itself.*

He took a slow bite, the pale yellow wedge heavy in his hand. He chewed for a moment, then tried to hide the deep satisfaction on his face.

He hid the satisfaction poorly.

'Tell me a factory can make that,' Hannah said. And then, she pointed at the clock. 'Tell me a factory can make *that*.'

She knew what he was tasting. She knew the sharp, tangy opening notes, the gradual creamy finish, the buttery aftertaste. She knew the grass that fed the cows that gave the milk, how even the soil itself added to the rich flavour Mr Luxford was experiencing.

'Let it never be said about me that I can't recognise good craftsmanship,' Mr Luxford said eventually, hiding a compliment for Hannah in a compliment to himself. She knew it was the most he would offer, and she smiled to receive it.

'Even still,' he continued. 'I'm not so easily persuaded…but I'll be patient with my other offers, and I'll consider your proposal.' He bit into the wedge of cheese once more, and Hannah nodded goodbye.

But perhaps, she thought to herself as she left the shop, *there will be more to say in days to come.* If she could truly slow Mr Luxford's decision, then maybe, *just maybe*, she would have a proper sum of money before he accepts another offer. A proper sum of money from a proper rich husband—*whom we have yet to properly find.*

Sylvia knew she wasn't going to find a proper gown at the second-hand store—she had told herself to keep expectations low *several* times on her walk over—but she somehow couldn't stop herself from being disappointed at the dismal selection of clothes on the rack.

'Do you have any more in the back?' Sylvia asked Betty, which earned her a nudge in the ribs from Violet. 'I only *mean*,' Sylvia hurried to salvage the interaction, 'that these are all so *lovely*, I simply *must* know if you have more of them.'

Betty raised her eyebrows, unconvinced. 'You know how to get to the modiste. Go along then, if you want something more suitable to your tastes.'

Violet giggled. 'I can even fit you myself!'

'I'll make do,' Sylvia grumbled. She shuffled through the rack as Betty shared some recent work with Violet, a child's dress that had nearly torn in two.

'You can't even tell!' Violet gasped, astonished. Sylvia silently wondered if she'd ever get that excited over a glass of milk or a wedge of cheese.

Unlikely.

'The trick is…' Betty started. But Sylvia's attention was pulled instead to a shimmering blue gown in the corner, deep and vibrant as sapphire, that stood out among all the rest. She pulled the fabric into her hands and felt at home.

'That one came in yesterday,' Betty said. 'The niece of a resort owner, moving to the country and downsizing her wardrobe. It didn't even need mending.'

It was the nicest gown in the shop by far, and Sylvia would have been happy to find it—if she had more than two weeks of farm wages in her hand.

Sensing Sylvia's concern, Violet spoke up: 'Let me help.'

Sylvia gasped. 'You wouldn't.'

'Well, first of all, I *would*—'

'No, sorry. Of course you would. I mean *you can't*.'

Violet walked over to Sylvia and placed a gentle hand on her shoulder. There was so much in Violet's eyes when she looked at her sister. Hope, Sylvia could tell, but sadness too.

'If this is what it takes to get us back home, then *yes*, Sylvia, yes I can.'

Sylvia had never been the sentimental type, but as she stared at her sister she felt a tug at the base of her throat, that tell-tale sign of oncoming tears. She hugged Violet, tighter than she ever had before.

'Thank you,' she whispered. And then she pulled away, fighting to keep her face dry.

They paid Betty for the dress, for some thread, and for some scraps of lace and tulle, then they hurried through the rainy streets of Heene.

Sylvia knocked on the Wickershams' door. When Hannah answered, her eyes travelled between the damp sisters, the shopping bags in their arms, and the desperate expression on Sylvia's face. She let out an exasperated sigh.

'Please,' was all Sylvia said.

'All right, come in.'

The air beyond the threshold was warm and sweet, saturated with the rich scent of cinnamon and fruit and baking dough. Sylvia longed to turn left into the kitchen, but instead she hurried up the narrow stairs to stash her new dress in Hannah's wardrobe.

'Those are…impressive,' Hannah said when the gowns had been hung.

Sylvia was eager to remove her damp grey dress and try it on. She looked about the room, then frowned. 'Where's your mirror?'

'Haven't got one.'

Sylvia continued to scan the room, as if she hadn't heard what Hannah said. 'But…surely you can afford one.' The Wickershams were far from the life Sylvia was trying to live, but they were also pretty far from the life Sylvia *currently* lived.

'Yes, and we have a family one downstairs, mostly to check for stains.'

Sylvia heard the undertone of annoyance in Hannah's voice. 'You must think I'm terribly vain,' she said with her chin raised high.

Hannah laughed. She *laughed.* Sylvia crossed her arms, defensive and exposed.

'Of course I think you're vain,' Hannah said through her laughter. 'Isn't that what you're trying to be?'

'Not at all,' Sylvia said too quickly. 'A lady must be beautiful but *unaware* of her beauty, effortless in the effort she exerts upon her figure.'

Hannah raised her eyebrows. 'Did you memorise that from an etiquette book?'

'No.'

'I think you did!' Violet said with a gasp. 'I remember, from *Lady Hasting's Guide to*—'

'Whose side are you on?' Sylvia jabbed Violet's shoulder, but it didn't stop Violet and Hannah from devolving into giggles.

'So tell me if I'm correct,' Hannah said eventually. 'If a man decides you are beautiful, it's a compliment. But if *you* decide you're beautiful, it's vanity.'

'Precisely.'

After a moment of pause, Violet tilted her head. 'That *is* a bit strange, now that I think about it.'

'That's not...' began Sylvia, her cheeks flush with embarrassment. 'There's plenty about *your* life that makes no sense, no sense at all... Just because the two of you have real jobs doesn't mean you're better than me.'

Hannah and Violet stopped laughing.

Hannah turned to Violet and said, with forced easiness, 'I think whatever Aunt Charity was baking is done by now. Would you bring up a plate?'

Relieved, Violet nodded and left the room.

'I think there's been a misunderstanding,' Hannah said.

'Truly!' Sylvia huffed. She tried to tell herself that Hannah's opinion of her didn't matter. As long as she could find a man who thought her pretty enough, captivating enough, refined enough…that was the only opinion she needed to secure.

Yet she couldn't stop herself from feeling like Hannah's approval mattered more.

'I didn't mean…' Hannah sighed. She opened her palms, then closed them. 'I don't think I'm better than you just because I know how to make cheese, Sylvia. And I know Violet doesn't think she's better than you either. But…' She looked uncomfortable, like she wasn't sure if she should keep going. 'Do *you* know that, too? Do you know that the reason I'm good isn't because I have a job, it's just because… I exist? Being good—being appreciated, being cared for, being loved—these aren't things you have to earn.'

Sylvia stiffened. Her whole plan to get out of Heene was to *earn* a husband, to convince a man that she was worthy enough to be his wife. Hannah knew this.

'A gentleman with a fortune won't just agree to marry me because I *exist*,' Sylvia countered. Hannah stepped forward then, toward Sylvia, and it wasn't until Hannah brought her thumb to Sylvia's cheek did Sylvia realise she had started to cry.

'I'm not—' Sylvia started. 'I mean, I don't know why I'm…'

She let her shoulders drop beneath Hannah's gaze. She let her whole body relax, like it was melting, like Hannah's irises were the sun itself and Sylvia was encased in ice. Hannah pulled her into a hug and Sylvia thawed, unable to hide, anymore, from a very painful truth:

Sylvia didn't just want to find a husband to restore her family to the comfortable life they had always known; she wanted to find a husband so she would have proof that she was valuable, important, and worthy of being loved.

How else could I have those things, she thought, *if I don't have to earn them?*

Hannah pulled away so they could see each other, and Sylvia's body ached at the sudden separation.

'We're going to find you a husband,' Hannah said, 'but even *before* you have a husband to tell you so, you've got to know that you're already smart, and you're already beautiful, and—'

'You think I'm beautiful?' A sly smile played at Sylvia's lips.

Hannah sighed, her eyes looking at everything in the room but Sylvia. 'Yes…' she said sheepishly. 'And admitting so might not be my favourite thing in the world, but I pride myself on being an honest person. So, Sylvia, I think you're beautiful. *And*—before you get too excited—I think you're annoying and strange and bewildering. But the point is—you are *good*. Not because I say so, and not because some future husband will say so, but because you just are.'

Sylvia didn't know what to say. Of all the things she had strived to be, *good* was never one of them. It seemed too unattainable—she could scheme and strategise her way into becoming anything else, but *good*...?

'Gooseberry tarts!' Violet entered the room with a tray of fresh dessert, saving Sylvia from having to respond. But the relief was short-lived. Sylvia found herself missing the moment, wishing it hadn't ended so suddenly. There was so much more that could have been said between her and Hannah, so much more that could have been done.

These are dangerous thoughts, she told herself. Getting close to someone she would know for a mere fortnight was a wretched plan. Hannah was helping her get *out* of Heene, which meant Hannah could only ever be an accomplice. Not a friend.

But as she sank her teeth into a flaky tart, as she tried on the gown, as she let Violet make adjustments—as she walked home in a light shower of seaside rain—Sylvia couldn't let go of the fact that her favourite moments in Heene were those with Hannah by her side. She wanted to pretend it wasn't true, but more than that she wanted to walk back to the farm first thing tomorrow. She wanted to stand across from those shining amber eyes, to hear that soft and steady voice. She wanted to know and be known by someone who called her the one thing she had never before cared to be:

Good.

'I can't help you write a love letter if you won't even tell me her *name*,' Hannah said for the third time that morning.

'Stop calling it a *love* letter,' Amos huffed. 'She barely even knows I exist.'

'It sounds like she looks forward to your deliveries. And it sounds even *more* like you're disappointed I'm taking charge of deliveries today.'

Hannah paused to count the bundles of cheese she had loaded into the cart. Each resort had their usual order, and now that June was well underway there was no shortage of families on holiday to feed. The wealthier families sent their staff to market to stock their kitchens, but special events called for special orders—and by the looks of Hannah's cart, special event season had finally begun.

Special events with potential suitors, Hannah thought. Soon the dark, quiet shoreline would come alive with candles burning late into the night, flickering in the windows of tourists who needed elaborate soirees to mark every birthday, every marriage, every newborn heir to every made-up title.

'It sounds like *you're* a bit eager to take charge of deliveries today,' Amos countered. He loaded the last of the butter into the cart.

'I *told* you—I have to teach Sylvia the route, so eventually she can do it on her own and *we* can have more free time.'

'And *I* told *you*—I'm more than happy to take her myself.'

'But you don't know how to work with her. She's very…particular.'

'Are you worried I won't like her?'

Hannah eyed the road to make sure Sylvia wasn't near. 'Why would I care if you don't like her?' But then, before he could answer: 'Is that why you won't tell me the name of your mystery paramour? Because you think I won't like her?'

Amos blushed. 'I— That's not…' He groaned. Then he looked up, and Hannah followed his eyes—Sylvia had just turned the corner, and would be close enough to hear them in less than a minute.

'Is she an Anglican?' Hannah asked. 'Because you know I don't care about that, not like our parents do.'

'It's more complicated than that—'

'Or is she not a *she* at all? You've never been with a man before but it's not too late to—'

'*Hannah.*' Amos lowered his voice. 'You're never this talkative with me. Not unless you've got something to hide.'

All the words Hannah had planned to say next evaporated. She wasn't the type of person to hide things, especially not from Amos. Sure, she kept her cheese-making to herself. And she didn't exactly *advertise* the fact that young women occasionally climbed up and down the lattice beneath her bedroom window. But overall she was an honest person, and being able to say that about herself was important to her.

She would never hide something from Amos. At least, not on purpose.

If I'm not being honest with him, she wondered, *it must be because I'm not being honest with myself.*

'I know that look,' Amos said with a grin. 'You're *introspecting.*'

But Sylvia was too close for Hannah to say anything back, so she simply stuck her tongue out at Amos, then turned around to greet Sylvia.

'Welcome to delivery day!' Hannah said with too much enthusiasm.

'The load looks heavy today,' Amos said. 'I really don't mind—'

'Nonsense.' Hannah reached for the handles and tilted the old yellow cart onto its wheels. 'You have a letter to write.'

She pushed the cart into the road and beckoned Sylvia to follow.

Neither of them spoke for a moment, which Hannah didn't mind. The squeak of wooden wheels and the high-pitched squawk of herring gulls were enough noise for her. But Sylvia, Hannah had learned, was not so comfortable with long pauses in conversation.

'Where's our first stop?' Sylvia asked.

'A lodging house in Little Heene, the smaller field near the shore. I think...' She tried to remember the few scraps of information she knew about Ella Hogge. 'I think your mother used to live around there? It's all changed so much since then. The place we're going to now is having a hard time keeping up with all the new resorts.'

She wanted to keep telling Sylvia about the history of Heene, but Amos's voice rang clear through her mind: *You're never this talkative. Not unless you've got something to hide.*

She tried to focus on the sounds of Little Heene, the sounds of doors opening and closing, horses biting into carrots, a child fumbling out of tune through a pianoforte lesson. But now that Amos had put the thought in her head, she just couldn't stop thinking it: *What am I hiding from myself?*

Hannah could have let Amos take charge of deliveries. She had *insisted* it be her, even when Amos had offered, even when she knew how heavy the cart would be on such a humid day. She could already feel sweat prickling through her undergarments and onto her light grey dress.

No, Hannah didn't need to take this errand for herself—the truth was, she *wanted* to. Despite the heat, despite the heaviness, despite the myriad other ways she could be spending her day, she just wanted to be around Sylvia.

They approached a large building that looked like it could use several new coats of paint.

'Hannah Wickersham!' Mr Pyle said as he opened the back door. 'And you must be one of the Queensburys.'

'Sylvia's learning the delivery route,' Hannah said, then turned to Sylvia. 'So now that we're here, I take out the ledger book and check with the customer that everything is in order.'

'It's always in order with the Wickershams.' Adam offered a friendly smile, then loaded his small order of butter and cheddar into his basket.

'And then we take payment,' Hannah said, drawing a coin purse from her apron. 'Unless…'

'No, no, not at all.' Adam reached into his pocket, then began counting coins. 'I have everything today.'

Hannah took the coins and recorded the transaction in her ledger, tilting her head to the side so Sylvia could watch over her shoulder.

Then she hoisted the cart back onto its wheels and marched onward.

'What did you mean back there?' Sylvia asked. 'When you said *unless*.'

'Sometimes people can't pay on time,' Hannah said. 'So in that case, you'd write *payment pending* in the ledger and we'd follow up with them eventually.'

Sylvia paused, thinking. 'But when is *eventually*?'

'Whenever they can.' Hannah realised that late payments must be a foreign concept to Sylvia. Her family had always had enough money for anything they wanted to buy, any time. 'What do you think of that? A world where we all just trust the payment will come eventually.'

'I think it's kind,' Sylvia said in a quiet voice, and Hannah smiled to herself. Perhaps Heene was rubbing off on Sylvia after all.

'Now, some people here absolutely have enough,' Hannah continued. 'Like our next stop: Alister Coyle, owner of Worthing's most popular oyster bar. Have you been?'

'Have *I* been?' Sylvia said incredulously. 'To Worthing's most *popular* oyster bar, in the state I'm in right now?'

'No, no.' Hannah laughed. 'I mean before. Your family must have spent a holiday in Worthing at some point.' She still wasn't sure why she wanted so badly to be with Sylvia today—learning more about her felt like a good place to start.

'We were Brighton people in the summer.' Sylvia shrugged. 'My mother wasn't keen to revisit the past.'

'Were you ever curious, though? About where you come from?'

'I come from London,' Sylvia said.

So much for getting to know her, Hannah thought.

Sylvia changed the subject. 'I can take a turn with the cart. I'll have to do it myself eventually.'

'And risk getting splinters on your velvet-soft hands?' Hannah was surprised by the bitterness in her own voice.

Sylvia stopped walking. 'So one minute I'm *good*, and you're holding me in your bedchamber,' she said, 'and then the next minute you're back to teasing me about something I can't even help?'

Hannah let herself get defensive. 'There are worse things than being teased.'

'What is your problem with me?' Sylvia's voice was strained.

'I don't have a problem with you,' Hannah said.

'But you have a problem with my *velvet-soft hands*?'

'It's not…' Hannah stopped pushing the cart. 'Don't you realise you're exactly the kind of person that is ruining this town?'

The silence that hung between them now was not the kind that Hannah enjoyed, the peaceful kind that brought her comfort. This silence was buzzing with tension, with accusations and expectations. It was barely silence at all.

'I know,' Sylvia said.

Hannah wasn't sure she had heard her correctly. 'You know?'

Sylvia crossed her arms and looked at the ground. 'I didn't know *before*, but now…' She shifted uncomfortably.

'But now?' said Hannah. She had expected Sylvia to brush off Hannah's comment, or fight back, or do any number of things that could confirm for Hannah that *she did not like Sylvia Queensbury.*

But instead, Sylvia uncrossed her arms and looked at Hannah with wide, vulnerable eyes. 'The Pyles gave us a basket of baked goods not long after we moved in. And someone else—another neighbour, I'm not even sure who—left a jar of honey and some second-hand stockings on our doorstep. They don't even *know* me, and—' She paused, collecting herself. 'And it's still more than what was given to us after my father died. None of our old friends offered to help. They couldn't even spare their used stockings. So yes, Hannah, I am starting to figure out that *people like me* aren't the kind that you would want in your town…or the kind you would want to be friends with.'

'Then why do you want to go back?' Hannah asked. 'Why go through all this—the scheming, the fortune-hunting—just to return to the very people who spurned you when you needed them most?'

'Because I won't let them have the last word,' Sylvia said. Her voice was hard, resolute, unwavering. 'I want them to know that the Queensburys can do just fine without their help. And—I didn't know this before, but now… I want to do things differently. I'll get a husband who can fund your cheese shop, then after that…there has to be plenty of other shops, and farms, and families that could use a donation.'

Hannah didn't know what to say. She had never seen this side of Sylvia. She hadn't let herself imagine that Sylvia might have some *Heene* in her after all.

'So you don't have to like me,' Sylvia continued, 'but if you could at least—'

'I do like you,' Hannah said without thinking. 'I just wish we…met under different circumstances. If you had—I think if you had grown up here, if your mother had never left, maybe we…maybe we would have been friends.'

Maybe, Hannah didn't say, *we would have been more.*

Sylvia nodded. 'And if you had grown up with me— or if you had been in London my first season—we… well, maybe I would have had a real friend.'

Hannah remembered when Sylvia had first shown up at the farm, and her father had reminded her that Sylvia, like everyone, had the inward light. She was more than just her upbringing, more than just a product of the society that raised her—a society that abandoned her the moment she didn't have enough money to fit in.

A society that, Hannah realised, had probably been waiting a long time for the opportunity to send Ella Hogge and her daughters back where they belonged.

Hannah felt suddenly protective. *Okay*, she thought. *Sylvia can belong—at least for now.*

'Maybe we can be friends anyway,' Hannah said. 'Even if it's only for a few weeks.'

Sylvia walked toward Hannah, arms extended for an embrace. Hannah's heart quickened...until she realised that Sylvia was only reaching for the cart. 'I'd like that,' Sylvia said. 'But only for a few weeks.'

'Of course,' Hannah agreed. And she meant it—she really did hope that Sylvia would soon find a suitor, that she herself would soon have a cheese shop. But was that really all she hoped? Hannah was no stranger to temporary friendships, and she knew all too well what those temporary friendships could become...

They continued on their route until the smell of oysters was too strong to ignore. Sylvia parked the cart at the restaurant's service entrance, then strolled along the side of the building, peering in the windows.

'I should be in there,' Sylvia said wistfully. 'And you should too, of course. Everyone should get to dine in a place like this.'

Coyle's was a fine establishment indeed, with polished tables, live music, and deep blue upholstered booths. The menu boasted dozens of sauces and seasonings—and prices that seemed to increase every time Hannah stopped by with deliveries.

'I can get twice as many oysters for half the cost at a market stall,' said Hannah. She stood next to Sylvia, and together they peeked through a window.

'But surely they aren't as tasty.'

'I can't say for certain—I've never liked oysters. But my mother's been to a fancy place like this one before and she swears you can't tell the difference.'

Sylvia smiled like she had just heard something improper. 'Really?'

'Oh yes, the whole thing's a scam.'

'No, I mean—you don't like oysters?'

As far as Hannah knew, each person having their own personal food preferences was not nearly as shocking as Sylvia's face would suggest.

'I don't like oysters…do you?'

Sylvia looked around, as if someone might overhear her. 'No!' She giggled.

Hannah wasn't sure what was happening, but she giggled too. 'And this is funny, because…?'

'Because *everyone* likes oysters,' Sylvia said. 'It's just what you do! You go to a ball and someone comes around with a tray of oysters, or you get invited to a restaurant, and you spend the whole time talking about the *depth of flavour* and… I always thought there was something wrong with me, that I found them so disgusting!'

'So you would just eat them anyway? And pretend you liked them?'

'Of course!'

Hannah was swept up in Sylvia's laughter. There was so much joy in this moment, this giddy secret of Sylvia's that she was finally allowed to share.

'Sylvia,' Hannah said. 'There is nothing wrong with you. And I bet plenty of other people at those parties were pretending to like oysters too.'

Sylvia wrinkled her nose. 'They're just so…*slimy.*'

They fell into more giggles. 'They really are!'

'I would be happy,' said a stern voice behind them, 'to place my dairy orders elsewhere, if being near oysters is such an unpleasant experience for you.'

Hannah's stomach dropped. The last of her laughter died in her throat. She slowly turned around to see the smarmy smirk of Alister Coyle, his arms crossed and his head held high.

She wanted to reach for Sylvia's hand, but all she could do was tremble in place.

Chapter Eight

Sylvia grabbed Hannah's hand.

She had done it without thinking, and without wondering why. She didn't know Mr Coyle, and had no reason not to trust him—if anything, he should be the *most* trustworthy person in all of Heene, given his success in business, his ability to rise above his station. He was a familiar character to Sylvia.

And as she thought harder—in those fleeting seconds between what he had said and what Sylvia would say next—she realised that was exactly why she had grabbed her friend's hand. Because Sylvia might not know this man, but she knew his type; and that meant, for the first time since meeting Hannah, she could really help.

'That's quite acceptable,' Sylvia said, giving Hannah's hand a squeeze before letting go. '*We* would be happy to fill our dairy orders elsewhere, if being near people who don't agree with you is such an unpleasant experience.'

The smug expression on Mr Coyle's face faltered. This was the part of being a lady that so many gentlemen didn't understand—the more a woman studies how to flatter a man's ego, the more she learns how to wear it down as well.

'You aren't a Wickersham,' he grumbled.

'I might as well be.' Sylvia stood and offered a small curtsy, facing her adversary despite wanting to turn and look at Hannah. She was feeling...well, she couldn't quite place it. Her heartbeat had quickened, but she wasn't nervous. Her stomach felt tight, but she wasn't afraid.

'I work for them,' she continued. 'And I'll be a regular on the delivery route. But don't concern yourself with my palate—I'm happy to take your money even if you don't like butter. That's how business works, yes?'

His eyes travelled the length of her body. Sylvia had to suppress a shiver. She instinctively took a step in front of Hannah, who was standing now with one hand on the cart.

'You're one of the *Queensbury* girls,' Mr Coyle finally said, his lips arching into a self-satisfied smile. Sylvia didn't like how he said her name, how he taunted her with it, like it was supposed to be an insult. 'Peddling butter is quite the fall from the life *you* used to live,' he continued, clasping his hands behind his back.

'I admit I am more familiar with the *inside* of a fine

establishment like yours than I am the *service door*.' She raised her chin a fraction of an inch. 'Though I can't say how you have time to run the place, given your proclivity for gabbing with your vendors.'

Mr Coyle frowned. He cleared his throat. 'Let's discuss business, shall we?'

Sylvia stole a glance at Hannah, whose eyes were wide with gratitude and awe. Sylvia's heartbeat slowed, and the tension in her body eased. She realised then what she had been feeling, what had taken over her senses since the moment Mr Coyle first spoke:

Sylvia was feeling protective.

Sylvia was feeling protective *of Hannah*.

But there wasn't time for a thought like that, not now. Not when it might lead to any of the other strange, inconvenient, Hannah-related thoughts she'd been having recently, like how pleasant their closeness in the herb garden had made her feel, or *that day with the damn butter...*

Hannah stepped forward now, her confidence returned somewhat, to do business with Mr Coyle. 'We've brought two pounds of...' Hannah started, but Sylvia stopped listening, lost in her own thoughts.

Catching a husband is a kind of business, she realised. She had spent her whole life learning how to market herself, how to be both vendor *and* product in the marriage mart. She had never thought to apply those skills to anything else.

No one in her life had encouraged her to do so.

'Until next time,' she heard Mr Coyle say. She watched him shake Hannah's hand—the hand *she* had squeezed, just a moment earlier.

'What an unpleasant man,' Sylvia said after the door had closed behind him.

Hannah nodded in agreement, counting the coins he had given her.

'Are you—' Sylvia started, then second-guessed herself. She wanted to ask if Hannah was all right, but… *What reason would Hannah have to open up to me?*

Hannah put the coins away but didn't move toward the cart. She stood silently, watching a flock of gulls fly toward the shore, a small frown on her face.

Sylvia couldn't hold her tongue any longer. 'You're starting to worry me,' she said with a nervous laugh. 'I mean…are you all right?'

Hannah kept her eyes on the sky when she answered. 'I don't like confrontation. I tend to freeze, or get stuck inside my own head, or—I'm not sure, Sylvia. It's just a flaw I've always had. It makes me feel…' She looked at Sylvia, then looked down at her feet. 'It makes me feel weak, and unreliable, if I'm being honest.'

Sylvia's heart ached thinking that Hannah—perhaps the most competent, skillful, hardworking person Sylvia had ever met—felt inadequate in any way.

'Stop with that,' Sylvia said. 'We're friends now. And that means no one is allowed to speak ill of you—even *yourself*.' She took Hannah's hands in her own. 'You are one of the strongest and most reliable people I know.'

'You haven't even known me that long,' Hannah countered, but her hands relaxed in Sylvia's grip.

'I just happen to be an excellent judge of character.' Sylvia knew it was more complicated than that, of course. She may not know Hannah that well, but she knew Hannah—*truly* knew her—better than she knew most people. She had never had any close friends in London. She had never let anyone get close enough to hurt her, close enough to learn something about her they could use against her. She was so used to seeing every gentleman as a potential prize and every lady as a ruthless competitor.

Hannah was something new entirely. Hannah was a friend.

'And also,' Sylvia admitted, 'getting to know you isn't as unpleasant as I thought it would be, so I find myself enjoying your company.' She knew the compliment was far too flimsy as soon as she said it. 'I find myself enjoying your company *very much*.'

Hannah tightened her fingers around Sylvia's. 'I… feel the same way.' Reluctantly she pulled her hands free and returned to the cart. '*And* I suppose I ought to thank you. I've never seen anyone talk to Mr Coyle that way.'

Sylvia dropped into a dramatic curtsy. 'Why—you are very welcome. I can't help but notice,' she said with a sly grin, 'that I seem better suited to the business side of butter than the actual *making* of it. Perhaps—'

'You are *not* getting out of farmwork just because you have a smooth tongue.'

Sylvia stuck out her smooth tongue toward Hannah, and the two of them giggled. They carried on in that way for the rest of the delivery route, laughing, bantering, and even—occasionally—complimenting one another.

Usually, Sylvia didn't want each day to end because it meant she'd have to retire to her cramped cottage and eat bland, mushy beans. But now she had a better reason for wanting the day to last longer—a much better reason.

Now she had Hannah.

Today was the day.

Today was *the* day, and Hannah nearly tripped running down the stairs with excitement.

'Have a bite to eat?' Aunt Charity called as Hannah sped through the kitchen.

'There must be a batch ready,' her father sighed as she left the house and ran toward the cellar below the cheese shed.

He was right—there *was* a new batch of cheese ready, one that Hannah had been waiting on for over a year. Cheesemaking was a slow and patient profession, and of course Hannah relished each moment—but days like this were extra special.

Everyone in the house would want a taste, but they knew to leave this moment, this first encounter, all to Hannah.

'Hello,' she said as she swung open the door. She walked down the dim stairs, a single candle in her hand. She could feel the temperature drop with each step, the cool stone walls beckoning her from below the ground. This was the cellar her grandfather had built, when Heene itself was barely a village. This was where fresh wheels of newly pressed cheese went to rest for months, sometimes years, and sometimes more, ageing into colours and flavours and textures that defied the rapid pace of an increasingly industrialised England.

Here in this cellar, Hannah stood witness to the slow magic of homegrown cheesemaking, that strange and wondrous alchemy that humans have studied for thousands of years.

She said a prayer.

Walking deeper into the cellar, Hannah's senses were flooded with the sharp and tangy scent of cheddar. She was confident that anyone could hand her a block of cheese and, without opening her eyes, she could tell its age. Salt, cream, mould, and earth all mingled in the subterranean air, and Hannah shivered with delight.

She selected a round, thick wheel from the far shelf to bring up for tasting. Assuming all was well, the rest of the wheels in its age group would be prepared for market and their various orders in town.

The weight strained her arms as it always did, but far less than when she had first taken up the profession as a young girl. She delighted now in her own strength, in the bulge of her muscles as she carried the clothbound wheel to the kitchen.

'Best day of the year,' Amos said from his seat at the table. He leaned back, the chair's front legs hovering several inches off the floor.

'You'll be saying the same thing when the Stilton's ready at Christmas,' Hannah said.

'There can be more than one best day of the year.' He grinned, and Hannah had to agree.

Everyone else in the family took their seats for this beloved ritual.

'Go on,' her father said. 'Tell us the story.'

Hannah peeled away the strips of fat-soaked muslin to reveal a rough, mottled rind. 'At the very start of September—not this past September, but the one before—I gathered a very special batch of milk. It was still summer, so all those fresh Heene grasses were adding their flavour to the cheese, but it was nearing fall when the cream gets richer.' She peered around the table as the last of the cloth fell from its wheel, taking in everyone's eager faces. 'I don't need to tell *you* lot that when it comes to dairy, timing is everything.'

Her mother handed her a large knife, which Hannah used to slowly slice the wheel in half. She parted the cheese and revealed its golden centre.

Everyone leaned forward and inhaled.

They were quiet for a long while.

Amos was the first to speak. 'Savoury,' he said.

'Like broth,' added Aunt Charity.

And then they all spoke, words climbing on top of each other.

'Nutty.'

'Caramel.'

'A hint of horseradish.'

'Grass and clover and ocean waves.'

Pride swelled in Hannah's chest. She was proud of Henry and Grace and Willow, the cows who gave the milk. She was proud of her whole family, who tended the land and fed their community. And she was proud of herself—she was proud that she chose to use her short and blessed time on earth for something so wonderful as cheesemaking.

And then, as all that pride and gratitude and love washed over her, she remembered someone else. Someone who wasn't at the table, but should be.

'We need to wait,' Hannah decided.

'Obviously,' Amos said. 'It needs to breathe for… what, half an hour?'

'No,' Hannah clarified. 'We need to wait a bit longer. Until Sylvia gets here.'

She looked at the mantel clock. Sylvia was set to arrive in just under two hours, and there was really no *reason* why they should wait for her, but… Hannah wanted her to be there. Hannah wanted her to be part of this family ritual, to share in the joy of this moment.

And, of course, she wanted Sylvia to be impressed.

'Well, don't just sit there,' her father announced. 'Plenty of work to do until then.'

They rose from the table and went about their tasks; Aunt Charity turned to mending torn clothes, Isaiah to the morning milking, and Rachel to churn some butter.

Amos stood in the kitchen, staring at Hannah as if he expected her to speak.

'Is there something I can help you with?' she asked eventually.

'Oh, I don't know, is there something I can help *you* with?'

'I suppose you could help me carry the rest of the cheese—'

'Hannah.' This time he spoke softly, gently. And then he let them stand in the silence, their favourite way of communicating.

When her defences eventually lowered, she put words to what they had just wordlessly shared. 'You know how I get…nervous, when talking to people I don't know well, or—or people I don't particularly like.'

'I do.'

'Well Sylvia…she just doesn't. She's *confident*, and personable, and she sort of, er, stood up for me yesterday. During a delivery.' Hannah twisted her fingers together. 'So when she's not so busy being *shallow* and *frustrating*—'

'Yes, yes, skip ahead.'

'What I mean to say is, when she's being *herself*, I do confess that I…' Hannah mumbled the end of her confession so quietly Amos couldn't hear.

'What was that?' He cupped his hand dramatically behind his ear.

Hannah mumbled a bit louder: 'I fancy her.'

'I didn't quite catch—'

'I fancy her!' She threw her hands into the air. 'Are you happy?'

'Very,' Amos said with a satisfied smile. He reached for an apple on the table and took a bite. Despite her stubbornness, Hannah did feel better—lighter, truer, clearer—and she resolved to stop hiding her feelings for good, both from Amos and from herself.

'And she's leaving soon,' Hannah said. 'Which would keep things from getting complicated.'

'Is she?' Amos asked between bites.

'Of course. She's not made for Heene.'

'No, but she's made *from* Heene.'

'She doesn't act like it. Toss me an apple.'

'Maybe she *didn't* act like it.' He lobbed an apple into Hannah's outstretched hands.

'All I'm saying is that *when* she leaves—'

'*If*.'

'*When* she leaves, I won't be bothered, because I've done this before.' She took a deep breath. 'Something romantic *and very short term* isn't entirely out of the question...but I don't even know if she fancies women!'

'You'll just have to find out then.'

Hannah wanted to protest. She wanted to say that Sylvia wasn't worth the trouble. But she thought of Sylvia's creamy blond curls, her slender fingers pushing butter into a mould, her mossy green eyes...

She sighed. 'I'll just have to find out then.'

The next hour and a half passed quickly, a blur of tedious but necessary chores. Rebecca called out when she saw Sylvia down the road, and everyone gathered at the kitchen table once more.

'Sylvia,' Amos said from his seat next to her. 'You should know that very few people who aren't Wickershams have ever experienced what you're about to experience.'

'If I remember correctly, Sylvia's mother came by a time or two,' said Aunt Charity. Rebecca shot her a look that Hannah didn't understand.

She cut the round halves into neat wedges, sunny orange around the edges and brilliant yellow in the centre.

'It's an honour, genuinely,' said Sylvia. She sat with her usual perfect posture, her hair styled as if she were dining with the queen. Hannah desperately wanted to know what those gilded locks looked like wild and unpinned.

Once everyone had their cheese, they prayed in silence for a moment before sinking their teeth into twenty-one months of patiently aged cheddar.

The first flavour was sweetness, a soft milky caramel that danced upon Hannah's taste buds for only a second before the full essence of the cheese came through. The second flavour was comfort—savoury, earthy, meaty—like a family hearth or a bonfire on the beach.

Hannah watched Sylvia's face as she moved through the flavours, from light to brothy to mildly acidic.

'Well done,' said Isaiah, and Hannah smiled. A *well done* from Isaiah Wickersham was as good as an *excellent* from anyone else.

'You make the whole family look good, Hannah,' her mother said before her second bite.

Then let me try something new, Hannah wanted to say. *Let me show you what else I can make!*

'I've never had cheese like this before,' Sylvia said, and Hannah's heart leapt to hear it. 'And I've had…

well, I must have had so much cheese. It's always out at dinner parties, at balls…but I never…'

'Nothing ever commanded your attention quite like this?' Amos offered.

'No,' Sylvia said. Her eyes rose to meet Hannah's. 'Not like this.'

Hannah inhaled sharply, then broke eye contact to finish slicing the cheese. One by one the Wickershams left and returned to their daily tasks, until Sylvia and Hannah were left alone.

Hannah searched along the kitchen shelves until she found a large glass jar. 'We should have time tomorrow for a stroll. Violet's working on your blue dress, right?'

'Oh yes,' Sylvia raved. 'It looks good as new. Well, almost. Best not to look *too* closely. But from a distance, or for a quick conversation, no one will be the wiser.'

Hannah joined Sylvia at the table, then scooped thick, shimmering honey out of the jar and onto a bite-size triangle of cheese.

'Try…*this*.' She lifted the slice to Sylvia's lips.

'*Mmmm…*' Sylvia hummed with delight. She looked toward the ceiling and leaned back in her chair. 'Wow. When I'm able to host parties of my own…this will be on the table. Every time.'

'I'll hold you to that,' Hannah said as she spooned some honey for herself. 'I'll be looking for *Queensbury* on the ledger this time next year.'

'My name will be different by then, of course.'

Hannah shrugged. 'You could always go double-barrelled.'

'That's so uncommon.'

'But still, it happens.'

'I suppose it does, in rare cases.' Sylvia reached for the honey spoon herself this time. 'And why *must* we take our husband's last name, anyway? I've never really wondered...well, it's embarrassing to admit, but I never wondered about it until now.'

'It's not embarrassing.' Hannah traced her finger-nail along the woodgrain of the table's surface. 'I think it's wonderful, to question something for the first time, something that has been as normal as the air you breathe. It's brave, even.'

'I'd hardly call a question *brave*.'

'It is.' *This would be the perfect time to ask*...thought Hannah, her chest suddenly tight. But she couldn't just come with it, could she? *By the way, Sylvia, I fancy women, and I'm wondering if you do as well.* It's quite possible Sylvia didn't even know that women *could* fancy women.

That's unlikely, Hannah thought, losing herself to an imaginary conversation. Plenty of women—well, maybe not *plenty*, but certainly *enough*—had spurned their marriage prospects and moved in with each other instead. There were hatmakers down in Worthing, who'd been together for over a decade; there was Anne

Lister, somewhere up north, who took to wearing gentlemen's accessories and courting fine ladies; and there was even a duchess, or perhaps a duke's sister... Hannah couldn't remember the details, but she *knew* she'd heard a fanciful piece of gossip about a pair that caused a stir in London just a few months earlier.

'Anyway,' Hannah said, shaking her head and returning to the present moment. 'Have you ever wondered if you...truly enjoy men's company?'

Sylvia took a slow breath, thinking. 'No, it never seemed a question worth asking.'

'Why is that?'

'Well... I'm *supposed* to enjoy men's company. I wouldn't want to *be* the kind of woman who didn't. Because that would mean...' Her voice trailed off. She took another bite of cheese, and Hannah was impressed at how much silence Sylvia was holding. She was usually so quick to speak, but not today.

Eventually, Sylvia continued: 'That would mean spending my life with a husband I did not love.'

'But have you ever *fancied* a gentleman?'

'No.'

'Not once?'

'I have to assume I just haven't met the right one yet. My mother...she tells me of how she just *knew*, with my father. And I've heard stories like that from so many women, where they find a love match and...

and everything just makes sense. I'll meet that person, I know I will, but it just doesn't...'

'Make sense yet?'

'Exactly.' Sylvia had finished her portion of the cheese, and with it their reason for staying in the kitchen.

But Hannah didn't want to go back to work just yet.

'Have you ever fancied...anyone?' she asked. 'Even someone who isn't a gentleman?'

'You mean like a footman?'

'No, no,' Hannah laughed. 'I mean someone who isn't a *man*, any man, *gentle* or not.'

Sylvia laughed too, but quietly, awkwardly. 'Well that would be *quite* inconvenient, wouldn't it? If I fancied someone who wasn't...well, who couldn't be my *husband*.'

'Attraction is many things, but *convenient* isn't one of them.' Hannah glanced at the mantel clock, then back to Sylvia.

'Nothing about my life is convenient anymore,' Sylvia sighed. 'So if I *were* to fancy a woman, I suppose that couldn't make things any *worse*.'

'It might even make things better.' This was the furthest Hannah would let herself go, the most she would let herself say.

Sylvia nodded slowly. 'It might.' She stood from her chair, pulled down an apron from a hook in the wall.

'It just might.' Hannah took an apron herself and fol-lowed Sylvia out the door.

'And maybe—' Sylvia added, but stopped herself. She shook her head, then looked around the farm and noticed no one was tending to the herb garden. She walked away, leaving Hannah to find something else to do.

For the rest of the day, those two words—those two sparkling words, bursting with hope—trailed across Hannah's mind like shooting stars. They stayed with her as she carried the cheese from the cellar, as she filled the delivery cart, as she ate and drank and milked the cows. They stayed with her as the sun set, as she sank into bed, as she closed her eyes.

And maybe, Sylvia had said.

And maybe, and maybe, and maybe...

Chapter Nine

Sylvia Queensbury had one singular, shining goal to accomplish today: secure an invitation to a weekend event.

In her daydreams, of course, she was invited to *multiple* events, each host more desperate for her presence than the last. *We've all been anticipating your triumphant return to society*, they would say. *Oh, how we have missed you.*

Looking at herself now in the mirror, Sylvia couldn't stop herself from hoping that her old acquaintances would welcome her back into their social calendars with no mention of whatever gossip they'd heard about the Queensburys.

'I wish it were *me* in that dress,' Rose whined. She was sprawled out on their large shared bed, hair in a messy bun. 'It's been *so long* since I looked like that.'

'You've never looked like this,' Sylvia said, twirling in front of the mirror. 'You've never been *out* in society.'

'But *still*.' Rose twirled a strand of hair that hung over her forehead. 'I'd *at least* like to wear a necklace.'

'If everything goes according to plan,' said Sylvia, turning to face all her sisters. 'You will have a *real* necklace, several of them, not this…strand of *costume* beads.'

'I think it's rather convincing,' Violet said from her place beside Sylvia. She was putting her final details on the dress, scraps of lace and sequins discarded by the modiste for their imperfections—which Violet had managed to hide brilliantly. Sylvia was impressed that her sister had become such a talented seamstress, but surprised she had put so much work into learning a skill she would never need to use again.

Your face is the best part! signed Mary, bouncing on the balls of her feet next to Sylvia. She was proud of the cosmetics she had made from basic kitchen in-gredients—the oil and saffron and other stolen goods the twins had swiped from their place of employment added a subtle red tint to Sylvia's lips and cheekbones. Sylvia wasn't pleased that her sisters had resorted to thievery on her behalf, but there was also something… *exhilarating* about her ruse becoming a family opera-tion.

Or, more accurately, a sisterly operation. Ella Queensbury had not been invited to join the fortune-hunting team, and Sylvia was growing increasingly concerned that if Ella *were* to be invited, she would want nothing to do with their plan.

Sylvia decided to broach the topic with her sisters. 'Did any of you notice… Mother's hair, yesterday?'

'You mean that it was *down*?' Rose asked.

'I don't see anything strange about keeping your hair down at home,' said Violet dismissively.

'Yes, but it wasn't *just* at home,' Sylvia clarified. 'I think she wore it that way to market, entirely un-styled! And this morning, after she left the house, the papillote iron wasn't even hot—no curls today either, apparently.'

'We're the only ones in Heene who spend this much time on our hair,' Violet said. 'Would anyone care if we just…stopped?'

Sylvia bristled at the suggestion. *Of course* she knew that the Queensburys wore their hair differently from the rest of Heene, but *that was the point*.

Rose rolled across the bed toward Sylvia. 'We *would* get more sleep if we didn't have to wake up early to curl our—'

'Enough,' Sylvia said. 'We cannot forget who we are.' But she thought of Hannah. Her *friend*—a word she never thought she'd use in this godforsaken place. She softened her tone and said to her sisters: 'But I suppose there's no harm in enjoying ourselves while we're here.'

When Sylvia finally stepped outside, she was relieved to find that Heene was cloudy. A cool shade stretched out along the shore. *Thank goodness*, she thought, fingering her necklace. *I'll need all the help I can get—atmospheric or otherwise—to pass these beads off as pearls.*

Hannah was already waiting for her when she arrived at the border wall.

'If I didn't know better,' Hannah said, 'I would be *convinced* that you're a genuine member of the *upper crust*.'

Sylvia curtsied, comically low, and grumbled, 'You think I don't know that *upper crust* is an insult used by the lower classes.'

'Now that *you* are part of the *lower classes*,' Hannah said, grinning, 'the insult is just as much yours to use.'

'Fair enough.' Sylvia stood tall. 'But really, how do I look?'

She hadn't worn the pale blue dress since her first days in Heene, back when she refused to acknowledge that she'd ever have to wear anything else. Its original adornments had been plucked and pawned, but Violet's new additions gave the dress the dignity it deserved. She felt at home in the fine fabric, the weight of earrings tugging at her lobes a reminder that *who she was* had not been entirely lost.

'Gorgeous,' Hannah said, leaning against the stone wall. 'If you're into this kind of thing.'

'And who *isn't*?' Sylvia asked.

'I just think it's all a bit much. Sometimes I wonder if more money goes into *looking* rich than actually *being* rich.'

Sylvia opened her mouth to speak, but couldn't find the words. Now that she knew the price of bread, she could hardly make the case that the gowns and shoes and jewellery of the peerage was the best use of the nation's wealth.

'I don't mean to be unkind,' Hannah clarified. She stood from the wall and took a step toward Sylvia, offering her hand. Sylvia clasped her own around Hannah's palm, the light fabric of her second-hand gloves separating their skin. She hadn't worn this particular accessory in ages, and she assumed they would feel as natural as they did the month before.

But already Sylvia missed the naked warmth of her gloveless hands against Hannah's.

Attraction is many things, Hannah had said yesterday.

Many things, thought Sylvia now. *But could it be… this?*

She had met women before who lived as Hannah had suggested—fancying other women instead of taking a husband. But they were mostly older women, long past their marrying prime. At some point in her life Sylvia had made the assumption that the few women who paired with each other were doing so out of necessity, not desire: they were lonely spinsters in need of companionship, or well-to-do widows who didn't need the money a second husband would bring.

It was a fine way for a woman to live her life, but only if she didn't have or need better options. Sylvia had never considered that courting a woman could be her *first choice.*

She cleared her throat. 'Shall we?' She let her covered hand slip from Hannah's and walked through the wall's opening. They entered Worthing, this time— unlike any time before—trying to *attract* attention rather than hide from it.

'You'll want to stay a few feet behind me, and— *goodness*, I completely forgot to compliment *you*!' Sylvia looked over her shoulder, where Hannah followed in a charcoal grey dress and crisp white apron. Her hair was pulled into a tight bun beneath a simple white bonnet, the neatest her hair had ever been. Her transformation had not been as drastic as Sylvia's, but still…there was a tidiness about her, an attention to detail, that communicated how hard she was trying to help Sylvia achieve her goal.

Sylvia was moved, and gave her friend a conspiratorial smile. 'You look like the perfect lady's maid. No one will know the difference.'

'Unless they've seen me during deliveries,' Hannah said. Sylvia faced forward again, and on they walked.

'I am ashamed to admit,' said Sylvia, 'that this lot

wouldn't recognise your face if they had seen it a thousand times.'

'And yet they are your friends?'

Sylvia paused. '*Friends* is…perhaps too strong a word.'

Soon they were surrounded by shops and shoppers, buildings painted in cheerful pastels and tourists carrying their newly bought goods. The smell of fresh food and flowers wafted from the bakery, the butcher, the market. She heard the high-pitched bell on the hat shop's door, the clang of construction on the highly anticipated Royal Baths. A cluster of young women and their lady's maids entered the jeweller's; a gentleman stepped out of the Pyles' stationary shop, carrying a neatly wrapped package; and a child skipped ahead of his parents on his way to the toymaker's.

Worthing was so full of life today, and Sylvia soaked it all in.

Just ahead, she caught sight of three pairs, each with their arms linked, each lady holding a dainty parasol. She recognised the tallest woman in the group immediately, chestnut ringlets bouncing beside her pale face—Augusta Beaumont, primed to be the most desirable catch of next year's season.

One couple in the group split off to enter the shoemaker's shop, and Sylvia recognised them too: Augusta's sister Arabella and her new husband, the younger son of a baron. He seemed excited at the prospect of getting new shoes.

Arabella seemed bored out of her mind.

'Is that *Sylvia Queensbury*?' Augusta gasped.

Sylvia's heart raced. This was everything she had prepared for. This was the moment her plan really took off, the moment her life changed—or changed back—forever.

'The one and only!' Sylvia flashed a smile then stood still, letting Augusta walk to her.

'I haven't seen you in *months*,' the youngest Beaumont daughter said in a sugary tone, too sweet to be sincere.

'I haven't *been out* in months,' Sylvia replied. 'We've been keeping a low profile until all that *dreadful* gossip about my *terrible* uncle has disappeared.'

'Of course, of course.' Augusta nodded. 'You remember my cousin from the north, Mr Hemstreet?' She gestured to the gentleman at her side, who offered a toothy grin. Sylvia couldn't remember his first name.

'And my brother, Phillip.' Augusta's quieter counterpart finally spoke: Catherine, middle child of the illustrious Fitzroy family, known for their extravagant parties and generous patronage of the arts.

Surely Phillip—future viscount and heir to the Fitzroy fortune—didn't need a bride with a dowry.

Sylvia curtsied. 'Such a delight to see you all again.'

The two gentlemen offered subtle bows.

'You simply *must* tell us where your family is living these days,' Augusta said, clasping her hands together. Sylvia knew that whatever she said next would spread from Miss Beaumont to every other person in their age group on holiday in Worthing. But before Sylvia could speak, Augusta leaned to the side and looked over Sylvia's shoulder. 'And who is *this*?'

'My lady's maid,' Sylvia said quickly, then glanced behind her to notice Hannah's curtsy—just as they had practised, but a little clumsy. 'She's been with our family for ages. Perhaps you don't remember.'

'Perhaps not...' Augusta squinted her eyes.

'Anyway,' Sylvia continued, 'we travelled here for some privacy during mourning and decided to stay for the summer holiday. Just until we decide where we'd like to settle more permanently. And how about you? I heard about your sister's engagement—*so* wonderful—and didn't it happen at *your* family's ball, Catherine?'

'Yes, and it was *so* romantic,' Catherine said. She was shorter than Arabella, with sandy blond hair and round cheeks. She twirled her parasol. 'I can't *imagine* how you're faring in the sun, without cover. Would you prefer we stand in the shade?'

Catherine didn't let the insult show on her face, so neither did Sylvia. The clouds were clearly cover enough, and the group was very much in the shade already. Catherine wasn't observing that Sylvia had no parasol—she was suggesting that Sylvia couldn't *afford* a parasol.

'I find the sunlight healthy,' Sylvia said with her head held high. 'Our physician recommends it, in fact. My countenance grew quite frail in mourning.'

'Fascinating,' said Mr Hemstreet. 'I haven't heard that before.'

'Well I'm *so* glad we all spotted each other, because I'm trying to spread the word that my mourning period has ended and I'm fit to return to the social scene.' Sylvia smiled awkwardly at Phillip Fitzroy, who very clearly had disengaged from the conversation.

'Oh, we'll be sure to mention your name…*if* we hear of anything,' Augusta said.

The sun was still behind a wall of thick white clouds, but Sylvia felt like it was burning through her. She knew an *immediate* invitation wasn't guaranteed, but…she was starting to panic.

'I'm surprised your family isn't hosting anything this weekend,' Sylvia said to Catherine, just the slightest bit too loud.

'We're just *so tired* from the London season,' answered Catherine. *'So tired.'*

The door to the shoemaker's shop opened, and Arabella unfurled her parasol. Sylvia made a mental note to purchase one of her own the next time she got paid.

'We must be off,' Augusta said. 'So much *planning* to do for the wedding!' She turned to join her sister, then faced Sylvia to add: 'We had to delay it, of course, since my family had already planned a holiday on the Continent for all of May.'

And then, all Sylvia could see of Augusta, Catherine, Phillip, and Mr Hemstreet were their backs.

'She's not telling the truth,' Hannah said when they were out of earshot.

Sylvia took a moment to process what Hannah was saying. She could tell, of course, that Catherine and Augusta were hiding something, but she just didn't want it to be true.

'How do you know?' she asked.

'Because I checked this morning.' Hannah took a few steps closer to Sylvia. 'Two wheels of our new cheddar are going to the Fitzroys for a Friday-night ball.'

Sylvia lowered her shoulders. She felt her stomach twist, her throat tighten. She had known there was a chance she wouldn't be welcomed back into society on her first try, but she had hoped…

She had hoped the people she used to know just liked her for *her*, not for her money or status.

And why should I hope that, Sylvia asked herself, *when they don't even know me, not really?*

'You're better off without them,' Hannah said. 'Back to the farm?'

'No.' Sylvia stood in place for one heavy breath, then continued forward. 'I'm not giving up.'

'But they—'

'But they lied? But they were unkind?' Sylvia turned around to face Hannah. 'That's what my people do. That's the game we play. I need them to know—' Her voice caught, and she paused to compose herself. She would *not* cry. 'I need them to know that they don't get to decide who's in and who's out. They feel so grand right now, but when I make it back, when I'm dancing and hosting again, I'll… I'll outshine them all, Hannah. I'll prove they were wrong about me, and I'll have their respect, and they'll regret ever belittling me and I'll *outshine them all.*' She spun on her heel to face forward again, all too aware of Hannah's concerned gaze on her back.

And then she smiled. She felt a spark of hope ignite within her chest. She felt lifted from her pit of despair, because just a few feet away, exiting the library just as she was nearing its door, was her mystery man, the one who'd spent the last several years away in France.

'It's him,' Sylvia whispered over her shoulder. She watched as Hannah's eyes found the man, her eyebrows raising.

'Decently handsome, I think,' Hannah said. 'Quite tall.'

'And quite *single.*'

But how to approach him? A lady was never supposed to initiate a conversation with a potential suitor…such boldness would make her look *desperate*. No, she needed to get him to speak to her first.

Sylvia looked around, assessing her resources. All she had to work with was…the breeze. But no matter—she waited for a strong enough gust of seaside air, then slipped a glove off her hand and let it go.

'*Please, please…*' Sylvia begged the glove to land just in front of his feet, waited a beat, then hurried in its direction.

'*Oh dear!*' she said innocently. She watched his hand scoop the glove from the ground, then tilted her face up just as he was standing. He would remember this moment as entirely spontaneous, but for Sylvia it was choreographed to perfection.

'It's you!' they both said at the same time, then laughed.

'I was hoping to find you again,' he said, offering Sylvia a charming smile. 'May I?' He held out the glove, then fit it delicately onto Sylvia's hand. Their fingers touched, and Sylvia felt…well, nothing *yet*, but surely once they got to know each other better this kind of touch would send shivers through her body.

Like how it feels to touch Hannah. The thought slipped into her mind without permission, and she banished it as quickly as it had come.

She cleared her throat. 'You remember me, then.'

'Remember you? My lady, if I may speak freely, how could I forget a face as fair as yours?'

Sylvia lowered her head and placed a hand over her heart. 'You are too kind, Lord…?'

'Marshall,' he said, then bent into the perfect bow—not too shallow, not too deep. 'Lord Henry Marshall.'

'I've just met a Henry!' Sylvia said. 'She's…well, never mind that… I'm Miss Queensbury.' She dipped into a perfect curtsy. 'Miss Sylvia Queensbury.' Somewhere behind her, Hannah was very clearly trying to smother a laugh. Of course it was terribly funny that Sylvia's suitor shared a name with a cow, but at least Sylvia had the decency to wait until later to laugh about it secretly. Hopefully with Hannah.

'The Queensburys!' Lord Marshall said. 'You have sisters, yes? You'll have to forgive me. I'm not one for gossip, so during my time on the Continent I lost track of the noble families, who is related to whom…'

'That's just marvellous,' Sylvia said, barely containing her glee. 'I mean, I've never been one for gossip either, and it must have been so refreshing to spend that time away.'

'It was refreshing, yes,' he agreed. Sylvia noticed the crinkle around his eyes when he smiled, how genuinely happy he was to see her again. 'And how is your collection?'

It took Sylvia a few seconds to remember. 'The shells! Oh yes, I had *such* success the day we last saw each other. I found some excellent pieces. You must be good luck.'

'Maybe we can search for seashells together some time,' he said, and then bashfully added: 'If you'd like, that is.'

'I can think of no better way to spend an afternoon.'

Lord Marshall reached into his pocket and checked his watch. 'I'm late for an appointment,' he said apologetically. 'But…what are you doing this Friday? I'm sure a lady such as yourself has a full social calendar by now, but if you happen to be free…'

She turned to face her lady's maid. 'Hannah? Do I have any appointments this Friday?'

Hannah pretended to think for a moment. 'I do believe you've had a few invitations, but none that you've decided on as of yet.' *Bless her for committing to the role.*

'I may be free,' Sylvia said, locking eyes with Lord Marshall.

'I've been invited to the Fitzroy ball, and I have a *plus one.* I don't presume you would fill your dance card with me all night, but it would be an honour to at least escort you in my carriage. And…' there was that crinkly-eyed smile again, warm and tender '…to share in your first dance.'

Sylvia held in her excitement and pretended to weigh her options. And then, after making him wait: 'I shall accept your offer.'

'Wonderful,' he said. 'I'll arrive at seven. Where are you staying?'

Where am I staying?

The first and only resort she could think of was the one where her sisters worked. 'The Linfield House. I'll be waiting outside.'

'I'm already counting down the days.' Lord Marshall gave another bow, then hurried down the street.

Sylvia looked up at the sky and let her face stretch into a triumphant grin. She slowly spun around and walked toward Hannah, who was smiling too.

'I did it,' Sylvia said, her voice a mix of joy and disbelief.

'You did it,' Hannah agreed.

'*We* did it.' Sylvia took both of Hannah's hands in her own, then remembered they were in public and dropped them. 'We did it.'

'Come to supper,' Hannah said, the smile still wide on her face. 'We deserve to celebrate. Have a bite of honey cheese with me.'

Sylvia wanted to say no—she had avoided spending time with Hannah outside of farmwork and fortune-hunting—but she was *happy*, and something about being happy made her want to stay by Hannah's side.

'Yes,' she said, and they set off in the direction of the farm. She felt light and airy the whole way, like she was floating above the ground. She smiled widely at the passersby she recognised and even, when they reached the Wickersham farm, out at the dusty expanse of cattle and pasture. Hannah helped Sylvia out of her jewellery and lent her a dress for an afternoon of butter-making. They talked and laughed and let their hands linger longer than necessary when passing tools between them. As the sun settled on the horizon, Sylvia rested her head on Hannah's shoulder, and she claimed it was from the exhaustion of churning the butter barrel but they both knew it wasn't.

And then it was supper. Hannah had already gone ahead to help Aunt Charity prepare the meal. As Sylvia walked along the winding dirt path to the main house, she felt her stomach rumble with anticipation. She could hear the sounds of mirth pouring from the windows, the sounds of a family enjoying each other's company. She smelled thyme and cream and something savoury, and her stomach rumbled even louder.

The door was already open, and she stepped inside ready to take her place at the table. But then she paused, surprised to see seven chairs instead of the usual six. And from that seventh chair came a familiar giggle, a familiar head of blond hair leaned against Amos's shoulder in just the way Sylvia had leaned against Hannah's an hour earlier.

Sylvia gasped.

'Violet?'

Chapter Ten

There was a bird's nest in the rafters of the barn, and the babies within were nearly old enough to begin flying. If they were waiting for some motivating force to nudge them out of the nest, then Hannah imagined Sylvia's current rant—which had just surpassed the ten minute mark—might do the trick.

'…and I *know* he's kind, and patient, and all the qualities a woman could hope for in a husband…' Sylvia continued, as Hannah nodded along. She was only half listening and gave most of her attention to the cheesecloths they were rinsing in a warm basin. '…but Violet just wasn't *raised* for a life of working. She's trained to host parties, and play charades, and walk in the park… She's not trained to be a *farmer's wife.*'

'A farmer,' Hannah said.

It took Sylvia a moment to realise she'd been interrupted. 'Excuse me?'

'She wouldn't just be *a farmer's wife*, she would be

a farmer in her own right.' She knew this wasn't the point of Sylvia's monologue, and she knew that Violet and Amos had only been seeing each other for a week or so—but the distinction mattered, at least to Hannah. 'You can't run a farm with just one farmer. They both wake up early to milk the cows. They both plough the fields and harvest the produce and even slaughter the meat. There's no such thing as a farmer's wife—just two farmers, married to each other.'

Sylvia blinked. 'I... I've never thought about it like that before.'

'But *anyway*,' Hannah said before Sylvia could start back up again. 'They've only just begun to see each other. Violet has come to supper two or three times. They haven't even *kissed* yet.'

'Well, *of course not*,' Sylvia said sternly. 'They aren't married.'

Hannah laughed.

Sylvia did not.

'Oh...' Hannah said, wringing the cheesecloth in her hand a little too tightly. 'Is that...important, to people in your class?'

'Is it not to yours?'

'Kind of...it depends on who you ask.' Hannah felt out of her depth. She wasn't the best source of information on social mores—she had never cared enough about what people thought of her to follow them. 'People out here value their privacy. Some are *very* insistent that you shouldn't even be *alone* with a person who isn't the same sex as you, and others don't see marriage as having anything to do with our God-given bodily urges. We all just…let each other be.'

Sylvia flicked her hands into the basin, droplets rippling across the surface. 'And which are you?'

'I'm the latter,' Hannah said as Sylvia began to stack the damp cloth. 'My father, Isaiah, he's my father in every way that matters…but he didn't— Wait, you know how babies are made, yes?'

'*Yes* I know how babies are made,' Sylvia said quickly.

'Good. Right. Yes. Anyway, he's not my father in *that* sense. He can't have children of his own, so when he met my mother and she was already pregnant…it was a convenient match. They're not perfect, of course, but they genuinely get along.'

Sylvia nodded, smoothing her hands over the stack of cloth. 'Do you know him? The man your mother knew before Isaiah?'

'No, and that's never mattered to me.' Hannah twisted water from the final cloth, her hands rough and red. 'It takes one night to make a child, but it takes a lifetime to raise them.'

They gathered their laundry in a basket and brought it to the clothing line behind the barn. 'Hannah…' Sylvia said as they were walking. 'I've been meaning to ask—the ball will end quite late on Friday, and I don't want my mother to ask where I've been…' She bit her lip nervously. 'Can I stay the night here, with you?'

Hannah's stomach did a somersault. *As friends*, she reminded herself. She tried to contain her enthusiasm when she finally answered. 'I'd like that.'

Sylvia exhaled in relief. 'Excellent. Because I must admit, I'm *far* more excited for that part of the night than the ball itself.' And then she laughed, surprised at what she had just said. 'Don't tell Lord Marshall, of course. Or Violet…or anyone. In fact, forget I said it altogether.'

Despite Sylvia's instructions, Hannah would not forget what Sylvia had said.

She would not forget *at all*.

Sylvia could tell from the moment she woke up that the most important Friday of her life would *not* be going smoothly. There was an uneasy feeling low in her stomach, a twist of nerves that made her squirm. There was an ache in her lower back that made her wonder, at first, if she had slept strangely. She rolled over to face her sisters, all asleep, the low light of dawn blue across their faces. This was not her usual waking time.

And then, the cold dread of realisation crawled through Sylvia's body. She gripped the bedsheets with angry fists and whispered through her teeth, *'Not today!'*

Her fears were confirmed when she snuck out of bed and lifted her nightgown: Sylvia had started bleeding.

She closed her eyes and leaned her head against the wall. 'Not today, not today…' she continued to mumble to herself. 'Literally, *any other day*…'

But her fate was sealed. She would have to dance through cramps and soreness, with fabric tied between her legs.

The rest of the day passed in a tedious blur of butter churning, herb harvesting, and dairy equipment cleaning. She didn't have much time to chat with Hannah until they were both upstairs getting ready for the ball, half-dressed in their outfits for the evening and enjoying a plate of toasted cheese.

'Eat slowly,' Hannah instructed, eyes alight. 'Really *savour* each bite, and see if you can notice all the flavours.'

Sylvia was no stranger to good food. She had dined on the finest fish, duck, and roast beef that England had to offer. She had tried soups and sauces prepared by the most in-demand chefs in all of Europe. She had filled her plate with venison hunted by the Duke of Wellington himself. But she couldn't remember any of it. She had never stopped to savour the food on her tongue.

But Hannah was teaching her how. She bit into the toast and its toppings, comically slow at first to make Hannah laugh, and let the texture spread across her tongue. She noticed the subtle sharpness of the mustard, the sweetness of the butter, the comforting fluffiness of the melted cheese.

'Wow,' Sylvia said. 'I've never thought about food this way before.'

Hannah smiled, and Sylvia realised just how many of her sentences had been starting like that recently. *I've never thought about...*

Hannah had a habit of opening Sylvia up to new experiences, new perspectives, new feelings—feelings that were becoming increasingly difficult to ignore.

Hannah moved behind Sylvia to finish buttoning her gown. Her fingers were steady on Sylvia's back, which made Sylvia feel steady herself. When Hannah finally finished and removed her hands, Sylvia felt unmoored. She longed for the simple tether of Hannah's touch to return.

'I don't exactly know how dance cards work,' Hannah said, 'but I think it's safe to say that looking like *this*, yours will be full.'

Sylvia beamed. There was no mirror, but the candlelight on the window gave a faint reflection. They stood in front of it now, Sylvia wrapped in peacock blue fabric with stitches of gold thread, Hannah in her same outfit from their promenade. They flickered like ghosts in the warped glass, the night sky blurring their edges so Sylvia couldn't tell where she ended and Hannah began.

They donned cloaks and hurried wordlessly to Linfield House, arriving just before the Marshall carriage.

And *what* a carriage it *was*—glossy black exterior, silver family crest, plush crimson upholstery, room to spare. Henry Marshall was as gentlemanly as expected, extending his hand to both Sylvia and Hannah as they stepped inside.

'I'm surprised your sister isn't joining you,' he said when they were seated, the three of them and his younger brother. It wasn't *strange* to only be accompanied by a lady's maid to a ball, but mothers, aunts, and sisters were more common chaperones.

'She isn't out yet,' Sylvia said. 'This would have been her first season, but after my father passed— *aah*!' A pang of cramping gripped her abdomen, and she bent forward.

'I'm terribly sorry for your loss, I had no idea—you don't have to talk about it, really.'

Sylvia nodded, then felt Hannah's hand on her shoulder for *one, two, three* seconds—no longer than appropriate. Henry launched into a conversation with his brother about finance, about hunting, about expensive brandy—occasionally pausing to explain terms to Sylvia that she already knew.

'You make a *distilled* drink by...'

Sylvia swore that once this man was her husband, she would interrupt his ramblings and show off just how much she knew. But for now, she was *courting*

Lord Marshall, and in that stage Sylvia could never let him feel like she knows as much as he does—or, God forbid, *more.*

On their way out of the carriage, Hannah whispered in Sylvia's ear: 'I much prefer *my* Henry…'

Sylvia smothered a laugh behind her glove.

The Fitzroys' holiday house was almost as grand as their country estate—large and decorative, with sculpted shrubbery lining the path to a tall, polished door. The gentle melody of a string quartet drifted through open windows and pierced right through Sylvia's heart. She inhaled, held her breath, and closed her eyes. She was *homesick.*

'What's wrong?' Hannah said quietly.

Sylvia let a subtle shiver travel down her body. 'Nothing,' she said, ready to link her arm with Lord Marshall's. 'Nothing is wrong—*everything* is right, finally.'

With every step she took toward the house, she settled more into her old self. The familiar sight of swirling couples in a candlelit ballroom welcomed her from the windows. The butler greeted her at the door and she almost *hugged* him with how happy she was to see a butler again. As Lord Marshall tied a dance card to her wrist, she felt in her heart that, even after all she'd been through, *she still belonged in this world.*

'If you don't mind…' Lord Marshall said as he wrote his name in the first and last lines of the card. He gave her that charming smile of his, the one that pressed a small dimple into his left cheek. She was struck by the sudden fear that she might be dreaming, that none of this was real, that she was about to wake up in the bed she shared with her sisters and whatever spider had decided to crawl beneath their blankets that night.

But then she was on the dance floor, moving her feet as she hadn't in months. Somehow, *thank God*, she remembered each step of the quadrille as expertly as if she hadn't missed a day. The chalked dance floor below and the crystal chandelier above were so *real*, so wonderfully, delightfully, blessedly real.

'You're enjoying yourself,' Lord Marshall said. She hadn't even realised she was smiling, distracted by her own elation.

'How could I not be?' she responded. 'You're the finest dance partner I've had in months.'

'I believe I'm the *only* dance partner you've had in months.'

'Then you'll have to check in with me at the end of the night, and see where you stand.'

But when Sylvia thought about the end of her night, chatting with Lord Marshall wasn't the part she looked forward to most. She wondered, briefly, if she could find Hannah in between dances, and she almost tried after she and Henry had parted ways—but a scathing whisper caught her attention just as she was leaving the ballroom.

'...*the eldest Queensbury girl...*'

Sylvia turned her head in the direction of the voice just in time to catch two older women disappear behind their fans. She recognised them, but only distantly. One was the mother of someone she had danced with over a year ago, a lanky gentleman who had brought her flowers once. Jack? James? She chided herself for letting Heene erode her memories.

The other was an old friend of her mother—but maybe *friend* wasn't the right word after all. She was a countess from the north who had spent afternoons taking tea with Ella for years, but who hadn't written a single letter since they'd lost the estate.

No one had.

Sylvia kept telling herself it was because they hadn't shared their address with anyone back home, but deep down she knew their old neighbours could have found a way to reach out if they'd wanted to.

'Miss Queensbury?' A quiet and nasally voice grabbed her attention. She spun to see Phillip Beaumont, tall and thin and eating a scone.

'Mr Beaumont,' she said with a curtsy. 'Such a pleasure to see you here this evening.'

'I feel the same way.' He glanced around, then leaned in close. 'My sister was terribly rude to you the other day. I'm glad you found your way here regardless.'

Sylvia wanted to ask why he didn't make his feelings known earlier, perhaps in front of his sister as she and Catherine were *actively being rude to Sylvia*, but her dance card was far too empty to justify such boldness. She pinned a grateful smile on her face instead.

'I'm sure the ball simply slipped her mind.'

'We both know that's not true.' He winked. 'Is there room on your card?'

Two country dances later, she and Mr Beaumont had developed quite the rapport. He was clumsier than Mr Marshall, but the conversation flowed smoothly, and soon Sylvia was laughing as he caught her up on all the London drama she'd missed last season. There was a particularly fascinating story about a duke who lost his bride to a rakish painter—his own sister, no less—that Sylvia couldn't wait to tell Hannah later.

But as the night wore on, Sylvia was finding fewer and fewer things she was excited to tell Hannah about when they were finally alone together. Most of the conversations she had with people were…more boring than she'd expected. Her feet were sore from dancing in thin-soled shoes, and her cheeks hurt from smiles that were increasingly hard to conjure.

The glamour of the night was wearing off, and Sylvia didn't understand why.

'What's wrong with me?' she asked Hannah hours later when they returned to the Wickersham farm. The carriage ride home had been mostly quiet, all four passengers ready for sleep. She and Hannah had crept up

the stairs and fumbled into nightgowns, then propped their pillows against the wall so they could sit next to each other.

'I mean, at first I felt *wonderful*,' Sylvia continued. 'I was *ecstatic* to be back where I belonged, I was *jubilant*, I was…all the words, Hannah! All the words for wonderful.'

'But?'

'But then…' Sylvia shrugged. She stared at the lone candle on Hannah's bedside table. 'It took more effort than it used to. It took real *effort* to make polite conversation, to dance, to keep my face locked in a friendly smile, to manoeuvre myself into dances and out of the scandalised stares of people who knew I shouldn't have been there…'

Hannah's fingers glided across the bed sheets and pressed lightly against Sylvia's. 'Did it take more effort than it used to? Or are you just noticing, for the first time, the effort it always took?'

Sylvia wasn't ready to answer that question. 'Surely putting up with a husband I don't care for takes less effort than churning butter.' She shifted beneath the blankets, bringing her knees to her chest and moaning through a cramp.

'Let me make you some tea, for the pain.' Hannah squeezed Sylvia's hand, but when she tried to let go, Sylvia held on tighter.

'No,' Sylvia said. Tea sounded lovely, but being

alone in the dark with her thoughts…that was scarier than all the aches that pulsed through her body. She leaned her head against Hannah's shoulder. 'I shouldn't be this sad. Tonight was a success, really. I have *two* potential husbands—though I shudder to think I may become a *Beaumont*. The plan is working. I just have to figure out what to do next.'

'A stroll along the beach?' Hannah suggested. 'A trip to the oyster house?'

'Yes, those would work. And then…'

'And then…?'

Sylvia sank lower into the bed, her head against Hannah's arm. She was too tired to be anything but honest. 'And then I don't know. I've never gotten past the initial courting phase with anyone. I've never— I mean, I've never even had to contemplate *kissing* someone before. But if our scheming is successful…'

'Do you *want* to kiss people?'

Sylvia was surprised. Hannah asked the question like there were real choices other than just *yes*. 'Of course. Everyone wants to kiss people.'

'Not everyone.'

'Okay, well—I hadn't considered that before. But yes. I'm at least *curious* to know what it's like. But what if—what if I were to *kiss* Henry—'

'I wouldn't recommend it—'

'I'm not talking about the cow!' The conversation broke into a fit of laughter. Their bodies shook, and

the bed squeaked, and by the time they were breathing calmly again they had somehow fallen flat onto the bed. They lay next to each other, their noses almost touching. Hannah's irises glowed in the darkness, like pools of gold catching the flicker of candlelight.

'What if I kiss Henry,' Sylvia said quietly, 'and I mess up? What if I'm not good at it? And it makes him not like me anymore?'

'Hmmm…' Hannah hummed, thinking. Sylvia resisted the urge to feel embarrassed. *Hannah's my friend now. I can trust her.* 'Well,' Hannah continued, 'we could—oh, nevermind…'

'No, tell me,' Sylvia said. 'Please.'

Hannah stared at Sylvia. The expression on her face was serious, and Sylvia could tell she was weighing the reasons to share—or not share—whatever idea she had come up with.

Hannah's face shifted into a casual smile. 'We could practice, if you want. Together.'

'We could practice…kissing?'

'Maybe it's too much—it's just that I have experience with these things, and I wouldn't mind—but if you don't want to—'

'It's an excellent idea,' Sylvia said. She heard the eagerness in her own voice without fully understanding it. She laughed nervously. 'I mean, I must learn somehow, right? Might as well…do it with someone I trust. Someone who won't judge me.'

Hannah shifted her body slowly, resting her hand on Sylvia's cheek.

'You *won't* judge me, correct?' Sylvia clarified.

'I won't judge you,' Hannah said. 'It's simple, really. You just part your lips, and lean in, and let your body…take over.'

Sylvia inched closer, the tip of her nose touching Hannah's with the lightness of a feather falling to earth. 'But there must be more to it than that?' she asked, her voice barely above a whisper.

Hannah paused. 'It's not like…learning a new dance. It's more like…you *become* the music.' She gently ran her fingers through Sylvia's hair. 'Can I show you?'

'Yes.'

Hannah closed the space between them and pressed her lips into Sylvia's, soft and sumptuous and hungry. Shock waves reverberated through every inch of Sylvia's body. She parted her lips and felt the warmth of Hannah's face, Hannah's fingers, Hannah's everything.

Sylvia sank into the pleasure of her first kiss. She tried to pay attention to the mechanics of it—how Hannah moved her lips, her teeth, her tongue—but any attempts at thinking straight were crushed by her sweet and sudden arousal.

How do you know when you fancy someone? Sylvia had asked Hannah weeks ago. The memory floated to the surface of her mind before diving back under in a wave of pleasure.

Have you ever swam in the ocean? Hannah had asked in response.

Sylvia knew what it meant to *be* in water. She had taken a plunge in the salty waves of Brighton, but only with the help of a professional dipper. She was held the entire time, as all proper ladies were expected to be.

Tonight, something new roiled deep in Sylvia's core. Her tongue lept from her mouth into Hannah's; their legs tangled like seaweed caught in a current; their chests rose and fell like the waves of high tide.

This was no dip into cautious waters. This was diving into the wild sea.

Sylvia was swimming.

And she had no desire to return to land.

Chapter Eleven

Hannah had no memory of falling asleep. She wasn't sure when, or how, she had eventually drifted into unconsciousness. She didn't even remember her dreams, or if she'd had any. All she knew was that *right now* she was tangled in bed with Sylvia, their limbs woven together like beanstalks, and that *hours ago* when the sky was still dark they had been like that too.

The sun crept ever upward as dawn gave way to morning. Amos would be milking the cows by now, and the rest of her family would be getting dressed. Sylvia slept so heavily against Hannah's shoulder that Hannah had lost feeling in her arm, but to move now would mean starting a day filled with so many things that weren't *this*.

A rooster made the decision for her. Sylvia shifted at the sound, pulling a blanket over her eyes to block the light.

'What time is it?' she mumbled, then pressed her cold feet against Hannah's calves.

Hannah shivered, but didn't move away. 'Time to get out of bed.' She slowly peeled the blanket off Sylvia's face, her creamy blond hair a mess of half-formed curls.

Sylvia groaned and clutched her abdomen, then folded at the waist. 'No thank you,' she said, still clinging to sleep.

Hannah sighed, stroking her hands through Sylvia's hair. Of all the excuses Sylvia could have come up with not to work, this was the one Hannah would never refuse.

'I'll get you some tea, and something to eat.' She gently removed herself from beneath Sylvia's body, stepped into stockings and an old beige robe, and went downstairs.

By this point in the day, Hannah's usual nighttime lovers would have snuck out of the house. Sylvia was *not* currently sneaking out of the house, and she was also not Hannah's lover. *Kissing practice*, Hannah told herself. *That's all it was.*

She daydreamed about her cheese shop as she prepared breakfast in bed for Sylvia, the one she would finally be able to afford when their plan was complete. Kissing Sylvia had not been an *expected* part of that plan, but Hannah could easily convince herself it was important nonetheless. *It would be irresponsible*, she thought, *to let Sylvia get married without even knowing how to kiss...*

Hannah brought her tray of tea and cake upstairs. Sylvia was already sitting, arms wrapped around her legs, forehead pressed against her knees.

'Ginger tea will ease the pain,' Hannah said as she joined Sylvia in bed. 'And so will the caraway seeds in the cake. And...' Hannah lifted a hot stone wrapped in cloth from her pocket, then balanced it on Sylvia's abdomen.

Sylvia looked like she might cry. 'You don't have to take care of me.' She sniffed.

'Of course—I can stop, if you want, or I can leave—'

'No,' Sylvia said, placing one hand over Hannah's. 'It's just... I'm not used to showing people when I'm in pain. Especially not *this* kind of pain. It's improper.'

Hannah felt the urge to lean over and kiss Sylvia's cheek. She settled for wrapping an arm around Sylvia's shoulders instead.

Hannah hadn't realised just how much *discomfort* people like Sylvia tolerated for their lavishly *comfortable* lifestyle. It all seemed so pointless, here in Hannah's bed. Such a small group of people holding on to so much of the country's wealth, and they were not even free to be themselves. They could let it all go— *they could share it with the rest of us, some of whom badly need it.*

'You're not a burden,' Hannah eventually said. 'You know that, right? And next time I'm feeling ill, you can return the favour.'

Sylvia curled her body around the hot stone in her lap. 'I'd like that,' she said quietly. 'I knew about ginger tea, but the caraway seeds…you teach me something new every day, Hannah Wickersham.' Then, Sylvia let her grimace of pain shift into a mischievous smile. 'And you teach me something new every night.'

A sudden heat ran through Hannah's body, but she was used to feeling ablaze the morning after kissing a beautiful woman.

What she was not used to was making beautiful women breakfast in bed.

'You're a quick learner,' she said with a wink, then poured Sylvia a second cup of tea and dressed for her day. She had a meeting with the Heene Society of Artisans and Shopkeepers to attend, which should take her mind off Sylvia for a while. There would or would not be more kissing practice later, and either way Sylvia would be gone in a few weeks' time. Hannah would move on with her life, never having grown attached enough to miss Sylvia for more than a day.

This arrangement had always worked for Hannah. She had no reason to believe it wouldn't work now.

Sylvia officially had her very own parasol. It was lacy, and delicate, and worth way more of her week's wages than she was comfortable spending. She justified the cost by telling herself that once she was Lady

Marshall, she would have enough money to purchase a hundred parasols on a whim.

'How are you feeling?' Hannah asked as they walked into Worthing.

'Much better,' Sylvia was happy to report. 'The first two days are always the worst…though much *less* worse than usual, thanks to you.' She handed Hannah a small basket of raspberries she had picked from the bushes near her house.

Hannah smiled, but her mind was clearly elsewhere.

'How was the meeting?' Sylvia asked. 'Any updates with the cheese shop?'

Hannah sighed. 'No…and there wasn't a lot of good news going around. Another resort here, another mineral water spa there…'

'Worthing has mineral water now?'

'It does not. But it turns out you can put just about anything in an advertisement.'

'Ah, I see.' Sylvia nodded. She wanted to ask more questions about the meeting, but the only questions her mind could come up with were about Hannah's lips against her own…

'I think I see him, over there?' Hannah pointed to a tall figure a dozen yards away, and sure enough Henry Marshall was walking in their direction.

Sylvia didn't want her time alone with Hannah to end so soon. *Was I any good at kissing?* she wanted to ask. *Do I need more practice? I probably need more practice. We should—*

'Ready to collect some shells?' Hannah asked. 'Amos has requested that we bring him the most *interesting* shell we find as payment for all our farm work that he's covering today.'

'What makes a shell interesting?'

But Hannah was already dipping into a curtsy. Sylvia turned to face her suitor, transforming into her old self.

'My lord,' she said. 'Such a lovely day for so fine an invitation.'

She had been lucky—*extraordinarily lucky*—that Mary had overheard the woman at the front desk wondering why Linfield House had received a letter for someone who was *not* staying in one of their suites. That letter, in elegant penmanship, had expressed Lord Marshall's continued interest in spending time with Sylvia and suggested a date searching for shells.

'I'm delighted you were available to join me,' he said, polite as ever.

Sylvia studied his face, pleasant enough to look at, convincingly genuine in its joy. His eyes were the warm brown of rainy-day soil, and his floppy black hair gave him a boyish charm—one that was quickly tempered by his stately top hat. Sylvia sensed a balance in him, the kind of balance ladies like herself always hoped for in a husband: he was refined but dashing, restrained but fun.

Arm in arm they strolled along the sand, stopping every few feet to examine the shells beneath their feet. Hannah trailed behind them, carrying in her basket whatever they decided to keep.

'What are you most excited to enjoy next season?' Lord Marshall asked.

Sylvia thought for a moment. 'I was quite the champion at charades, back in the day. I should like to reclaim my crown.'

'Now, *that* I must see,' he chuckled. 'I have yet to meet someone who could best me in the game.'

'We'd make an excellent team, then,' Sylvia said, charmed to find something she had in common with her suitor. 'That is, *if* you're as good as you say you are.'

'You'll just have to find out in person. Tell me, does Countess Cowper still throw those excellent parties of hers?'

'Yes! Such splendid times. And what a magnificent home; the marble archways and the—'

'Gilded wall panels!' he said excitedly. Sylvia beamed—here was someone with an eye for quality and a taste for opulence. He was speaking her language.

'When I get to decorate a manor someday, it'll look just like that.'

'Except without the—' he started.

'Green curtains! Please tell me you're about to say green curtains.'

'They're dreadful! The colour of crocodile skin.' They laughed together, and Sylvia settled deeper into his arm. *This* is what marriage could be like. The hot sparks of desire may well have been absent, but Sylvia by no means felt cold. Perhaps the warm embers of companionship would be enough.

'Have you ever seen a crocodile?' Sylvia asked. 'A real one, not just a drawing?'

'Oh yes. I've seen wonders, travelling as much as I have.' He stopped, bending down to observe a vibrant orange variegated scallop.

'*Mimachlamys varia,*' Sylvia said proudly. She had been reading books about shells ever since she got his invitation. 'And in excellent condition too.'

He held the flat shell between his thumb and index finger, its sunny ridges fanning out like a halo.

'Keep it,' he offered, then placed it in Hannah's basket. 'Have you done much travelling?'

'I've been to Scotland,' Sylvia said. 'But not the Continent, not yet.'

'I should like to take you to Paris,' he said abruptly. 'You would find it…*exquisite.* All the latest fashions, the finest food…'

Sylvia tilted her parasol so he wouldn't see her face, the unrestrained smile and wide-open eyes that betrayed her excitement. She knew it was still wise to pursue Mr Beaumont as a back-up plan, but it was impossible now not to put all her hope in Lord Marshall.

'That would be a dream come true,' she said, resetting the parasol.

'So many places I could show you…there's this oyster bar overlooking the water, my favourite place to dine in all of Europe. You'll *adore* it.'

Sylvia grimaced. She would never *adore* an oyster bar, but Lord Marshall didn't need to know that. He wasn't interested in Miss Sylvia Queensbury—he was interested in the future Lady Marshall, who would travel with him to his favourite places, dance with him to his favourite songs, host his favourite friends at parties, and toast with all his favourite drinks.

This was the kind of future Sylvia was made for. It had never felt unbearable. The slight discomfort she was experiencing now changed nothing. It made her no less capable of being who she wanted to be.

'Ah!' Lord Marshall exclaimed, digging his fingers into the sand. 'I was hoping I'd find one of these…'

He lifted a small stone into his handkerchief, then rubbed it clean of sand. He gave it to Sylvia, its cool damp surface pressed into the fabric of her glove.

'Keep it with you,' he said, 'and think of me.'

Sylvia stared down at the heart-shaped stone in the centre of her palm. It was smooth and grey, speckled with white, nearly exact in its symmetry.

He must really like me, Sylvia thought. She pressed her thumb against the rock and let her own heart swell with the feeling of being so *wanted*.

'I'll treasure it always,' she said. 'I must admit, I am growing quite fond of you, Lord Marshall.'

'Please, call me Henry.'

She smiled, twirling her parasol between her fingers. *If only Augusta and Catherine were walking by*, she thought to herself.

If only they could see me now.

Sylvia was convinced that every Worthing ball she attended was cursed. On the morning of her first ball, she had woken up aching and bleeding. On the evening of her second, she left the Wickersham house with Hannah on her arm only to see her own mother standing at the gate, hands on hips, eyebrows raised. Even in the pale light of dusk, Sylvia could see the deep frown lining Ella Queensbury's face.

Sylvia froze. She gripped Hannah's arm tighter. 'Is it too late to go back inside?' she whispered.

Hannah gave her a sympathetic look. 'I think I should let you—'

'But—'

'—let you two talk.' Hannah didn't force herself away from Sylvia; she stood there, steady as always.

After a few painfully awkward seconds, Sylvia finally slipped her arm from Hannah's and walked toward the gate.

'Mother!' she said, as though nothing in the world were wrong. 'It is *such* a delight to see you. I was just about to—'

'Your next words better be *go to the Elwes ball.*'

Sylvia was relieved—she had no idea what lie she was about to come up with, and now she didn't have to.

'Don't be cross—'

'I don't *want* to be cross, Sylvia. But I also didn't *want* to run into Lady Fitzroy today, who asked why I hadn't accompanied you to her ball, and *then* asked if I would be joining you at Marino Mansion this evening.'

Sylvia gasped. She *audibly gasped*, which clearly vexed her mother even more.

'Before you ask—I didn't tell her about our situation,' Ella said. 'I told her I was simply too grief-stricken to return to society, and then *I left* before she could ask any more questions. But she saw how I was dressed, Sylvia.' She sighed, running a tired hand through her untied hair. 'Whatever you're up to…you're going to get caught eventually.'

'Come to the ball with me,' Sylvia said impulsively, though she knew it didn't make sense.

Ella made a face of utter disbelief. 'Come to the ball? Dressed like this?'

'We could find you something—'

'I don't care if you found me a gown made of solid

gold—I don't *want* to go to the ball, I am done with balls. But the thing I've been asking myself—the thing I haven't figured out yet—is why *you* are going.'

Sylvia wanted to sink into the ground beneath her feet. She'd rather the earth swallow her whole than have to continue this conversation.

She said the first words that came to mind. 'I haven't been in a real *mansion* in so long, I just wanted to feel at home again.'

'Right.' Ella nodded. 'I considered that. But then I saw your dress. That must have been, what, a week of wages? Two? You don't make a purchase like that for just one ball.'

'But it's a *fancy* ball. It's hosted by *the* Robert Elwes…he met *Jane Austen*! And the mansion is only four years old, it's built in the latest style—'

'You sound like you're reading the description of the party you'll hear in tomorrow's paper. You're just listing facts. I don't—' Ella's voice caught. She looked away, blinking, and Sylvia was struck by a terrible feeling of familiarity. She recognised what her mother was doing, the way her eyes remained fixed on the sky, the way her breathing was slow and deliberate.

She recognised what her mother was doing because *she* did it too, all the time.

Ella was trying not to cry.

Her voice was small when she faced Sylvia again. 'I don't know why you're lying to me. I didn't raise a liar.'

Resentment flared in Sylvia's chest, then burned through the rest of her body in seconds. It was her turn to be cross.

'You're right,' she said. 'You didn't raise me to be a liar. You didn't raise me *at all*.'

Ella opened her mouth to speak, but Sylvia wasn't done yet. She had *never* spoken to her mother like this, or her father, or any adult at all.

'You did what every other lady of the *ton* did for her children,' she said. 'You hired me a decent governess, paid for my education, bought me all the gowns and jewels and makeup I would need to be pretty enough for society, then set me on the path to marriage so I could begin the cycle all over again.

'So if you're wondering what I'm doing, Mother,' she continued, running out of breath. 'I am simply doing what I was raised to do. Not by you, not by Father, but by the whole of England.'

Sylvia locked eyes with Ella, daring her mother to look away first.

'You're right,' Ella said eventually, her shoulders dropping. The crease across her forehead disappeared.

Sylvia wasn't sure she heard correctly. She was… *right*?

'I just wanted to be…' Ella's gaze drifted off once more, not to stop tears, but to look for something— something Sylvia wouldn't be able to see, something in the past. 'I just wanted to be like everyone else.'

The anger that burned inside Sylvia fizzled out, leaving a sad trail of smoke in its place. She wasn't used to seeing her mother this vulnerable.

'When I fell in love with your father, I didn't realise how *different* things would be in London. I knew I'd wear nicer clothes and do less work, but it wasn't until I got there that I—' She shook her head, searching for the right words. 'I just thought it would be easier to do what everyone else was doing until I could find my own way, but then... I never found my own way.'

'But that's what I'm trying to do now,' Sylvia said. 'I'm trying to find my own way...*my own way out of Heene.* I haven't just been attending balls, I've been—I've been entertaining suitors. Ones who could restore our family to its proper place.'

Ella's eyes went wide. She bit her lip. She crossed, then uncrossed, her arms.

The crickets chirped and the owls sang.

'And your sisters?' Ella asked. 'They know? They approve?'

'Yes,' Sylvia said, growing anxious at how much time was passing.

'I think you're making a mistake.'

'Did you make a mistake when you got out of Heene? When you married Father?'

'No, but—'

'Then you don't get to tell me I'm any different.' Sylvia looked behind her, to the house, where Hannah was peeking through a curtain. 'Hannah!' she called, straightening her spine.

'Sylvia,' her mother said quietly. Sylvia didn't interrupt her, but if Ella had anything more to say, she decided not to say it.

Hannah came to the gate awkwardly, her eyes to the ground. Sylvia linked their arms together and moved them swiftly onto the road. She kept a quick, frustrated pace, only turning around once to see if her mother had left.

Strangely, Ella was walking into the Wickersham house.

Sylvia didn't have time to wonder why, and she *certainly* didn't have time to dwell on the conversation she'd just had.

'What kind of hors d'oeuvres do you think they'll have tonight?' Sylvia asked, too enthusiastically.

'Sylvia…' Hannah said, her tone delicate. 'Do you want to talk about—'

'No,' Sylvia half shouted. And then, softer: 'No, I'm sorry. Perhaps later. I don't want a bit of sadness to spoil a lovely night.'

But Sylvia was feeling so much more than *a bit of sadness*, and she knew Hannah could tell. She knew Hannah wanted to keep asking. She knew Hannah probably would.

But tonight, Sylvia didn't want to dwell on her mother's disappointment and all the big, messy, complicated feelings that came with it.

Tonight, Sylvia just wanted to be okay.

'We'd better get going, then,' Hannah said, linking her arm around Sylvia's. 'We don't want *being late* to spoil a lovely night either. Now, tell me, what food do you think they'll have at the ball...'

Sylvia smiled. She listened as Hannah asked her all sorts of distracting questions, and together they talked about all sorts of ordinary things. Sylvia just wanted to be okay, and Hannah understood that about her. Hannah *knew* Sylvia, and Sylvia wasn't used to letting people know her. She wasn't used to it, and she had never sought it out before.

Walking toward the glittering lights of Worthing, Sylvia let herself be known.

Chapter Twelve

For the first time in over a year, Sylvia Queensbury had a full dance card.

For the first time in all her life, Sylvia Queensbury didn't want one.

The beauty and charm of Marino Mansion was everything she had hoped it would be, of course, but Sylvia could see through the shiny veneer of polite society in a way she hadn't before. She saw gold cufflinks and diamond necklaces and wondered how many families they could feed. She saw smiles exchanged by people she *knew* hated each other, or envied each other, or spread gossip about each other…and she saw too, that she was about to do the same.

'Who are you dancing with tonight?' a young woman asked, one whom Sylvia didn't recognise. A group was gathering around her, not to sneer and smirk but to admire, to be in her presence. No doubt they had seen her with Lord Marshall on the beach.

'I can hardly keep track,' Sylvia said, lifting her

wrist to view her card's crowded list of names. 'But—and *don't* tell him I said this—the dance partner I'm *most* looking forward to seeing is Henry.' She waited for one salacious beat as the women's eyes went wide. '*Oh dear,* I've spoken out of turn! I mean *Lord Marshall.*'

Nothing about the interaction felt genuine. That wasn't unusual for events like this, but now that Sylvia knew what *genuine* really felt like…

Another woman in the group spoke up. 'I've got Lord Marshall on my card too.'

'And I as well!'

That's to be expected, Sylvia told herself. He was an eligible lord, and he could dance with whomever he wished—but only Sylvia had his heart-shaped stone.

A waltz began and the crowd of ladies dispersed.

'Miss Queensbury!' Sylvia heard a bellowing voice behind her. She turned to see Lord Bogsworth, the oldest gentleman to claim a spot on her card.

Sylvia curtsied. 'I trust you are having an enjoyable night, Lord Bogsworth.'

'Enjoyable enough,' he said through his thick grey moustache.

Sylvia forced a smile and told herself—again, and again, and again—that nothing about this night was different from what she was used to. Dancing with gentlemen who are old enough to be her great-grandfather was all part of the process.

Sylvia stepped into Lord Bogsworth's arms and tried not to flinch at his surprisingly strong grip. He smelled like stale mustard, and the only way Sylvia got through the dance was by imagining what she and Hannah would get up to after the ball was over. *If things go well with Henry tonight*, she thought, *I'll have to ask Hannah for more kissing practice, just in case...*

The song was mercifully short. She decided to get a drink—or better yet, to find Henry and have him fetch a drink for her, preferably within eyesight of Catherine, or Augusta, or anyone else who needed a reminder that *Sylvia belonged in this room.*

But when she did find Henry, he was already bringing lemonade to another woman.

No matter, she told herself, then checked her dance card. *My time with him will come, and I shall make the most of it when it does.*

It took the taste of a dozen hors d'oeuvres, the clumsy but winsome flirtations of Phillip Beaumont, and several conversations with people who didn't seem to mind the scandal her family had gone through— but eventually, Sylvia was swept up once again in the grandeur of her old life. She felt *lovely*, just as she had wanted to on her walk to the ball.

By the time Henry Marshall approached her for their dance, Sylvia was ready to put on a show.

'Good evening, Henry,' she said, loud enough for

anyone nearby to hear. She extended her arm and let him kiss her hand. 'Have you been enjoying the ball?'

'Not as much as I'm about to,' he said with a smile, as he escorted her to the dance floor. On the way, Sylvia locked eyes with Catherine Fitzroy and gave her a wink.

Catherine frowned.

This particular dance was lively, leaving little room for intimate conversation—but Sylvia could say plenty with just her eyes. She focused on Henry's deep brown irises and willed the rest of the party to fade away. He looked at her in the same way she was looking at him: communicating a dictionary's worth of words without even opening his mouth.

Interest, she heard from his unmoving lips. *Affection, want, desire.*

The song ended and she asked for a drink. Men just *adored* fetching drinks for women, from the simplest lemonade to the bitterest wine—it made them feel useful, agentive, in charge. Henry would pursue her, and she would let herself be pursued.

'Thank you,' she said when he returned. 'I am quite in need of refreshment.'

'I believe it,' he said. 'I've barely seen you off the dance floor. You're in high demand tonight.'

Yes, Sylvia thought. *Let him think there's real competition.*

'Oh, you know this crowd,' she said, playing modest. 'I wasn't around for the season—they're just interested in a new face, that's all.'

Slowly, gently, he lifted his hand and cupped one side of Sylvia's jaw. '*This face* is so much more than just *new*.' And then he dropped his hand, before anyone could notice, and cleared his throat. Sylvia felt... well, she didn't feel the spark of attraction she'd been hoping for, but maybe love took longer to develop than she'd expected. Maybe her story would be different from her mother's.

'If that was meant to be a compliment,' she said, 'then I must admit I quite like your face too.'

Henry opened his mouth to speak, but he was interrupted by a gentleman Sylvia had agreed to dance with at the beginning of the night but whose name she could no longer remember.

'Miss Queensbury! Such a delight to see you enjoying society again.'

'Oh—' she began. This next suitor's smile was too eager, and he smelled strongly of cigars. Before she had time to settle into her old, deferential self again, she said: 'I was actually just telling Lord Marshall how I've grown faint from all this dancing—you know how we ladies can tire *so easily*—and he was about to escort me to my chaperone so I can rest.' She linked her arm in Henry's and left the ballroom.

'Good call,' he said when they were out of earshot.

'Robertson's drowning in gambling debt. Better stay away from him.'

So much for not gossiping, Sylvia thought. But she smiled gamely and said, 'Well, that just won't do—I only dance with upstanding gentlemen.'

They reached the back of the house, where wide glass doors opened to a sprawling yard. 'I take it you're not really faint, then?'

'No, not all. I just…' Sylvia didn't know how to finish that sentence. It was true that she didn't want to dance with Robertson—she didn't like the way he had looked at her, like she was a particularly appetising leg of lamb that had been set on his plate—and the thought of sustaining *another* conversation with *another* random gentleman was becoming increasingly boring. But she also knew there was more to her desire to leave the ballroom than just that.

She knew that she missed Hannah, and she knew there was no way Hannah had stayed inside on a night as lovely as this.

'I can feel my ribbons coming loose,' she lied, 'in the back of my dress. I just need to find my lady's maid…'

Henry's eyes darted into the dark night that stretched beyond the light of the mansion. 'I could come with you—'

'It wouldn't be proper,' Sylvia said. She knew that sneaking off with Henry Marshall could advance their courtship...but when she thought of putting her kissing practice to use in that way, she felt a knot tighten deep in her stomach.

And, she reminded herself, *Henry is too much of a gentleman to desire something like that anyway.*

'I'll be all right,' she assured him.

He hesitated, but said, 'If you insist.'

Then Sylvia was on her own.

The sweaty warmth of the mansion gave way to the cool night air as Sylvia stepped through the threshold into a wide courtyard.

She expected Hannah to be nearby, sitting on the ledge of the fountain or lying in the grass to gaze at the stars. If a woman *had* to go outside at night, she was never to venture further than where the nearest window's light could reach.

Hannah, apparently, did not know this rule.

Sylvia moved to the edge of the light, peering into dark trees and hedges that populated the mansion grounds. *'Hannah?'* she whispered loudly. *'Hannah, are you out here?'*

She looked around to make sure no one was watching, then ventured onto a thin stone path that took her farther and farther from the comforting sounds of clinking glasses, laughing dancers, and a busy string quartet.

'Hannah?' she said, a bit louder this time.

A few more seconds passed. She was starting to doubt if Hannah was out here at all.

A loose stone shifted beneath Sylvia's foot. A creature scurried in the distance. 'Hannah?'

'Sylvia!' Hannah said suddenly, appearing behind her. Sylvia spun, her heart beating loud and fast. She clutched her chest.

'Oh, sorry,' Hannah said, placing her hands on Sylvia's arms to steady her. 'I didn't mean to frighten you.'

'Where did you come from?' Sylvia's body, tense from surprise, eased considerably at Hannah's touch.

'There's a garden.' Hannah pointed down a turn in the road behind them that Sylvia had missed. 'This place is *huge*—there's so much to explore—I've been—' She was talking quickly now, her excitement moving so fast her words could barely keep up. 'Oh, let me just show you.'

Hannah took Sylvia's hand and led her down a tree-lined path. It wasn't long until they reached a clearing, a grove of shrubs and flowers and short trees with wide leaves. The sounds of the ball were completely gone now, the crash of ocean waves a whisper in the distance.

On her first night in Heene, Sylvia had detested the grating screech of crickets outside her walls. The nocturnal *hoots* and *hollers* had kept her awake and kept her on edge. But here, on this peaceful patch of open land, this trimmed circle of grass with its ring of benches and bushes, Sylvia heard no grating screech. Instead, she heard those same crickets chirping a tune like a choir of bells. She heard the clear trill of a lone nightingale, the low rumble of mating toads.

And then, the lead performer in this grand orchestra, the line of melody swelling up as the symphony carried on below: *Hannah's voice.*

'Isn't it marvellous?' she asked, full of wonder.

'Yes,' Sylvia said. 'Yes it is.'

Sylvia gave her full attention to Hannah, beholding the beauty she could see now that her eyes had adjusted to the night. Her bonnet was missing and her bun untied; wild waves of amber fell past her shoulders.

Sylvia had never once been this captivated looking at a man.

Hannah smiled, letting her eyes sweep over the garden again before landing on Sylvia. And then she frowned, suddenly concerned. 'Why did you leave the party?'

'Oh, right,' Sylvia said. She had forgotten there was anywhere else in the world she could be than right there. 'It's so noisy, and hot, and… I just needed some fresh air. A moment of rest.'

Hannah eyed her suspiciously. 'But isn't *this*,' she gestured back at the mansion, now just a sliver of light in the distance, 'all you've been working toward? Isn't it what you want?'

'Yes, of course,' Sylvia said. 'But I...well, I've never had a *friend* at these events before, someone I could confide in and get through the night with. I didn't know what I was missing—I didn't know there was anything *to miss.* I just wish—I wish you could be in there with me. But you can't, so—here I am.'

Hannah smiled slowly. 'Here you are.'

A moment of charged silence passed between them. The heaviness in Sylvia's stomach—the knot that had formed when she'd imagined kissing Henry—unravelled. She felt loose, untethered, drifting toward Hannah and wanting to—

'I danced with a man who smelled like mustard,' Sylvia said, trying to distract herself from the light, tingling sensation she felt in her own lips, eager as they were for more...*practice.*

'I don't mind mustard,' Hannah said.

'No, but not in a good way. Like *stale* mustard, or *mouldy* mustard.'

Hannah laughed. 'That's oddly specific. And definitely unpleasant. What was his name?'

'Lord Bogsworth,' she said, doing an impression of his stuffy voice.

Hannah wrinkled her nose. 'I have something that will take your mind off old mustard.' Sylvia followed Hannah to a tree, then watched her reach into its boughs and pull down an indigo-coloured fruit, cradled gently in her palm.

'This is a *fig orchard*?' Sylvia gasped. She accepted the gift from Hannah and sank her teeth into the plump, juicy fruit, moaning in delight. She closed her eyes and relished the taste, the sweet pulp on her tongue.

When she finally opened her eyes, she found Hannah staring at her lips.

Sylvia could deny it no more—the molten hot desire that pulsed through her body, that defied all reason, that threatened to disrupt everything she knew about romance and lust and *desire*.

She held the bitten fruit to Hannah's mouth. 'Your turn,' she said.

Hannah obliged, biting into the fruit as juice dripped down Sylvia's hand, wrist, arm. For the second time in a row, Sylvia forgot there was anywhere else in the world she could be other than right here. All she knew was the curve of Hannah's lips, the sparkle of glow-worms in the dark grass, and the pale moonlight streaming through branches like a dozen wedding veils caught in the trees.

'Hannah,' Sylvia said. 'It's been so long since we last...*practised*, in your bedchamber—I think I need another lesson, to refresh my memory—'

Hannah didn't need any more instructions than that. She pulled Sylvia in for a hungry kiss, and Sylvia let the fig fall from her fingers. She gripped Hannah's hips and rocked into her body, their lips dancing to a song no one else could hear.

Hannah slid one hand up Sylvia's back to the base of her neck, then leaned their bodies against the bark of the tree. Sylvia felt a desperate pressure building in the core of her body, and somehow she knew—*just knew*—that in all her years of courting gentlemen, *this* was the feeling she had been waiting for.

Hannah broke away to kiss Sylvia's cheek. 'Is there anything else you want to learn?' she whispered.

Sylvia inhaled sharply. 'No,' she said. 'I mean—*yes*. There's more I want to *do*, but…' She bit her lip. She knew that what she was about to say could not be un-said. 'I don't want you to teach me so I can just run off and shag Henry Marshall. I want…oh God, Hannah, I don't know how else to say it—I want *you*.'

Hannah smiled, her eyes ablaze with mutual desire. 'Are you sure?'

'Yes—I don't know what it means, I don't know if I fancy women, or just you, or if I'm ever going to want to kiss a man, but—' She shook her head, banishing the last of her doubts. 'I don't care what it means. I just know that I've never felt this way before and I want to taste—I want to *savour*—every last second of it.'

'All right then,' Hannah said. 'Jump.'

'Did you just say *jump*?'

'Trust me.'

Sylvia did as she was told. As soon as she had left

the ground she was grasped by Hannah, who spun her until her back was against the tree, her legs parted and wrapped around Hannah's waist.

'*Oh,*' Sylvia said. A dizzying tension spread across her body. 'Oh *yes—*'

The last word barely escaped before she was sighing deeply, before Hannah's warm lips travelled downward toward Sylvia's breasts. Hannah, Sylvia knew then, was just as eager as she was.

Sylvia felt the tip of Hannah's tongue slip below her neckline, then dug her fingers into Hannah's hair.

'May I?' Hannah asked, fingers cupped around Sylvia's breast.

'Yes,' Sylvia breathed, then melted into the pleasure of Hannah's hand pressing and pinching and stroking her, drawing desire to the surface of her skin in a way that made her whole body ache.

She wanted more.

Sylvia squeezed her legs, then tugged on the layers of fabric that separated her from Hannah. She pulled her skirts up until she could feel the fresh night air against a part of her that was growing damper by the second.

Hannah moaned and kissed Sylvia all over, her breath hot against Sylvia's chin, her neck, her ears, her forehead. Sylvia did as Hannah had told her all those days ago—she gave her body over to its own rhythm, let herself dance without being told how.

She clenched her thighs until her muscles quivered.

'*Sylvia,*' Hannah mumbled, her eyes closed. Sylvia wanted to do whatever she could to hear her name in that same tone of voice, over, and over, and over again.

She pushed her pelvis forward, writhing with pleasure as the heat of Hannah's torso pressed against her naked vulva. 'What else can we do?' Sylvia asked.

'What else?'

'I mean… I know there's *more*. I may be inexperienced but I'm not *naïve*.'

She studied Sylvia's face, considering her options. 'If you want, I can…touch you. I mean, more than I'm currently doing. I can use my hand and rub, kind of like this…' She placed the pads of her fingers over Sylvia's nipple and moved them in a firm, steady circle. 'But between your legs instead.'

Sylvia nodded. Her lower body throbbed with *want*. 'I'd like to try that, yes.'

Hannah smiled, biting her bottom lip. And then, she stepped away from the tree and set Sylvia back on her feet. 'I'll be right back.'

Sylvia watched Hannah walk a few steps to the fountain in the centre of the garden, lean down, and rinse her hands in its water. A chill ran across Sylvia's skin now that she was no longer wrapped in Hannah's warmth. She leaned against the tree and smelled the fragrant air, eyes trained on Hannah as she returned from the fountain, drying her hands on her dress.

'I missed you—' Sylvia began, coyly, but already Hannah had scooped her off the ground. Sylvia wrapped her arms around Hannah's neck and kissed her forehead, laughing all the while. There was a special joy in being *held* that Sylvia hadn't known was possible.

Hannah bent her knees until they were both in the grass, reclined against their sturdy tree. Sylvia's whole body tingled as Hannah worked her hand up the inside of Sylvia's leg, her touch light and gentle but no less *restless*.

'Tell me if you like what you're feeling,' Hannah said as she leaned in to kiss Sylvia's neck. 'And tell me if you want to stop.'

'Have you ever known me *not* to speak up?' Sylvia said, grinning, but she knew Hannah's words were important. Here at the base of this tree and tangled up in Hannah's limbs, Sylvia felt aroused and enchanted and so wet she could drown the grass beneath her— but most profoundly, most meaningfully, she felt *safe*.

'I trust you,' Hannah said…and then she moved her fingers the final distance across Sylvia's thighs to the outer folds of Sylvia's vulva.

If the crickets were still chirping, Sylvia couldn't hear. Every ounce of her attention was fixed on the cosy sensation budding between her legs. Hannah moved her fingers just as she had a moment ago, in slow, deliberate circles that left Sylvia gasping. Just when Sylvia thought this was as good as it could get, Hannah shifted her hand up just an inch to a bundle of nerves that Sylvia couldn't *believe* had been on her own body this *entire time*.

'Hannah,' she called, louder than she expected. Sylvia's back arched and her neck craned, hair snagging on the bark behind her. The updo would be ruined, but Sylvia didn't care. Her neat curls didn't stand a chance against Hannah Wickersham.

Pleasure bloomed across Sylvia's body, twining itself through every limb and ligament like an overgrown vine. She kissed Hannah's cheek and cursed as the blissful tension kept building: *'God damn,'* she said between panting breaths, which wrested a satisfied smile from Hannah's lips. Sylvia noticed how much Hannah was enjoying this too, how much Hannah was getting from giving. It made Sylvia want to give too.

Hannah moved her hand faster, her stiff fingers spinning in tight, urgent circles. Sylvia felt a droplet of sweat slink down the side of her face, her whole body flush and damp. Her legs began to shake, and just when she thought her body couldn't hold another ounce of pleasure—

'Mmmm!' She hummed a crescendo as all the ecstasy that had gathered in her body burst forth, a euphoric release that washed over her very soul. She shuddered, delirious and drenched, as Hannah slowed her pace to a gradual stop and her muscles melted back to their usual, unclenched selves.

Sylvia tucked her weakened legs beneath her skirts and curled into Hannah's arms.

'That was…' She tried to find the words, her breathing still heavy. 'I mean…you just…'

Hannah laughed. 'I'm sure they're all having *loads* of fun in there.' Hannah nodded in the direction of the mansion. '*Just* as fun as we're having.'

She was teasing, and Sylvia gladly took the bait. 'Not *one person* in that ballroom is having anything *close* to the amount of fun we are having.'

'Not even the mustard man?'

'*Especially not* the mustard man.'

They were both laughing now, peaceful and cosy beneath a canopy of figs.

Sylvia leaned her head against Hannah's shoulder, then curled a hand around Hannah's waist. 'I can't guarantee I'll be quite as…*skilled* as you…but if you'll give me a chance to try…'

Hannah kissed Sylvia's forehead. 'You'd be surprised how transferable the skills of butter-making are, Sylvia. The arm strength, the endurance, the ability to move in consistent circles…'

Sylvia smiled and dragged her fingers to Hannah's thighs.

Hannah kept speaking, her voice steady and sure. 'Another time. And I look forward to that time, really. But I'm so sleepy—in a good way, in a peaceful way, and I just… I want to listen. To the crickets. To the fountain. To the gentle beat of your heart. I want to sit beneath this tree and be at peace. With you.'

Sylvia was sleepy too, and maybe more peaceful than she'd ever been in her life. Hannah wanted to sit here and just *be still*, and Sylvia felt a sudden permission to crave that stillness herself.

They stayed that way for a while, like statues in the garden. They were quiet and tranquil and so very grateful to be in each other's arms.

After a long time had passed, Hannah said: *'Awake, O north wind; and come, thou south; blow upon my garden, that the spices thereof may flow out. Let my beloved come into her garden, and eat her pleasant fruits.'*

Sylvia looked at Hannah through drooping eyelids. 'What is that from? Usually when you use your *recitation* voice like that you're quoting the Bible, but that was clearly about—'

'It was the Bible.'

'But that was about *sex*. And—'

'I changed the pronouns around a little, but that's a true verse from the Bible.'

Sylvia's eyes opened wider. 'But…*eat her pleasant fruits? Blow upon my garden?'*

'It's a metaphor,' Hannah said playfully, 'for how much Christ loves the church.'

'No it isn't.' Sylvia started to laugh.

'Thy two breasts are like two young roes—'

'Hannah!'

'Thy lips, O my spouse, drop as the honeycomb...' Now Hannah was laughing too, their bodies fluttering together like flowers in a breeze. *'Honey and milk are under thy tongue.'*

'I can't believe that's in the Bible,' Sylvia said. She had never considered that bodily desire could be worthy of divine literature—*then again*, Sylvia thought, *I'd never considered bodily desire at all.*

'Now that we're not...*practicing* anymore,' she continued. 'Are we...are we *courting*?'

Hannah didn't say anything for a while, and Sylvia started to wonder if she had fallen asleep.

But then, Hannah spoke. 'There isn't a word for the kind of desire that society doesn't want to talk about.' She ran her fingers through Sylvia's hair, softly, rhythmically. 'But the closest thing I can think of is... I fancy you. And I wouldn't mind fancying you, like this, for a few more weeks.'

Sylvia wanted to nod her head, but she was too sleepy. She knew there was a chance she'd never feel this way for a man...for her *husband*, when she finally had one...so she decided not to focus on what this moment *meant*, and instead to just be thankful, *so thankful*, that she'd had it at all.

The dancers danced, the ocean roared, the planet turned. All the while, Hannah and Sylvia lay in their secret garden, silent and still, lips as sweet as honey and figs.

Chapter Thirteen

Hannah couldn't remember the last time she'd dug her toes into wet sand. Judging by the creases in the linen sheet she saved for beachfront picnics, it had been too long.

'Is this our first picnic since… *May*?' she asked Amos, who was spooning blueberry tart into his mouth.

'Mmm-hmm.' He nodded, his cheeks full.

'You're so busy these days, *wooing Violet.*'

He raised his eyebrows, but finished chewing before he responded. *'I'm* so busy these days? Wooing *Violet*?'

Hannah laughed, having anticipated this reaction. She kept teasing: 'I hardly even see you anymore… you're always off, gallivanting around Worthing—'

'You're the one *gallivanting*!' He grabbed a raspberry from their bowl of fruit and threw it in her direction. 'You can come for me after I've been to a *ball*, but until then, we both know who the busy one is.'

Hannah ate the raspberry. 'I really did think hiring a farmhand would give me more free time.'

'You thought wrong.'

'I thought wrong.'

Amos and Hannah were both smiling, eyes steady on the horizon. The ocean was calm today, the waves more like rolling hills than jagged mountains.

'How was it, though? The ball?' Amos asked. 'I've always wondered what that great big monstrosity of a house looks like on the inside.'

'It was a bit much,' Hannah said, politely dismissive of how extravagant the ball had been. It had been a hard sight to see, really: trays of artfully prepared food on full display, far more than could reasonably be eaten by the guests of Marino Mansion, all while families down the road struggled to buy bread. The gold wall sconces alone could pay rent for half of Heene.

But Amos knew this already. He was a romantic at heart, and she knew what he wanted to hear.

'I didn't stay long, actually,' she said, then paused to wave a seagull away from her plate of lemon biscuits. 'The ballroom was huge, and fancy, and noisy. I left to find some peace in the grounds. There were so many flowers, Amos, and hedges trimmed in the most interesting shapes, and there were fountains and statues, and I just stayed there, exploring, until—until Sylvia came looking for me.'

The more Hannah described the memory, the more

it set her heart ablaze. She burrowed both feet into the sand, like she was a hot air balloon and the memory of last night was enough fire to whisk her away.

'Sylvia came looking for you?' Amos asked. 'As in, she left the ball? She left her suitors to go find you?'

'Yes,' Hannah said, trying to hide her proud smile. 'That's exactly what happened.'

'Hannah Wickersham!' Amos placed a giant hand on Hannah's shoulder, giving her a playful nudge. 'She *so* fancies you.'

Hannah nodded, not sure how much she should say next. But then she looked at her cousin, at his radiant joy, at the smudge of blueberry filling on the corner of his smile.

'She fancies me more than she fancies that gown of hers, I can tell you that.' She took a long pause, savouring Amos's wide-eyed amazement, his impatient captivation. 'Grass stains aren't the easiest thing to get out of fabric that fine.'

He threw his head back and laughed. 'You're a regular rake, you know that?'

She shoved his arm. 'I am *not*.'

He finished his last bite of dessert. 'No, I suppose not. You care too much.'

'You say that like it's a bad thing.'

'It's not a bad thing. Not at all.' He dug his left foot into the sand, finding Hannah's toes. 'It just means...' Amos wasn't one for lengthy speeches, but Hannah could tell he was collecting the words for something wise. 'You choose your partners carefully, and for the right reasons. I've always admired that about you. And it hasn't hurt you, not…not very much, at least. Just know that if it does—if it hurts, this time—that doesn't mean you made the wrong choice. That doesn't mean you were wrong for caring.'

He cleared his throat and looked away. Hannah gave his words the silence they deserved, surprised at how verbose Amos had become this summer. All afternoon she had noticed in him a confidence that wasn't there before, a surety of words and feelings. Something had transpired in the past few weeks to help him grow, and Hannah hadn't been around to see it.

If she had to guess, she would say that *something* was love.

Hannah was so lost in her thoughts about Amos that it took her a while to actually process what he had said.

'Why…' she finally said, breaking the silence. 'Why do you think it's going to hurt this time?'

'Because she's going to leave.' He was talking about Violet, but he was talking about Sylvia too.

'Yes, but I'm used to that. I prefer it, actually. Keeps things simple.'

'But this time they don't have to.'

'Have to what?'

'*Leave*, Hannah. This time they don't have to leave.'

Hannah was quiet again, breathing to the rhythm

of the waves. Esther had left because of her father's employment. The woman before that had been a maid whose household grew bored with Worthing and left for Brighton instead. Hannah had never been made to feel abandoned or rejected, because Hannah had never been with someone who had the choice to stay.

Hannah found her cousin's hand and rested her own on top. 'You don't regret it, though? Being with Violet?'

'Not for a second. And you? Being with Sylvia?'

Hannah recognised, for the first time, just how different this situation was than the ones she'd been in before. She knew now that this one might end in more pain. It might leave a mark, even—the kind that lasts.

This new information could have changed Hannah's answer. Maybe it *should* have changed Hannah's answer. But she had never been the type to run from a good connection just because she couldn't stop its ending, and she wasn't about to change herself for Sylvia now.

'No,' she said. 'No regrets.'

With grains of sand still prickling between her toes, Hannah walked to the latest gathering of the Heene Society of Artisans and Shopkeepers. The coarse crunch in the bottom of her shoes took her mind off what she was about to do, and how nervous it made her. The basket Hannah was carrying felt heavy, not only with its bundle of specialty cheese but with the weight of opportunity and disappointment, of opening herself and her craft to the opinions of the assembly.

The batch she'd chosen was soft and creamy, three thick logs of gooey cheese held together by mould-ripened rinds as white as snow. She wanted to share the cheese with her neighbours, to show them what she was capable of, to gather support for the day—*someday soon*, Hannah hoped—when she would finally open her own shop.

She opened the door to the meeting house and thought about how confident Sylvia would be, if she were the one about to speak. But Sylvia was back on the farm churning butter, and Hannah was here.

The room was filled with chatter, and no one noticed her enter at first. She saw the usual attendees—the modiste, the clockmaker, the fruit sellers, the stationers—but she also saw some new faces: Katherine O'Toole and Beatrice Tupper, who together managed the hat shop, had never come to an HSAS meeting before now. She saw a seamstress, a baker, a lace merchant, and a man who owned a mackerel stall at market.

With this many in attendance she wasn't sure if a formal meeting would happen or if people would just keep talking business on their own, so Hannah took a deep breath and decided not to wait—she marched over to the nearest group and lifted her basket with both hands.

'We can't save Heene on an empty stomach!'

'I can't argue with that,' said Mrs O'Toole in her Irish accent. 'What do you have for us today, Miss Wickersham?'

Hannah handed the carefully wrapped discs of cheese to the people in front of her. She watched the surprise on their faces when they realised they weren't holding a standard slice of Wickersham cheddar, but something different—*very* different.

The fluffy white circle of rind on each cheese was speckled with wildflower petals, colourful bits of dahlia, rose, and dandelion. The smooth, pasty centre came mostly from goat milk she'd bought from a dairy farm in Littlehamptom, with just a dash of her own cow milk mixed in. This was a cheese to be proud of.

She left for the next group before this one had time to finish chewing their first bites. Hannah already knew how the cheese would melt in their mouths, coating their teeth with a mild floral flavour, notes of mushroom, and a peppery finish. She moved around the room handing out cheese, catching snippets of conversation along the way:

'I've been trying to patch up the roof, but...'

'Did you see the new perfume shop? I don't know the owner, but I heard...'

'Pay me back whenever you can, there's no rush...'

Soon the whole meeting house smelled like dairy

and flowers. Hannah had just one serving of cheese left, and just one person in mind to share it with.

'I'll be off, then,' she said to the nearest group. 'If anyone asks, I vote for keeping our buildings, opening more shops, and relying on each other to survive.'

'Hannah—wait!' exclaimed Mr Mercer, his voice earnest. 'This is fantastic.'

She offered an awkward, humble smile. Hannah didn't mind compliments, but she never knew exactly how to react to them. 'Thank you,' she said simply.

And then she walked through the door, trusting that whichever way the conversation went inside, her cheese would speak on her behalf.

Less than an hour later, she was curled up next to Sylvia in the herb garden, tugging the occasional weed from the dirt but mostly eating, and laughing, and… *kissing*.

'This is the most delicious thing I've ever tasted,' Sylvia said after her second bite of cheese. Her hair was down, loose and straight and dancing in the breeze. She licked the gooey cheese from her fingers, eyeing Hannah with a roguish grin.

'More delicious than this?' Hannah leaned in for a passionate kiss—but only after glancing at the house to make sure no one could see them through the window.

'Maybe it's an even tie,' Sylvia said when they broke away.

Hannah noticed the pile of weeds near Sylvia's

knees. All of them had been pulled correctly, their limp white roots dangling from thin green stalks. They were also, importantly, the *right plants*. Sylvia knew the difference between English thyme and oak-leaved goosefoot, which wasn't the case only a few weeks earlier.

Something about that pile of weeds made Sylvia seem like a regular part of Hannah's life, as steady as the grey skies above, the moist soil below, the house behind them and the family inside.

'I think your hair looks lovely, by the way,' Hannah said delicately, worried her words alone might cause Sylvia's hair to snap back up into curls.

'Oh,' Sylvia said, embarrassed. 'I should have—I mean, I just didn't want to get out bed early enough to—'

'I think it's lovely.' Hannah set her fingers at the top of Sylvia's head, then traced them down her pale hair.

Sylvia leaned into her touch, until her head was resting on Hannah's shoulder. 'Thank you,' she said quietly, though Hannah could hear the smile in her voice.

They fell into an easy rhythm in the following days. Lord Marshall was on a hunting trip for the next week, the Beaumonts had left for a cousin's wedding in the north, and a series of mid-July rainstorms kept Sylvia from promenading outside or venturing to balls in the only two decent dresses she owned. For the first time since Hannah met Sylvia, time moved slowly—and time belonged to them.

Most days started with milking or breakfast or tracking the growth of the summer's calves. As the sun moved lazily across the sky, Hannah and Sylvia would find excuses to do together work they really *could* have done separately. They told stories while skimming cream. They made each other laugh while folding laundry. They danced to the tune of songbirds while sweeping the barn.

And, on more than one occasion, they untied and unbuttoned and unfurled into naked pleasure, hands drenched in the syrupy warmth of each other's bodies.

There was one day in particular that stood out to Hannah, a beloved day amidst a beloved week. It began the same as ever, but soon they were in the kitchen helping Aunt Charity prepare a feast. By evening the table was full of soup and bread, sage-seasoned chicken and warm gravy, colourful millefruit biscuits for dessert. But it was also full of people: cheerful, chatty, laughing people. The Wickershams and Queensburys had all crowded into the kitchen elbow to elbow, every chair on the property dragged into the kitchen to accommodate the party of ten.

Aunt Charity had outdone herself with the absolutely delicious meal. Rose and Amos had a competition to see who could eat more biscuits. Sylvia skillfully held her own in a conversation with Hannah's parents about the dairy business, and Mary stole the show after supper with her razor-sharp charades skills. She and Sylvia were an unbeatable team, but the rest of them had just as much fun guessing and gesturing around the raging hearth. Ella and Rachel were awkward around each other at first, but by the end of the night they were so stuck in joyful conversation that their exhausted families had to pull them away. Violet and Amos held hands whenever they thought no one was looking.

Hannah's heart was as full as it had ever been.

'Do you remember,' she had said later that night, when everyone but she and Sylvia had gone to bed. 'When you asked about surnames, a few weeks ago?'

Sylvia thought about it for a moment, tangled up in crumpled sheets and low-burning candlelight. 'I asked why women take on their husbands' names.'

'Yes, well, I did some research.' Hannah had gone to the library. She had interviewed some of the older residents of Heene, the ones who kept family records. 'It turns out, it's only been this way for six or so centuries. Before that, there were all sorts of ways to name yourself, like after your place of birth or after your father's first name. *But*, one of the more common ways was by your profession. So if you forged iron for a living…'

'You'd be called Smith! That's why there are so many Smiths, then?'

'Exactly. All the Bakers in England come from men

who made bread, and all the Brewsters come from women who made beer.'

'I'm calling you Hannah Cheesemaker from now on,' said Sylvia.

And she did.

They called each other many things in the days that followed. New things. Exciting things.

'Pass me that cheesecloth, dear,' Hannah had said one morning by accident. But she didn't take it back, and Sylvia smiled.

'Oh, honey,' Sylvia had gasped through laughter—real side-splitting laughter, at a joke Hannah had told one night.

At market one day they overheard a Scottish couple call each other *hen*, and by the evening they were saying it too. Hannah started calling Sylvia *sunshine*, because of her hair, but the more time they spent together the sillier the names got. *How goes the butter-making, Queen of the Berries? Kiss me now, Royal Fruit.*

Can I stay the night, Hannah Cheesemaker?

The answer was always yes.

Chapter Fourteen

At the beginning of the summer, Sylvia had treated her time in Heene like a garden of weeds. Anything that started to grow within her—any comfort, any pleasure, any temptation to enjoy *anything* about her life here—was immediately plucked. But something had taken root in her these last few weeks, and when she looked at that garden now, she didn't see weeds.

She saw flowers, and herbs, and so much life.

Sylvia never forgot what she was working toward, not entirely, but after Henry left for his hunting trip it all seemed so far away. Without any immediate plans in their fortune-hunting scheme, she and Hannah just…stopped talking about the future. It loomed in the corner of every room, of course—that impending marriage proposal, the one they had worked so hard to achieve—but it was small enough that they often forgot it was there.

Blissful days with Hannah were accompanied by blissful days at home. Violet was entrusted with increasingly complex work at the modiste, and Sylvia would always remember the first time she saw someone in Worthing wearing one of Violet's signature patterns stitched onto a muslin hem. Rose and Mary had made real friends with other children their age in Heene, friends who took the time to learn Mary's signs. Ella had chosen not to revisit her confrontation with Sylvia the night of the Elwes Ball—which Sylvia was thankful for—but she'd begun to act differently after that night. She was more present, more attentive. She expressed real interest in her daughters' lives, and she hugged them often.

Sylvia described all this to Hannah one day, sitting in the wide branches of a tree. An hour prior, Sylvia had admitted that she'd never climbed a tree before, so Hannah cleared her schedule to give Sylvia a much-needed lesson.

'Sylvia…' Hannah said slowly when Sylvia had finished speaking. 'I think what you're describing is *happiness.*'

A robin landed on a nearby branch. A wide cloud drifted over the sun, painting all of Heene with shade. Sylvia received Hannah's words like an accusation— *Look how satisfied you've become, living below your station! Look how easily you've lost your ambition. Look how easily you've lost yourself.*

But Sylvia knew that voice belonged to no one but herself. She had gotten better at ignoring it, but she was afraid of what would happen if she silenced it completely.

'Sylvia?' Hannah had asked up there in the boughs, noticing as Sylvia stared at nothing in particular.

'You're right, I think,' Sylvia admitted, turning to face her. 'Happiness.' She said the word awkwardly, like it didn't belong to her. Happiness was the thing she would get *after* marriage, *after* returning to London and proving to her peers they were all wrong about her. After she restored each member of her family to their rightful place in society. To claim happiness *now*, before any of that had been achieved…it felt like cheating.

Sylvia felt decidedly out of practice when she and Hannah arrived that afternoon at the Queensbury residence to prepare for a promenade about town.

No one in Sylvia's family had touched the papillote iron in well over a week; as she raised it now, to her straight blond hair, it felt heavier than it had before. But still, she welcomed the neat rows of curls. Mary and Rose had such lovely waves when they let their hair go wild, but Sylvia's was limp and boring and straight as straw.

Like silk, Hannah had said one night.

Sylvia pressed the hot iron into her hair and sculpted herself back into the person she'd always been. She leaned over and kissed Hannah's nose. 'I've enjoyed this holiday with you,' she said. 'And I know we have more time together, but… I did make a promise to get you that cheese shop, and I intend to keep it.'

Hannah returned the kiss on Sylvia's nose. 'And I promised to help you find a husband. Despite how… *distracting* you can be,' she said, her lips so close to Sylvia's, 'I haven't forgotten my end of the bargain.'

They heard the front door open, and they pulled away from each other quickly. Sylvia picked up a small blue reticule she had recently purchased, then filled it with her most recent wages.

'I'll get something new for myself today,' she said as they stepped into the humid afternoon air. 'A brooch, or some earrings…something to get me back in the spirit of fortune-hunting.'

'An excellent idea, *Lady Marshall*,' Hannah said dramatically, offering her arm as if she were a gentleman. Sylvia curved her elbow around Hannah's, but only until the path reached Worthing.

With a deep breath, she opened her parasol and walked ahead, smiling and waving to people she recognised from the most recent ball. Some of them smiled and waved back—others lowered their eyes and whispered among themselves.

No matter, Sylvia thought when a passing lady snickered behind her fan. *She will have to accept me once I've restored my place. They all will.*

And they all will *soon*, considering all the attention Henry had been showing Sylvia—all the dances, the banter, the walks on the beach...surely a proposal wasn't far off...

Sylvia turned left into the jewellery shop, hoping to find something small and affordable but no less elegant. There was another pair of women in the shop already, two friends around Sylvia's age who were fawning over the tiaras on display.

Sylvia felt a pang of jealousy. These two could be friends in the open—they could accompany each other to balls, walk next to each other in public, share their gowns and gloves and jewellery.

Maybe, she told herself, *I can find another friend when I'm back in London, and they'll be just as close to me as Hannah is now...*

This thought wasn't as comforting as she'd hoped it would be.

'Miss Margaret,' said the jeweller, appearing from the back room. 'Your order is ready.'

He laid a velvet cushion on the counter, and Sylvia craned her neck to see the sparkling necklace on top.

'It's marvellous!' Miss Margaret exclaimed. She turned eagerly to her friend. 'Put it on me, will you?'

Sylvia watched Miss Margaret's friend undo the clasp of the delicate golden chain and gently lay the necklace in place. *It's rather strange looking*, Sylvia thought, *pale, irregular, and...familiar...*

A heart-shaped stone!

Sylvia smothered a gasp. The stone pendant on Miss

Margaret's necklace was identical to the one Henry had given her, down even to the white speckles in its smooth surface. *Surely a coincidence*, she thought... but of course she wasn't sure.

Her voice trembling somewhat, she said, 'Oh my, I've never seen such a thing before! Where did you get that stone?'

Miss Margaret blushed as she turned to show off her necklace. 'A suitor...isn't it charming?'

There are plenty of eligible bachelors in Worthing more than capable of finding heart-shaped stones, she thought. But were there?

'Miss Sylvia,' Hannah said slowly, her brows furrowed in concern, 'perhaps we should go—'

'Charming indeed,' Sylvia heard herself say. She stood frozen in place. 'So, so charming...'

'He's away on a hunting trip, of course,' Miss Margaret continued on dreamily. 'I'm going to surprise him by wearing the stone as a necklace when he gets back, and hopefully, well...' Miss Margaret turned to her friend, and the two of them giggled excitedly.

'Sylvia,' Hannah said, reaching for Sylvia's elbow. 'I really think we should go.'

This time, Sylvia let Hannah guide her out of the shop. The door swung shut behind them with a heavy *thud*.

Softly, Hannah said, 'Do you want to talk about—'

'There's nothing to talk about,' Sylvia snapped. She

lifted her chin and set off down the street. Hannah didn't say anything until they had finally looped back around and left Worthing, and even then she waited until they were nearly back at the farm.

'It's okay to feel hurt,' she said.

'What is there to feel hurt about?' Sylvia asked.

'Sylvia...' Hannah caught up to her and grabbed her hand. She held on tightly and didn't move, but Sylvia kept looking ahead. 'That necklace can't just be a coincidence.'

'And why not?' Sylvia stared at the trees, at the road, at the Wickersham fence—at anything but Hannah's kind and gentle eyes. 'Any gentleman could have given her a heart-shaped stone as a token of his affection, and any gentleman could be on a hunting trip.'

'Yes, that's technically true, but—'

'Then there's nothing to worry about.'

'Think about your glove, Sylvia. Do you remember when you tossed your glove into the wind, so it would fall at Henry's feet, and he'd have to talk to you?'

Sylvia didn't say anything.

Hannah continued: 'Do you really think it is only ladies who scheme?'

'I...' Sylvia started, but she couldn't bear to look away any longer. She let herself see Hannah's face— Hannah's soft, worried, compassionate face—and she couldn't keep up the act. She lowered her shoulders, and she sighed. 'I know. I know he probably has his tricks, and when he finds one that works he...he *re-uses* it, but for all we know *Miss Margaret* could be old news. That stone could have been from *weeks* ago, maybe *months*—'

'She said he's coming back for her—'

Sylvia removed her hand from Hannah's. 'She said *she's* going to surprise him, which doesn't mean he's coming back for her at all.'

'But—'

'Do you *want* a cheese shop, Hannah?' Sylvia said, the words stinging her throat as they left. 'Because I don't remember our bargain specifying that my husband had to be perfectly chaste.'

Hannah's face hardened. It was her turn to look away now. 'No, I suppose you're right. I just don't want to see you become...prey.'

'I'm hunting Henry just as much as he's—'

'You know it's not the same. He might not be looking for a wife—'

They were talking over each other now, their voices fast and heated.

'But he *can tell* I'm a respectable woman—'

'And Miss Margaret isn't?'

'*I don't know!*' Sylvia shouted. 'How should I know?'

She threw her hands in the air. She was frustrated—but not at Hannah.

Sylvia took a deep breath to steady herself. 'I'm

sorry,' she said. 'I understand your concern, I really do. It's why…' She opened her hand, and Hannah hesitated a moment before taking it back. 'It's why you're such a good friend.'

'There's always Phillip,' Hannah said, stepping closer.

'No—I mean, *yes*, there is—but I'm not giving up on Henry. He's newly titled and he needs a wife. He may have been…less than a saint with other women, but his courtship with *me* is entirely virtuous.'

Hannah looked doubtful, but she didn't argue. 'Anything for the shop, I suppose…'

'That's the spirit,' Sylvia said, squeezing Hannah's hand. 'Henry gets back the day after next, and when he calls on me—when he calls on me *first*, before any other woman—we'll know we have nothing to worry about.'

Sylvia was relieved, two days later, when that was exactly what happened. Henry requested she join him for dinner at his family's holiday home posthaste, which was certainly not the kind of thing a lecherous paramour would do. Meeting his parents made the whole courtship *real*, even more real than it had felt before.

She practised her posture in the mirror and imagined real diamonds dangling from her ears, genuine rubies strung across her neck. She practised her facial expressions: her polite smile, her flattered smile, her seductive smile. The expression of interest she'd have to wear while listening to Henry talk about his trip; the look of surprise she'd don when he described the size and stature of the bucks he'd killed.

She gathered her skirts and slipped out the bedroom window. She didn't want to walk past her family, sat around the hearth. She wasn't in the mood to be caught and chastised by her mother.

Tonight would be the third time Henry saw her in the sapphire gown, and she could only hope that as a man he couldn't be bothered to notice. She used her farm money to rent a carriage for the brief ride, and then she was there: the Marshall family's holiday home.

Sylvia was giddy as she climbed the wide stone stairs to the front door. *He wants me*, she told herself as a butler opened the tall wooden doors. *He wants me, he wants me, he wants me.*

I'm wanted, finally.

The butler guided her to the dining room. She breathed in the air, which smelled nothing like barn and sea; she marvelled at the silver sconces and thick velvet curtains; she glimpsed her reflection in the gilt surface of a decorative serving dish, her face and hair and eyes sapped of all colour but gold.

'Miss Sylvia Queensbury!' Henry said with enthusiasm as he joined her in the dining room.

'Lord Henry Marshall,' she said with a curtsy. 'I trust your trip went well?'

'Yes, yes, an excellent trip.' He was in his finest suit, his hair gelled into voluminous ripples. 'The venison you'll be tasting tonight is the finest I've ever caught.'

It was then that Sylvia noticed the table was set for only two.

'I'm eager to try it,' she said, but he noticed the way her eyes scanned the room.

'Oh, I see,' he said apologetically. 'You were expecting my family—of course. They're still away, in the country. I came back early to avoid my mother's matchmaking games. She's trying to set me up with this *dreadful* girl from *Wales*.' He spoke like the words themselves were sour. Then he moved closer to Sylvia. 'Your face…it has ruined all other women for me.'

Sylvia laughed nervously. She didn't love the fact that he complimented her by insulting other women. *But a compliment is a compliment*, she thought. *Right?*

'You'll get to see my face all evening,' said Sylvia.

'I'm counting on it.' He winked, then pulled her chair from the table so she could sit.

This is fine, Sylvia told herself. *This is just…the dinner before the dinner. He's preparing me for when his mother returns.*

His mother, who's trying to set him up with a different woman.

Sylvia fought with herself in her own head as a maid delivered two bowls of turtle soup.

Okay, so she's looking for a bride! I can be that bride.

A woman who can afford a soup like this will definitely be able to tell if I wear the same dress twice. I'll need to buy...

Sylvia noticed her fingers were fidgeting beneath the table, so she sat on her hands and focused on Henry. The maid poured dark red claret from a crystal jug.

'It's been ages since I've had a good *Bordeaux*,' she said, lifting her glass. They toasted, and Sylvia sipped what she could only describe as liquid luxury. 'You have excellent taste, Henry.'

He had spared no expense for their meal. They shared salmon and asparagus, drenched with melted butter that Sylvia wondered if she herself had made. Next came the venison—which she heaped with compliments—followed by almond tarts and plum cakes.

Henry talked about his hunting trip like it was some grand adventure, his life in peril at every moment. Sylvia had never been on a hunting trip herself, but she knew that gentlemen of the *ton* detested things like dirt and danger just as much as ladies did—even if they would never say as much out loud.

Still, she went along with his story, gasping and laughing at all the right parts, fearing for his safety and cheering for his ultimate victory.

When the meal ended, he took her hand. 'I have a whole gallery of paintings in the parlour,' he said suddenly. 'Would you like to see?'

'Oh yes,' Sylvia said, delighted to be among the world of fine art once more. She would visit so many museums when she became Lady Marshall. She would go to the opera, and the theatre, and every concert she would find. She had taken all these things for granted before, but once she got them back she would savour them the way Hannah had taught her to savour food.

Henry led her out of the dining room and through a dark corridor, then into a small parlour with navy blue walls and a grand chaise lounge. The room was decorated with vases and busts, mirrors and paintings, all the trappings of domestic comfort.

'Such a lovely room,' she said, her eyes adjusting to the dim lighting. She almost asked him to light more candles, but he spoke before she could get a word in.

'Now *this*,' he said, gesturing to a tall painting of a pale woman with dark brown curls, 'is the most expensive piece in my collection.'

'Do you collect artwork?' Sylvia eyed the softly painted woman, her skin clear and smooth as porcelain, brushed with rosy cheeks and shiny lips.

Henry didn't answer at first. He was standing behind her as she stared at the painting, trying to understand what this woman was feeling in her frame of bronze.

Sylvia noticed the hair on the back of her neck stand straight up a half second before she felt Henry's lips behind her ear. He kissed her, working along her hairline, one hand crawling up her shoulder and the other on her waist.

Sylvia froze. 'Henry…what are you doing?'

'Adding to my collection,' he said quietly.

She squirmed out of his hands and turned to face him. She had spent so much time alone with Hannah that she hadn't even noticed how unusual this meeting was, alone in the parlour with no chaperone, no butler, no maid.

'I think there's been a misunderstanding,' she said, trying to keep her voice light, even as she felt like a heavy stone was lodged in her stomach.

Henry only smiled. 'Don't worry, I've given the staff the night off.' He placed his hand on her lower back and pulled her toward him, close enough to smell the wine on his breath. 'And I won't tell anyone,' he whispered flirtatiously, his lips grazing her ear. His thumb snaked beneath the sleeve of her dress. 'Your reputation won't be any more ruined than it already is.'

Sylvia was shaking now, but she found the strength to press her hands against his chest and push him away.

'*Henry,*' she said sternly. 'We're not *married* yet.'

Henry Marshall had the audacity to look surprised.

Sylvia kept talking. 'This isn't proper, and I know you were raised better. It isn't the order of things—if you want—well, you're supposed to declare your intentions first and then—' She was struggling to find the right words. Sylvia wasn't used to feeling this helpless. She exhaled through her nose, frustrated, then crossed her arms. 'Unmarried ladies don't kiss suitors in empty parlours!'

'Sylvia,' he said, laughing through his disbelief. 'You aren't an unmarried lady. You're an unmarried *girl*.' Sylvia wasn't sure if he was speaking slowly or if the whole world had slowed down around her. 'You have no claim to any title, you have no dowry…surely you didn't think…?'

Sylvia's throat tightened. She blinked, and blinked again. *No*, was all she could think. *No no no no no.*

'Oh lord,' he said, eyes wide and slightly amused. 'Oh you really thought—'

'You said you would take me to France.'

'Not as my *wife*!' He tossed the word from his mouth like it was yesterday's rubbish. 'I know you've been playacting at wealth, what with your second-hand gowns and costume jewellery, but *certainly* you knew that the best you could ever be was a gentleman's mistress.'

Bitter tears stung the corners of Sylvia's eyes. Her breathing was shallow and her chest felt empty. Her legs quivered, caught between the urge to stay right here and the urge to put as much distance between herself and this man as possible.

She wanted so badly to be the kind of person who could say something brave. She wanted to place one hand on her hip and point the other in his face and say *Listen here, sir. I am Sylvia Queensbury, born and bred to be a proper lady, and you will treat me as such.* She wanted to slap him across the face, then turn and march through the parlour door, her shoulders back and her head held high.

But Sylvia Queensbury did none of these things.

Sylvia Queensbury ran.

On an ordinary night, Hannah wouldn't have been awake to hear the light tap of a pebble hitting her window. She would have been asleep, cosy beneath her warm quilt, breathing in time with the rhythmic staccato of rain on her family's roof.

But this was no ordinary night. Hannah heard the singular knock of a tiny stone hitting glass because Hannah was awake. She hadn't been able to fall asleep with all the worry that crowded her brain, all the racing thoughts of how everything in her life could suddenly go wrong.

Maybe Sylvia would get hurt travelling alone. Maybe Hannah's parents would stay disappointed in her after she wasted so much good milk on her Heene Society snacks. Maybe Mr Luxford would sell the shop to some wealthy developer. Maybe Sylvia would break Hannah's heart.

Maybe Hannah would let her heart be broken.

Hannah faced the window, streams of rain racing down its panes. She had been pacing for nearly an hour, unable to sleep, and now she moved in the direction of the sound. She waited, to see if it would come again.

Clink. Another small stone. She opened the window despite the deluge and stuck her head outside.

'Sylvia?' she called in surprise. Hannah could barely make out the figure that stood below her window in the dead of night, but through the rain she glimpsed a bright shock of yellow hair, a sagging wet ballgown, and the saddest eyes she had ever seen.

'Can I come up?' Sylvia's voice was hoarse. Hannah nodded, rummaged through her winter chest for a thick wool cloak, then hurried down the stairs as quietly as she could.

Cold, damp air rushed into the house when Hannah opened the door. Sylvia looked so frail. Her dress was heavy; the sleeves drooped over her forearms, and the bottom hem had clearly been dragged through the mud.

Hannah didn't know what to say, so she held open her arms and let Sylvia collapse into them. Hannah didn't mind that this embrace would soak her own clothes too—it wouldn't take long to get a fire going and collect all the spare blankets in the house.

'How could I have been so foolish?' Sylvia asked

after they had settled in front of the hearth. She had just finished telling Hannah the horrors of her night, naked and shivering beneath a grey wool cloak and an old cotton blanket. Every second of the story made Hannah's skin crawl.

Sylvia was wrapped up so tightly that nothing was visible but her face, her hair, and the tips of her toes pointed toward the fire. Hannah too was buried beneath several layers of blankets and quilts, a hot cup of tea cradled in her hands.

'You weren't foolish,' Hannah said. 'You were hopeful. Or maybe being hopeful *is* foolish, I don't know. But I do know that hope is generally a good thing.'

Sylvia stared into the fire. Her eyes were empty, flickering with the reflection of glowing flames. 'I just thought…'

Hannah noticed Sylvia's cup of tea, still on the floor, untouched. 'Drink something,' Hannah tried.

'He seemed so honest. He seemed so genuine. How is that possible, Hannah? How did I miss… Why didn't I see…'

'You wanted him to be honest, so you believed he would be. That's a natural thing to do.' Hannah lifted the cup from the floor and handed it to Sylvia. 'But the point—the *very important point*, that I'm not sure you're getting—is that this is not your fault. This is not your fault, Sylvia.'

Sylvia took the smallest sip from her cup, still not looking at Hannah.

'*Henry* is in the wrong here,' Hannah said firmly. 'Not you. *Could* you have been a bit slower to trust this man? Sure, maybe. Did you imagine subtext that wasn't really there? It's possible. There's a case to be made that you could have handled this situation differently…but I could have too.' Hannah felt her chest tighten, her jaw clench. She was feeling so many things—anger at Lord Marshall, care for Sylvia, exhaustion from being awake for so long—but the thing that rose to the surface now was shame. 'I shouldn't have let you go alone—'

'No,' Sylvia said, finally looking up. The skin around her eyes was puffy and red, and Hannah realised that this was the first time she had ever seen Sylvia cry. She didn't notice when the crying had started—when Sylvia came in from the rain, it just looked like her face had emerged from the storm—but now she saw the slow and painful path of Sylvia's tears, which had nothing to do with the rain.

'Hannah, no,' Sylvia continued, blinking, a new energy in her eyes. She took a full sip of tea. 'I wouldn't have let you come with me. I was so convinced his intentions were…*true*. I wasn't in the mood to listen to you—please, don't for a second think this is your fault.'

'Okay,' said Hannah. 'But you too. Don't blame yourself. Please.'

Sylvia nodded. She was awake now, really awake and present for the first time all night. 'Yes. You're right. It's not my fault. It's that…that…*bastard* Henry Marshall.'

Hannah laughed, more out of surprise than anything.

'I mean it,' Sylvia said, emerging a bit from her blanket cocoon. The knot of damp hair atop her head sagged to the side, and tears fell from her check to her bare collarbone. 'He is dastardly. He is wicked and cruel. He thinks I'm beneath him, but it's quite the opposite. *He* is *very much* beneath me.'

'I'll drink to that,' Hannah said, finishing her tea. And then she added tentatively: 'Maybe we'll have better luck with Mr Beaumont. And maybe this time you'll let me come with you.'

She held her breath for Sylvia's answer. She wanted to outright *tell* Sylvia that Lord Marshall was likely not an aberration, and that maybe Sylvia should re-think trying to claw her way back into a society that had turned its back on her. She wanted Sylvia to see that maybe life in Heene wasn't so bad after all.

But Hannah was afraid to say all of that out loud. She was afraid to admit that she wanted Sylvia to stay.

And, deep down, she knew that Mrs Phillip Beaumont could do more for Hannah's future as a shop-keeper than Miss Sylvia Queensbury ever could.

Sylvia's shoulders slumped. 'If Phillip requests my presence at his home, you have my word I won't go without you. But…' She inched across the floor until she was close enough to slip her feet into Hannah's blankets. 'I'm getting tired, Hannah. I'm getting so tired of pretending to be someone I'm not.'

Hannah scooched forward too, so their bare legs were touching. 'What would life be like, if you stopped pretending?' The fire roared next to them. Hannah felt warm inside and out.

'I guess…well, I guess it would be sort of like… last week.' Sylvia leaned her head back and stared at the ceiling. 'I'm just so confused about everything,' she said. 'I don't know what I'm supposed to want. I don't know what the right answer is. I don't know anything at all.'

'You don't know *anything*?'

Sylvia looked at Hannah. She smiled for the first time in hours. 'I know at least *one thing*.' She took a long, dramatic sip of her tea, making Hannah wait.

Hannah lifted the bottom of Sylvia's blankets and crawled underneath, head first, into the darkness. She was swept up in the scent of embers and rain and Sylvia. She kissed Sylvia's bare hip, her shoulder, and then, emerging from the mountain of blankets, her cheek.

'What do you *know*, Sylvia?' she whispered. 'What's the *one thing*?'

Hannah trailed kisses from Syvia's cheek to the bridge of her nose.

Sylvia wriggled her arm out of the blankets to place her teacup on the floor, then wriggled her arm right back in to be with Hannah. 'I know that I love you,' she said, earnestly and tenderly. 'Tonight has been… terrible, really. And I still don't know how I'm going to save my family, or fund your shop…but I know that I love you. It's the one thing that feels clear.'

Hannah had never expected Sylvia to say those three words. She had never thought to consider what she might say in response, or if she might want to say them first, or if loving Sylvia had any bearing on their bargain—on their future.

But when Hannah looked inside herself, she saw that they had been there all along:

'I love you,' Hannah said. 'I love you too.'

And she kissed the tip of Sylvia's nose, and she pulled the cloak tight around them, and the pale light of early dawn filtered in from the kitchen window.

Sylvia yawned. They shuffled upstairs and fell into bed. The sun tried its best to brighten their room, and the rooster cried his usual tune, but Hannah and Sylvia slept like it was the darkest and quietest of nights.

The sun could rise and fall and rise again for all they cared.

They were not beholden to time. Not anymore.

Chapter Fifteen

Sylvia shivered as the cold ocean lapped against her knees.

'Are you sure this is safe?' she called out to Hannah, who was already several yards ahead of her and floating peacefully in the sea.

'Safe enough!' Hannah called back.

Sylvia was hesitant to keep walking. Hannah had assured her this was the shallowest and most secluded part of the beach, but Sylvia couldn't shake the feeling that she was about to step off a sandy cliff and plunge into the salty depths of the ocean while every single resident and tourist in Worthing watched.

Sylvia could have stayed where she was, the top half of her flannel bathing gown still dry, but the longer she stood still the more seaweed she collected around her ankles.

'Fine, fine… I'm coming!' she called out reluctantly.

This whole thing had been *her* idea after all. Two years prior, she'd debuted into society at her very own ball; the time had come, Sylvia decided, to debut once again—only this time into her new life in Heene. She wasn't resigned to staying there *forever*, but she had made peace finally with the fact that her time in Heene would be longer—maybe even much longer—than she had planned.

'Well, there's only one way to make a debut in a seaside town,' Hannah had said after Sylvia pitched the idea. 'You introduce yourself to the fish.'

Hannah's talk of swimming lessons in the open sea had excited Sylvia at first. *How hard could it be?* But now that she was cold and grimy and clumsy, wading into an impossibly big body of water, she was starting to have regrets.

'The faster you go, the warmer it gets!' Hannah called as she swam toward Sylvia.

Orange streaks of hair clung to Hannah's face. Water droplets magnified her freckles. She looked absolutely wild, and Sylvia couldn't resist—she floated forward until only her toes could reach the sand, her lips meeting Hannah's with eagerness and warmth.

Hannah scooped Sylvia into her arms and Sylvia felt weightless, like Hannah could jump and they would both just float into the sky.

'I love you,' Sylvia said, still surprised that these words were hers to say now, hers to share with Hannah.

'Yes,' Hannah said, a look of wonder spread across her face. 'You really do.'

The waves were tame today, and Sylvia bobbed along to their gentle rhythm. Hannah gradually let Sylvia go, until only their hands remained together.

'Oh dear,' Sylvia said when she stretched her legs into pure nothingness, no ground beneath her feet. She kicked frantically, holding tight to Hannah's wrists.

'You're okay,' said Hannah. 'Slow down. Long, slow kicks. You're not running. And then…' She twisted her arms from Sylvia's grasp. 'Move your arms, like this.'

Sylvia tried to mimic Hannah, bending and stretching one leg at a time, pushing her arms in wide circles. The water rose up to her face, stinging her nose and leaving a salty burn in her mouth.

As soon as it was clear Sylvia wouldn't drown, Hannah asked, 'What do you like about me?'

'Er…what?' Sylvia managed to say between gasps.

'If you talk about something, it'll take your mind off what your body is doing, and then your body will do it better. I don't enjoy making cheese when someone's watching me… I'm much more anxious I'll mess up. So, stop watching your body.'

Sylvia thought about Hannah's question, but she didn't have to think long. 'I like how…comfortable you are being yourself,' she panted. 'I like how you know who yourself even *is*. I admire…how you're just *you*.' Something scraped against Sylvia's calf, a rock or a shell caught in the tide. She startled, then steadied herself again by looking into Hannah's eyes. 'You are kind, and strong, and solid as the ground beneath my feet. Well, not right *now*. There isn't any ground beneath my feet right now. And this, *this* is kind of how I felt before I met you, I think.' Her breathing was steadier now. 'I was always treading water to keep up with everyone else. When I met you, it was like standing on solid ground for the first time. And that scared me. It seemed…boring, maybe? Or too easy? It felt unearned. But then…or now…'

Sylvia watched the wispy white clouds, low in the sky, drift behind Hannah. She kept talking: 'Now, I love that constant, safe, immovable ground. I love who I am when I'm standing still. I love…you.'

Sylvia felt very shy all of the sudden, and dipped her face below the water. She closed her eyes and felt the water billow against her cheeks, her forehead, her ears. She leaned her head side to side, feeling the heavy sway of her loose hair. In that moment the only thing she knew was the vast and endless sea.

Hannah was right after all, Sylvia thought. *This did feel like a proper debut.*

Sylvia lifted herself up and inhaled, blinking water from her lashes. Her limbs moved freely and smoothly, replacing the panicked jerking she had been doing earlier.

'What do you like about *me*?' Sylvia asked.

'Hmmm?' Hannah was floating on her back, her ears half underwater.

'It's obvious why I would fancy you. But it's not so obvious why you would fancy me.'

Hannah tilted her body forward to face Sylvia again. They drifted closer, their arms and legs sliding against each other with each movement.

'Why isn't it obvious?' Hannah asked.

'Because I'm *awful*,' Sylvia said. 'Or at least, I used to be. When I first showed up in Heene, I was so...so *pretentious*. I was lazy and shallow and I wasn't—' She paused, feeling vulnerable. 'I wasn't kind.'

'That's not true—well, maybe it's *a little* true.' Hannah bit her lip. 'I think that deep down you were scared. Your life was changing so fast, and it felt like everything was falling apart, and it was easier to pretend to be rude than admit that you were really just scared, so that's what you did. Once you started to just...*live* your life, to find yourself... I couldn't help but fancy you.'

She drifted closer to Sylvia as she talked. 'You are confident. You're protective. You're ambitious, which you sometimes use for scheming—but only *sometimes*.' Hannah paused to think. 'You're less like solid ground and more like...the sea. You're brave and exciting and disorienting. You sweep me away.'

Sylvia felt like her heart was dancing. She kissed Hannah suddenly, but they both sputtered away when a wave of salt hit their mouths. Together they swam back to shore, laughing and limbs aching.

They stretched out on blankets and dried beneath the sun, which hadn't shown its face in days. Sylvia looked around to make sure no one was near, then leaned over to kiss Hannah's neck, her chin, and finally her lips. Hannah smoothed her fingers into Sylvia's thick, salty hair, their bodies pressing grooves into the sand below.

They stayed like that for a long while, lost in undulating bliss, until the tide rose and reached for their ankles.

'Maybe it's time we head back,' Sylvia suggested, but neither of them moved. They let the ocean pool around their feet and soak the fringe of their blanket.

'I know there's work to do,' Hannah said, taking a moment to shake the sand from her hair. 'But…sometimes it just feels hopeless.'

Sylvia thought Hannah was one of the most hopeful people she'd ever met. 'What do you mean, hopeless?' Sylvia asked.

'Well…' Hannah started, then sighed. 'I had a meeting the other day, with the Heene Society of Artisans and Shopkeepers…we're too busy to gather often, and I didn't realise how much had happened since we last met. It was *weeks* ago, and…the Pyles—the younger Pyles, not the ones you're staying with—they sold their lodging house. Their family has lived in Heene as long as anyone can remember, and they sold their lodging house to someone from out of town, someone who wants to develop it into a resort for who knows how much money.'

'And that's...*bad*, right?' Sylvia asked.

'Of course it's bad!'

'Right, right... I'm still getting used to this way of thinking. Can you...remind me why, exactly? Why this is upsetting news?'

Hannah laced her fingers into Sylvia's. 'I'm happy for the Pyles. They had some debt, and one of their children is sick, and this...will help them sleep easier at night, to be sure. But why does help have to come at such a cost? The upsetting news isn't that they have the money they need, it's that the only *way* for some of us to get the money we need is to sell our buildings, and to watch them be replaced with resorts *we can't even afford to use.*'

Sylvia stroked her thumb against Hannah's palm. 'And you're worried that will happen to all of the buildings?' she asked.

'I am.' Hannah nodded. 'Some people think I'm overreacting. My parents are certainly sceptical. But spa towns make money, and when something makes money, people want it to grow. And if Worthing keeps growing—'

'There won't be any room left for Heene,' Sylvia realised. 'That's why you want your own shop. Something no one can take from you.'

Guilt crept over Sylvia's body like the cold rising

tide. In failing to secure a match with Henry—*however much that wasn't my fault*, she reminded herself—Sylvia had broken her promise to Hannah. Sylvia had broken her promise to the woman she loved.

'I'm not giving up,' she continued. 'Maybe I was too hasty thinking I could find a husband on my first go…maybe I need another year of wages, and dresses, and jewellery…maybe I need to build more connections in Worthing…'

'Or maybe,' Hannah said, 'Mr Luxford finds it in his heart to give me the shop despite his other offers. And if he doesn't…then there's always next year—which gives *me* more time to practice my curtsy.'

Sylvia didn't want to make Hannah wait another year for her dream to come true. She tried to think of something to say, some plan they hadn't considered, but a low rumbling in her stomach interrupted her thoughts.

'Maybe *now* it's time we head back,' Hannah said. 'To get you some food.'

'Yes, and…' Sylvia started, leaning close to Hannah's ear. 'There's one thing in particular I'm craving…' She trailed her lips along Hannah's neck until she gasped. 'And *that thing* is cheese.' Sylvia giggled. '*Your* cheese. Let's go.'

Sylvia sat up, but Hannah pulled her back. 'Wait,' she said. 'I want you to know… I appreciate how hard you tried. To find a husband, to fund my shop…'

This whole time, Sylvia had wanted a husband for herself—someone who could pave the way for her return to society and repair her family's reputation—but now…now a husband was so much more than that. A husband was someone who could make life better for Hannah, and maybe even for all of Heene.

'And when I *do* become Lady… *Whatever His Last Name Is*…' Sylvia said, continuing her thoughts out loud, 'I'll spend all his money on good causes. I'll give back to Heene. I'll make sure you always have a place to make cheese, and I'll… I'll think of people other than myself for once.'

'Be careful, Sylvia Queensbury,' Hannah said. 'Heene is making you *soft*.'

Sylvia kissed Hannah's cheek, her neck, her collarbone. 'I like plenty of things that are soft,' she said. 'Silk dresses…velvet hats…feather-stuffed mattresses…your body, *right here*.' She kissed the top of Hannah's breast, the subtle curve that rose before hiding beneath her neckline.

And then Sylvia's stomach rumbled again. 'As much as I'd love to stay here forever…'

Hannah sighed heavily, standing to shake the sand from her dress. 'Right…we promised each other a lot of things, but *forever* wasn't one of them—'

'No, not that—I mean it's time for *dinner*,' Sylvia said. She laughed, sort of, but she felt an unfamiliar tug on her heart. *What would forever look like, with Han-*

nah? But that particular thought was too dangerous, too distracting. She had come to Heene as a stranger, and as much as the decision to let go of Hannah some day pained her, it was a decision she had committed herself to. What kind of person would she be if she went back on her commitments to herself and to her family?

There was one person, though, she could let go of quite easily.

Sylvia found at the top of her blanket the small grey rock Henry had gifted her all those weeks ago. She felt the weight of it in her palm and wondered how many of these he had handed out, how many he had collected over the years just to keep in his pocket and conveniently 'find' on walks with his latest admirers.

Sylvia waded in the water until it lapped at her knees. She stretched her arm behind her back, inhaled, and shouted as loud as she could: *'Curse you, Henry Marshall!'* Then she launched his tiny heart of stone into the ocean where it belonged.

Hannah clapped behind her. 'He never deserved you,' she said when Sylvia was back on dry land. They folded the blanket and started the long trek up the beach and back to the farm.

Sylvia watched the seagulls, who have no need of titles and dowries and diamond rings, who fly freely through the air. She thought of the cows, and the weeds, and the tall sprigs of rosemary she had bundled together that morning, and how peculiar humans must seem to them. Life itself has already made so many things to care and worry about, but only in humans does one find the strange and ruinous desire to invent more.

Sylvia had finally been initiated into Heene, and she had permission to leave her old life behind. But every time she thought about it, *really* thought about it, she still felt a nagging sensation deep in her soul, like an itch she couldn't reach: *Isn't that just giving up? Isn't that just letting my family down?*

She didn't want to spend the rest of her life earning approval from the Catherines and Augustas of the world, but at least that life would give her *something* to earn. At least it would give her some tangible proof that she had made it, that she had won, that she was good enough.

Here in this private corner of the beach, there was no one around that could convince Sylvia she was good enough. There was only Hannah, and the best she could do was remind Sylvia again and again that she was loved.

Sylvia didn't know which life she wanted.

Well, that wasn't true—Sylvia knew exactly which life she wanted. She just didn't know which life she deserved.

Back at the farm, Hannah lingered by Sylvia's side for as long as she could. She had a dozen other things to do, and there were a dozen other tasks Sylvia could complete without Hannah's help, but for some reason Hannah decided this was the day she had to teach Sylvia how to make cheese dye from marigold petals.

'It's an old practice,' Hannah said as they scooped piles of dried petals into a pot of water in the fireplace. 'And now that you're going to be working with us for…longer than you expected…it's time for you to learn the real secrets of the dairy trade. Like the fact that cheddar isn't naturally orange.'

'Marigolds?' Sylvia said with mock outrage. 'What other *secrets of the dairy trade* have you been keeping from me?'

But Hannah was finding it difficult to focus. She was stuck in her own head replaying what she had just said out loud…*now that you're going to be working for us for…longer than you expected.* Sylvia had only ever committed to working on the Wickersham farm for a few weeks. Now that the fortune-hunting scheme had stalled, there was no guarantee she would want to stay.

Do I want her to stay?

'Hmm?' Hannah said when she noticed Sylvia looking at her. 'Oh. Right, yes. Secrets. Well…one time I added lavender instead. The purple was…quite faint, really, not at all as vibrant as I was going for. And I was so focused on the colouring that I completely fumbled the timing, and the end product was so hard I could have sold it to a bricklayer.'

'Did you try again?' Sylvia asked.

Hannah sighed. 'My parents said it was a waste of good milk. And they weren't wrong, but that's how all new things are made. You try, and you fail, and you try and you fail and then eventually something wonderful happens. But they told me to stick to the family recipes, so I listened…well, mostly.'

'Maybe we can try again sometime,' Sylvia said.

'If we ever get the shop going, I'd love to—'

'No, I mean… I mean now.' Sylvia added the last of the flowers to the pot. 'Or, not *right* now, but soon. Before any shops or husbands or trips back to London.'

It was time to let the flowers simmer and move on to other chores, but neither of them left their chairs.

'Does that mean…' Hannah asked, 'you're staying on the farm?'

'Where else would I go?'

'You could probably get another job, now that you have… I mean, now that you've learned some employable skills from—'

'Hannah.' Sylvia leaned over the arm of her chair and kissed Hannah's cheek. 'So long as I'm in Heene, I'm with you. And I wish…'

Now Sylvia looked away. 'I wish we could have a proper courtship, out in the open. I don't understand why courting a man for money is fine but courting a woman for love is…*unnatural*.'

'Anyone who says two women loving each other is unnatural has never met Henry,' Hannah said. 'The cow, of course—not the man.'

Sylvia looked confused, but then realisation dawned on her face. 'Are you saying that cows…?'

'Oh yes,' Hannah said, smiling. 'Cows are not so particular about who they mate with.'

'Then I think cows are quite sensible.'

'I agree.' Hannah was reminded that the cows actually needed some attention—and so did the cream, which was probably ready to be scooped, and so did the dozen other tasks she had put off to sit by the fire and make marigold dye with Sylvia.

But she was also reminded that every person who left her had planned to find a husband next. She didn't resent them for their choices—for many, it wasn't even a real choice—but here was Sylvia, openly and unashamedly wishing things could be different.

'And if we *could* have a proper courtship?' Hannah asked, surprised by her own courage. 'I mean—would you want to? If the law changed, and anyone could marry anyone. If the church changed, and it truly followed the part of the Bible that says *God is love*, or—'

'You're never this talkative,' Sylvia said. 'Not unless you've got something to hide.'

Hannah gaped, remembering how Amos had said

those exact words to her before she had confessed her feelings for Sylvia. 'How do you know that?'

'Because I know *you*.' Sylvia shrugged. 'And because Amos told Violet who told me.'

Hannah rolled her eyes. 'I will have words with him later.' But Amos, as usual, was right. Hannah was afraid to say what she was thinking out loud: *What if you stayed, Sylvia? What if our love was...permanent?*

The words ached within her, begging to be let out. This was the one thing she had never let herself hope for, the one thing that maybe she never would. So she buried it in hypotheticals and asked the next best thing: 'If a courtship like ours were acceptable— would you...really want to be with me?'

Sylvia watched the embers in the hearth. 'Has anyone ever done anything like that before? I mean, I've heard rumours, of course, but...even without the approval of society, is it something people do? On purpose? Is it something they *choose*?'

'Yes,' Hannah said. 'I've met them. And I've heard stories, too—stories from decades ago. Centuries, even. If you know where to look, what to read, and who to ask...people like us have always existed, Sylvia.'

That made Sylvia smile—and Sylvia's smile made Hannah's heart soar.

'It's hard to say what I would do if things were different,' Sylvia said. She opened her mouth to say more, but bit her lip instead. Seconds passed. Hannah wanted to ask what Sylvia was thinking, what Sylvia had stopped herself from saying—but Hannah had her own words that she would not say. They sat by the fire and let their unasked, unanswerable questions burn.

Still, Hannah let herself do something she had never done in a relationship before: she let herself hope. She let herself hope that she and Sylvia could maybe, somehow, stay together, despite the odds, despite all reason telling her otherwise.

She borrowed hope from all the women who had come before her—the ones who loved in secret, the ones who left their husbands, the ones who risked the wrath of church and state to stay in each other's arms—and she sent hope to all the women who would come next, the ones who might just build a kinder world. Her love for Sylvia was strengthened by this single thought, and her hope was strengthened too:

We have always existed. And we always will.

Chapter Sixteen

Hannah worked late into the evening. Her trip to the beach with Sylvia meant that everything she ought to have done that morning had to be completed after supper, so she spent her twilight hours turning cheddar and pressing butter and fixing the wheel on the delivery cart. She left the barn exhausted, ready for a long and peaceful sleep.

As she neared the house, Hannah heard the front door open and saw Sylvia set off briskly down the path, through the gate, and out onto the road. Except, it couldn't be Sylvia—Sylvia had gone home hours ago to spend time with her sisters. *Right?*

Hannah looked closer…and she realised this wasn't Sylvia at all.

This was Ella Queensbury.

Sylvia's mother had been to the Wickersham farm before. There was the night of the family dinner, when Ella had stayed late chatting with Rachel; and there was the night she had discovered her daughter's fortune-hunting scheme and stayed behind after Sylvia left for the ball. And now...well, Hannah wasn't sure what to make of this latest visit.

She knew that Ella and her own mother had been friends when they were younger, before Ella had been whisked away to London. But what sort of *friends* exactly?

'I'm home!' she called out as she stepped inside, but her mind was elsewhere.

Her mother was alone in the kitchen, peeling potatoes for supper. 'Care to join me?' she said, nodding at an empty chair.

Hannah grabbed a paring knife, took her seat, and set to work. They peeled in silence for a while.

But Hannah couldn't contain her questions forever. 'Why was Ella Queensbury just here?'

Her mother didn't say anything at first. When she did speak, it was with a nonchalant tone of voice. 'Reminiscing about old times. Catching up on everything that's happened since.'

'You knew each other, right? You were friends?'

'We were friends, yes.' Rachel had never been one to talk about herself in great detail. She preferred her actions to speak for themselves. *If you want to know a person*, she used to say when Hannah was young, *close your ears and open your eyes. Watch what they do, Hannah, especially if it's different from what they say.*

Hannah agreed. She didn't think anyone could truly

know *her* until they'd tasted her cheese. But she also knew that there were some things you could only learn from words.

'Were you *close* friends?' Hannah said.

Rachel smiled fondly. 'The closest.'

Hannah usually didn't mind silence, but this was too much, and she was too curious. She finished peeling the potato in her hand and then set down her knife. 'I want to hear what happened. I want to know…who you were to each other.'

Rachel just sighed. 'You know how the Bible says, *take therefore no thought for the morrow: for the morrow shall take thought for the things of itself*? I think it's the same for the past. Take no thought for the morrow and no thought for yesterday. My heart is set on today, on the present moment.'

'And I agree,' Hannah said. 'That's a good way to live. But today is built on a hundred yesterdays. I'm not sure we can understand the present without knowing how it arrived.'

Rachel laughed. 'When did you become so wise?'

Hannah placed a hand on her mother's knee. 'I learned from the best.'

'I don't fancy long-winded storytelling,' Rachel said, setting down her own paring knife. 'But these are the facts, Hannah: there was a time when Ella and I were inseparable. We grew up next to each other when there were half as many houses in Heene as there are today.

We were close as could be throughout childhood, always making flower crowns together and skipping along the sand when we weren't busy with household chores.'

Hannah noticed the wistful smile on her mother's face, the way her eyes went back and forth from Hannah to some place off in the past.

'Then we grew older,' Rachel continued 'And...we had such *dreams*, Hannah. We would lie in the grass and wait for shooting stars, and we'd wish for anything. Everything. Well-stocked kitchens and crowded tables, boats that could take us to far away places, diamond earrings and silver thread and gilded teacups.'

Hannah was surprised. 'I've never known you to want those kinds of things. Well, besides the part about the kitchen and the table—'

'Some things are more enjoyable as daydreams,' her mother said. 'I always knew that. It was fun to create these make-believe lives for ourselves, to tell stories about who we could be and where we could go. But I knew none of those things would really make me happy. What good is chasing after diamonds when I could spend my time laughing around a meal with people I love instead? But Ella...she really believed in the daydreams. And she almost had me believe in them too.'

Hannah tried to imagine her mother all those years ago, prancing about the shore with flowers in her hair, weaving tales of wealth and adventure. Rachel and Ella, the same age that Hannah and Sylvia were now.

The same age. Hannah had never put the pieces together before. She and Sylvia were also the same age—born in the same month! Ella had met her husband *here*, in Heene, then followed him out when the summer ended.

'What do you mean by that?' Hannah asked. 'What did you almost believe?'

Rachel bit her bottom lip. Her hands were clasped together on the table. 'You've never taken an interest in any of this before.'

'That's true,' Hannah said. 'But I just want to understand...' *how things might go wrong*, she wanted to say.

Her mind was turning. She was starting to wonder if *friendship* wasn't the whole of Rachel and Ella's story. She was starting to wonder if they had been in love.

She was starting to wonder how their hearts had broken, and how Rachel had picked herself up and made a happy life regardless.

'Sylvia and I have become close friends too,' Hannah said. 'And... I want to know where she came from, and where I came from. She hasn't talked to her mother about any of this, either, at least I don't think so. But I... I just *have* to know.'

Rachel sighed again. 'It started out as Ella's idea, but I joined in eagerly enough. Worthing was just starting to be worth anyone's time, and we wanted a taste of all that new glamour, all the exciting people and restaurants and attractions that were moving in next door. So we got dressed up and flirted with the first handsome men we could find.'

'Mother!' Hannah gasped, clamping her hand over her mouth. She was surprised, not ashamed. 'I'm sorry,' she rushed to say. 'I just can't imagine...'

Rachel offered a sly smile and a wink. '...that I had a different life before you?'

'No, I knew that, but—this is a *different* different life, if that makes sense. You're fascinating. And... I'm sorry I never took the time to learn that.'

Rachel laughed. 'Oh, Hannah. Seducing a man of the upper class is one of the least fascinating things I've done. But that's for a different day. The part you want to hear is that Ella found herself a man, and so did I. We spent a few weeks in our love affairs, then the weather got cold and we each had a choice to make. I was so surprised, *terribly surprised* when she told me she had gotten engaged. I never thought our lit-tle...*adventure*...would last beyond the summer. She asked me to come with her, to convince the man I was with to marry me...but that's not the life I wanted for myself. I said no. She left. And several months later, I got you.'

'Did you ask her to stay?' Sylvia asked.

'No.' Then a long pause. 'I'm not sure it would have made a difference if I had.'

'And you never wrote? You never visited each other?'

Rachel shook her head. 'Too painful. If I couldn't have Ella, the next best thing I could think of was to preserve the memory of who she had been…and to preserve the daydream of who we *could* have been, together.'

Hannah supposed that if she was busy with her own suitor while Sylvia was entertaining Henry, she and Sylvia wouldn't have had much time to have an affair of their own. She conjured up all the longing she felt for Sylvia, the yearning, the wanting, the raw desire, and imagined what it would feel like to never have acted on it. To always wonder what might have happened if she had.

Hannah pushed her chair back, slowly, then stood and walked to the space between her mother's chair and the fireplace. Hannah hugged her mother from behind, arms around Rachel's shoulders. They stayed that way in silence for a while. Hannah felt a tear fall on her forearm.

'All right,' Rachel said eventually. 'That's enough digging through the past for now.'

Hannah went back to her own chair to continue peeling potatoes. But Rachel said one more thing: 'We've patched things up, by the way. Ella and I. We've said what we needed to say. I wouldn't go so far as to call us *friends* again. That'll take some time. But we're on good terms. And, Hannah—' Rachel looked serious now. 'This is the most important part: I have no regrets about how my life unfolded. I stayed in the town that I love, and I married a good man, and I gave birth to the most brilliant, hardworking, compassionate daughter I ever could have asked for. This isn't the life of my dreams—it's so much better. All the shooting stars in the world couldn't change my mind about that.'

Now Hannah was starting to tear up. *When did I become so sentimental?*

'Thank you for telling me,' Hannah said, busying herself with her potatoes. She had a lot to process, and for that she would need silence.

But just as she was beginning to comprehend it all— her mother's heartbreak, her own parentage, the fact that if things had gone a different way she could have grown up like Sylvia or Sylvia could have grown up like her—the front door burst open.

Violet Queensbury ran into the kitchen. She was panting.

'Hannah!' she said.

Hannah and Rachel stared at Violet, who suddenly looked embarrassed.

'Oh dear,' she continued. 'That was terribly rude of me, sorry. Where are my manners?' She ran back outside, shut the door, then *knocked* on the door.

Hannah glanced at her mother, then called: 'Come in?'

Violet entered again. 'Thank you,' she said, talking very quickly. 'I just saw—well, I don't know if *you* saw, but I figured you would want to know, and I thought maybe you should hear it from someone you trust—'

'What did you see?' Hannah asked.

Violet stood still, then pulled out a chair and sat next to Hannah. Her eyes darted around the room and she looked for a moment like she might stand up again and ask if she could sit, but instead she took Hannah's hands in her own.

'Mr Luxford's shop is empty,' Violet said. 'He sold the building, packed up, and left town.'

No one said anything. *What?* Hannah wanted to ask, but very suddenly her mouth felt dry and her throat felt tight.

'He did what?' Rachel asked.

'He made a decision. I was walking back from the modiste, and I passed his shop, and usually I don't pay much attention to it but—'

Hannah was nodding, now, urging Violet to get to the point.

'—but it's hard not to notice when a shop is stark empty.'

'Okay,' Hannah said, gaining her voice back. 'Well, no one else has moved in yet, so that's good news.'

But the expression on Violet's face did not look like she had good news.

'Hannah…' Violet started, then took a deep breath.

'There's a sign on the window, with information on how to contact the new landlord. He didn't sell it to someone who wants to run a shop, just someone who wants to own the building.'

'Right,' Hannah said, hope still alive in her quickly beating heart. 'Who's the new landlord? Who did Mr Luxford sell the building to?'

Violet closed her eyes tightly, like she didn't want to see the name after it left her mouth. She scrunched up her nose, and Hannah realised half a second before Violet spoke that only one man in all of Heene could inspire a face like that.

Alister Coyle, Hannah thought.

'Alister Coyle,' Violet said.

Sylvia wasn't used to hearing sixteen horse hooves on the road by her house. A four-horse carriage had no business being in this part of town, so when she heard what *sounded like* a four-horse carriage down the road, she stood from the ground to see where the noise was coming from.

Sylvia had been planting seeds in her new herb garden, a project she'd taken on now that her family was going to stay in Heene for long enough to watch a seed grow into a bush. She shook loose dirt from her beige dress and walked to the edge of the yard, then leaned over the fence and stared down the road.

Sure enough, there it was: a shiny black carriage pulled by four reddish brown Cleveland Bays.

First, Sylvia wondered if the coachman was lost. Then she *knew* the coachman was lost, because he slowed to a stop right in front of her house. Her hands were still gripping the top of the fence when the man inside the carriage opened the door. He stepped into the sunlight, and Sylvia smelled mustard.

No… Sylvia smelled *stale* mustard.

'Miss Sylvia Queensbury!' said the small old man beneath his furry grey moustache. He removed his top hat and bent into a shallow bow.

'Lord Bogsworth,' she said, muscle memory guiding her into a curtsy.

He smiled, very pleased with himself. 'You must be wondering how I found you.'

Sylvia had not, in fact, been wondering how he found her. She was just surprised he was here at all. And, more importantly, she had gardening to get back to.

But Sylvia knew better than to contradict a lord. 'Oh, yes! You clever man. How did you know I was living all the way out here in Heene?'

He chuckled. 'I admit it wasn't easy, but you *have* been the talk of the town ever since your appearance at the Fitzroy ball. People were wondering how your family had risen back to prominence so quickly after the…*unfortunate* incident with your uncle.'

Sylvia suddenly felt suffocatingly hot, despite the curtain of clouds that covered the sun. She smoothed stray hairs out of her face and tried to look politely interested in Lord Bogsworth as he spoke.

'But I found it very suspicious,' he continued, 'that you were the only Queensbury to be seen in public. At the second ball I overheard some gossip that you had worn the same gown twice'—*why does that even matter to people?* Sylvia thought, frustrated that something she had learned to stop caring about was still so important to so many people—'and also that you were staying at the new Linfield resort. After our *charming* dance I decided to call on you, but there was no record of your family ever having booked a room.'

Yes, Sylvia wanted to say. *I know all this. Obviously I know all this.* Instead, she acted impressed. 'I had no idea you went to all this trouble just to call on *me*,' she said, as if she was unworthy of so much time and effort. 'How on earth did you find me *here*?'

'One of the staff thought I was simply confused,' he continued. 'Because there *were* Queensburys at the resort, but they didn't *live* there. They *worked* there!' He emphasised his words to really show Sylvia how smart he was. 'I won't bore you with the rest of the details, but that's how I traced you back to here. And are you wondering *why* I came all the way out here to see you?'

Sylvia was just about ready to turn her back on

Lord Bogsworth and walk into her house, manners be damned. She couldn't stand the way he prompted her to ask the questions *he* wanted her to ask.

'Why did you come all the way out here to see me?' Sylvia asked, her patience wearing thin.

He puffed up his chest. 'To ask for your hand in marriage, of course.'

Sylvia blinked. She wasn't sure what she had been expecting him to say, but it definitely wasn't *that*.

'Did I…hear you correctly?' she asked. 'Did you say marriage?'

'Indeed I did,' he said, chin tilted up. 'It's clear to me now that you were in search of a husband whose fortune could save your family. When you disappeared from the social scene a few weeks ago, it became even *more* clear to me that you had failed. But fear not—I am what a girl your age might call *flush in the pockets*. That's what they say these days, yes?' He laughed to himself. If he noticed the frown on Sylvia's face, he didn't say so.

'In plain language,' he continued, 'I have quite the fortune. I've had the rotten luck of having no heirs with whom to give that fortune, and I'm running out of time to change that luck. I need heirs, you need money. I don't need a dowry, and you…' he glanced at her dressed, covered in grass stains and mended holes. '…seem to have run out of options.'

Sylvia wanted to be angry. She wanted to be *cross*

with Lord Bogsworth. She wanted to take all the fury she had collected from her time with Henry Marshall and unleash it right now, telling this man off for his assumptions and his audacity and his blatant disrespect.

But she also realised that this man was handing her everything she had spent the last few months wanting. He was handing her everything she had worked for, everything she had failed to obtain. He was handing her a future. The future she deserved.

Bogsworth decided that too much time had passed without a response, so he cleared his throat.

'I'm flattered,' Sylvia said, rushing to find the right words. But she didn't know what the right words were—saying *no* felt impossible, but saying *yes* felt so much worse. 'This is just such a surprise, such a *delightful* surprise.' She forced a smile. 'I'm just at a loss for words.'

'I figured that might be the case,' said Lord Bogsworth, taking a moment to adjust his cravat and straighten his lapels. 'I understand that *the fairer sex* can be easily overwhelmed with emotion. And, though I'm *fairly* confident you have no other offers, I understand there *may* be others suitors you're considering. So I did not come expecting an answer today.' He pulled a crisply folded piece of paper from his pocket, then handed it to Sylvia. 'This is my address. You have until Sunday afternoon to make your decision, at which point there will be a *lavish* luncheon to celebrate our engagement. And trust me when I say—no expense will be spared.'

He bowed again, then turned to enter his carriage. Sylvia clutched the paper in her sweaty palm.

Today was Friday.

'Wait,' she said, just before he closed the carriage door behind him. 'If you know about my reputation… why marry me? Wouldn't it ruin you?'

He laughed. He *laughed*, long and hard, like Sylvia had told the funniest joke he'd ever heard. 'Oh, my dear Miss Queensbury,' he said at last. 'I have the kind of money that can make any problem go away. Don't you see? I have no heir. I have nothing to lose. And you, my dear girl, have everything to gain.'

He shut the carriage door. The coachman steered the horses away. Sylvia stood behind her fence, trembling and numb.

She decided the paper in her hand would make excellent fertiliser. She returned to her garden, feeling very detached from what had just happened, like it was a conversation that was meant for someone else and she just happened to overhear it. She scooped the soil with her hands and buried the address in the ground. She felt the softest whisper of guilt—*this is your family's ticket out. This is Hannah's cheese shop. This is the life you were always meant to live*—but she filled in the hole until she couldn't hear the whisper anymore.

Her mother seemed happy enough in Heene, at least for now. Rose and Mary had real friends, and Violet had Amos. Hannah still had time to convince Mr Luxford to sell her the shop for a reasonable price. And Sylvia—she had butter to make, and herbs to grow, and Hannah to love.

'This looks wonderful!'

Sylvia jumped at the sound of Violet's voice.

'How long have you been standing there?' Sylvia asked. She looked up at her sister, who was admiring the herb garden.

'Not long,' Violet said. 'I'm sorry, I didn't realise you were so focused. I just got home from the modiste…' Her voice trailed off and a look of worry fell over her face.

'Is something the matter?' Sylvia asked.

Violet knelt onto the ground beside Sylvia.

'I stopped at the Wickersham house on my way back,' Violet said. 'I went to tell Hannah that Mr Luxford has sold his shop to Alister Coyle.'

The numbness Sylvia had been feeling gave way to pungent dread. *No, no, no*, Sylvia thought. *Anyone but him.*

'I don't know Mr Coyle,' Violet continued. 'But from what I've heard…'

'He'll just sell to the highest bidder.' Sylvia grimaced. 'Even if it's twice as much as he paid Mr Luxford.'

Violet nodded. 'I'm sure you'll want to go be with Hannah…she's quite torn up about it. I asked if there were other shops for sale, and of course there are, but this was the only one even close to her budget.' Violet put her hand on Sylvia's shoulder in condolence, as if Sylvia was the one who had been hurt by this news. 'I'm really sorry.'

'Thank you for telling me,' Sylvia said. 'I'll head over soon.'

Violet left Sylvia alone. The sweet, cosy smell of cinnamon and sugar and freshly baked dough wafted from the door.

Sylvia turned her attention back to her garden, pressing her fingers into the dark, fresh soil. The dread had not left her body. It settled deep in her stomach like a bitter seed, sprouting and spreading until it consumed her. She dug her fingers deeper into the dirt until they reached the folded, crumpled, damp thing she had just condemned to a life underground.

Sylvia pulled the paper from its grave and smoothed it open.

Lord Bogsworth didn't know how right he was. Sylvia *did* have everything to gain from his proposal.

But more importantly, so did Hannah.

Chapter Seventeen

Hannah Wickersham had never been this uncomfortable sitting in silence before. Every small sound—every creak in the old wooden meeting house, every hurried footstep on the road outside—made Hannah open her eyes and glance at the entrance. When Sylvia didn't walk through the door, Hannah closed her eyes and tried not to think about the fact that *Sylvia didn't walk through the door.* Then there would be another sound and—eyes open, all over again.

Hannah didn't want to rethink her time in the ocean with Sylvia. She didn't want to comb through the two-day-old memory for signs that Sylvia's feelings were waning, that her attraction to Hannah was wearing off. She didn't want to search for evidence that Sylvia had said *love* too soon and was only just now realising that she didn't really mean it.

What Hannah wanted was to keep the memory preserved, in all its sunshine and sweetness and salty waves, unwarped by the sudden worry that *Friday had meant something different to Sylvia than it did to me.*

But no—Sylvia wouldn't have said yes to Hannah's invitation if she was losing interest in their relationship. Hannah knew there could be any number of reasons for Sylvia's absence this morning—maybe Sylvia woke up sick, or her muscles were too sore from swimming, or someone in her family needed help with some household chore.

Or maybe...

Hannah's thoughts circled back on themselves like this for an hour. By the time the meeting ended, she had spiralled into resenting herself for wasting what was supposed to be a cherished part of her week. Most Sundays she delighted in the hour of silence and prayer she shared with her community, the time they set aside from their busy lives to let the wisdom of God show them whatever they needed to be shown.

Hannah raced to the exit without talking to anyone. She could see in the faces of her neighbours pity over Mr Luxford's decision. She heard, or maybe imagined, their whispers as she hurried by: *How could he sell to such a traitor? We all know Mr Coyle won't be leasing to his own neighbours. You can't find anything better to put in that shop than Hannah's cheese. Were you there when she brought some, for all of us to try?*

Hannah didn't find much relief outside of the meeting house either. She didn't want to go home, to be anywhere near the meagre stash of money she'd been saving for the shop. But where else was there? And anyway, there were cows to milk and butter to churn and curds to slice…

'Where's Sylvia?' Amos said, jogging to catch up with Hannah. 'I thought you invited her.'

The sky above them was fuzzy with rain clouds, too light to bring a storm, just dark enough for a faint and soothing drizzle. The road ahead disappeared into mist.

'I don't know,' Hannah said, biting her bottom lip. 'She said she would be here. What if…'

'What if what?' asked Amos.

But Hannah wasn't ready to finish that sentence. 'She hasn't come to see me since Mr Luxford sold his shop, you know.'

'Two days ago?' Amos said. 'Hannah, if you're about to say that Sylvia left—'

'But what if she did?' The words came tumbling out before Hannah could stop them. 'What if she isn't coming back? What if—what if she just did what everyone always does?'

'*Everyone* doesn't leave, Hannah. I'm still here—'

'You know what I mean.'

'No,' Amos said firmly. 'I really don't. Because *some* people leave, but that's never bothered you before.'

'Sylvia was different,' she confessed. 'I realised too late that I want her to stay. And now…now she's not here.'

Hannah felt embarrassed to admit that she cared, *truly cared*, about someone who was always going to leave. She stared at the ground as she spoke, kicking pebbles to the side of the road. 'Sylvia wasn't around yesterday either. She didn't come by the house, not once, even though she *knows* about the shop, and she would *know* how heartbroken I'd be about it...'

'Do you regret being with Sylvia?' Amos asked.

Hannah kept her eyes on the damp ground, kicking pebbles to the side of the road as they neared the farm. 'You asked me this on the beach. You said it might hurt if she left...how did you know?'

'Because you brought her home for supper, Hannah. You've never done that before.' He opened his left hand and held it out, face up. 'Usually it's *life* over here—' he opened his other hand '—and your *lovers* over there. But with Sylvia...' Amos clapped his hands together. 'You let her become *part* of your life. You let your love for her become...ordinary. So ordinary, I think, that you stopped preparing yourself for its absence.'

Hannah sighed. She looked down at her brick-red dress and felt foolish; it was the nicest one she owned, which really just meant it was the only one without grass stains and loose threads, and she had worn it to look nice in front of Sylvia. 'Why did I let myself do that?'

'I can't answer that for you,' said Amos, 'but I can remind you that you *don't actually know* why Sylvia didn't show up this morning, or why she didn't come to comfort you yesterday. Maybe it has nothing to do with you. The only way to find out is to ask her. But if she *is* leaving, if she really is packing up just like the rest of them—well, I stand by what I said on the beach. You weren't wrong for caring.'

Hannah wanted to believe her cousin, but all her emotions just felt so muddled. Shame, hope, embarrassment, desire, sorrow…they swirled within her like a storm. She couldn't make sense of them, and right now she didn't want to.

Instead, she decided to throw herself into work the moment she got home and let the steady rhythm of life on the farm clear her mind. She spent hours in the barn, in the cheese shed, in the pasture, focused on whatever task was at hand. Every so often she would think about what Amos had said—*the only way to find out is to ask her*—and she would decide, each time, not to ask. Hannah didn't want to know why Sylvia hadn't shown up this morning, because Hannah already knew the clockmaker's shop was sold and that was just about all the heartbreak she could take.

Sylvia, however, seemed ready to decide that Hannah could take more.

'Can I come in?' Sylvia's voice was quiet—so was her knock on the barn's open door.

Hannah wasn't sure how much time had passed since she started working. The rain had stopped, and her arms were sore, and the butter she'd been churning was nearly done. She didn't look up when she spoke.

'Sure,' Hannah said over the rhythmic *thrum* of the barrel churn. She gripped the handle tightly, holding herself in place. If Sylvia was about to end their relationship for good—*which I have no reason to believe is the case*, Hannah reminded herself—then she didn't want to be looking at Sylvia when it happened.

'I'm sorry I didn't come sooner,' Sylvia said, stepping inside but keeping her distance.

Hannah kept spinning the churn handle—*one, two, three, four.* 'I missed you this morning,' she said.

'I would have been there, but—'

'And yesterday. After Violet told me about the shop, I figured it wouldn't be long until you came by too, but… I didn't hear from you at all.'

'I know, and—'

'I could have used some comfort,' Hannah said, pain rising in her chest no matter how much she tried to keep it down. There was nothing she wanted to say to Sylvia right now, but even more than that she didn't want to listen. She didn't want her worst fears to be proven right. As long as Hannah was talking, there was still a chance—a decent chance, a *probable* chance—that Sylvia had fallen ill over the weekend or was needed by her family.

So Hannah kept talking. 'I could have used *you*, Sylvia. I could have used your support, your friendship, your…' *your love.* 'If you were unavailable, you could have sent a message—'

'If you'd just—'

'Because you know how much this shop meant to me—'

'Hannah!' Sylvia almost shouted. 'Of course I know how much the shop means to you! That's what I'm trying to tell you—*I can buy you the shop.* Just—just look at me!'

Hannah slowed the barrel to a stop, then released her calloused fingers from the handle. She turned to face Sylvia.

'Oh…' Hannah started, stunned by what she saw. She blinked. She looked away, then looked back. Sylvia had the same buttery hair, the same angular face, the same mossy green eyes…but just about everything else was different.

Completely different.

'Where did you…' Hannah tried to ask, but she didn't even know what the right question was. Here was the Sylvia she knew only from stories, from the memories Sylvia used to share of her life before Heene. Here was the shimmering gown, the elbow-high gloves, the string of genuine pearls that Sylvia was always destined to return to.

Sylvia pinched her silver skirt with her satin-covered fingers, fidgeting with the fine fabric. 'I found a husband, Hannah. Just like we said I would do. After Henry… I had given up hope of returning to society quickly. I was ready to just…wait, here in Heene, and be happy while I waited. But then… I got another offer. A surprise offer. And I—'

But Sylvia was cut off by the sound of whistling. Amos entered the barn, returning a spade to the crate of gardening tools. He didn't notice them at first, but when he did, it only took him a second to realise what was going on.

'Oh, er…does that butter need moulding? Because I could—'

'Yes,' Hannah and Sylvia said at the same time. They glanced at each other, then Hannah followed Sylvia out of the barn. She squeezed Amos's arm on the way out, and said, *'Thank you.'*

There was no more rain falling from the sky, but droplets of water dripped from the trees as they walked to the shore. Hannah listened as Sylvia detailed the events of the last forty-eight hours. She explained the presumptuous manner in which Bogsworth showed up at her house, and the strange proposal that followed. She described his house, and all the gifts that were waiting for her there, and the elegant luncheon she had just come from. She told Hannah the facts of the story, that was all. Each moment gave way to the next and there were no emotions in between.

They had just reached the shore when Sylvia finished talking. The ocean looked so small today, most of it swallowed by the fog. Each wave seemed to come from nowhere.

'That's…a lot,' Hannah said. She'd been by Sylvia's side for most of their fortune-hunting, and it felt strange to hear the scheme had succeeded through a series of events Hannah had nothing to do with. 'I guess I'm just surprised. I mean, I knew—*we* knew—this was always going to happen, but it's moving so fast now.'

No one was lounging on this particular stretch of beach. They had it all to themselves, just the two of them and their damp, crisp footprints.

'This is what I wanted,' Sylvia said. 'It's what I asked for, what I *wished* for. And look—I mean, *really* look.' She held up a fistful of fabric from her skirt, thousands of blue-grey threads woven together beneath a glittering silver gauze. The hem was circled with lace embroidery, the bodice adorned with glittering beads. 'The pearls are *real*,' she continued, touching the double-strand necklace and large round earrings. 'When I put them on… I have missed this *so much*, Hannah. So much.'

Hannah could hear the relief in Sylvia's voice. She could also hear the crack of her own heart breaking, slowly, piece by piece with every word Sylvia said. She reminded herself again—as she had reminded herself so many times—that this was always how the two of them would end.

Isn't that better than Sylvia staying in Heene but leaving me anyway? Hannah wondered. *Isn't this the best possible way for our relationship to end?*

But Hannah didn't feel relieved.

'How does it feel to have your hair back up?' she asked. Hannah thought that maybe if she heard more about how happy this choice made Sylvia—how much Sylvia truly wanted this—then Hannah would be able to feel happy too.

'It was odd, at first,' Sylvia said, placing a hand on the back of her neck. 'But it's...nice, again. It's familiar. And I didn't even have to curl it myself—there was staff ready to attend to all that. My hair, my cheeks, my lips... I didn't lift a finger. It feels like—*I* feel like...' She trailed off, her sentence fading into the fog like the ocean and the birds and all of Heene.

'What do you feel like?' Hannah asked.

'I feel like I won.' Sylvia stopped walking. 'And Hannah, *you* won too. Like I said, I can buy you any of the shops up for sale right now. You...you've given me so much. And now—' Sylvia looked up at the sky, blinking fast.

'It's all right,' Hannah said. She knew this face—it was the one Sylvia made whenever she was trying not to cry. She reached out her hand to touch Sylvia's arm, but Sylvia pulled Hannah into a full embrace instead.

'Now,' Sylvia continued, her voice muffled in Hannah's hair, 'now I get to give you something too.'

Hannah smiled. She breathed in—and she was struck by the scent of unfamiliar perfume. Sylvia no longer smelled like Sylvia. Hannah wondered if her own mother had stood on this same beach all those years ago and hugged Ella goodbye and smelled something different too.

'Thank you,' she said eventually, letting go of Sylvia. 'It will be the most wonderful shop.'

'I won't get my cheese from anywhere else, you have my word.'

They were both smiling now, holding hands, unbothered by the light rain that had returned over their heads. They heard the rustling of waves in the distance, the call of a lone seagull. They were smiling. They were happy. They were both getting exactly what they wanted, nothing more, nothing less.

But Hannah was struggling to keep the smile on her face. She watched Sylvia's lips quiver at the corners and noticed the quiet pain in her eyes.

'This is what we worked for,' Hannah said.

'Yes,' Sylvia agreed, but she wavered when she said: 'This is what we both want…?'

'Of course.' Hannah made herself believe her own words.

'And I really mean it—I won't get my cheese from anywhere else. I'll come visit so often. I wouldn't be doing this…' She bit her lip, paused, then continued. 'What I mean to say is, Lord Bogsworth has a house in Worthing. That's one of the reasons why this arrangement works so well. You get your shop, we get to see each other, and I get to show everyone who scorned me that they were wrong.'

Hannah thought about what that kind of life would look like, spending her days waiting for Sylvia to show up in her glossy new carriage and whisk Hannah away like a fairy tale, only to drop her the moment Lord Bogsworth called her back to London.

You'll get busy, Hannah wanted to say. *Or you'll forget about me the moment you're back in London.* And though she knew these thoughts were probably true, she wanted—just for right now, on this beach, while she still had Sylvia in her hands—to pretend it could be otherwise.

The rain was falling harder now. Sylvia sniffed, her nose red, her slick hair plastered to her ruddy cheeks. Hannah couldn't tell if she was still crying, or if it was only the rain.

'We won,' she said, squeezing Sylvia's hands. She would go home after this, dry off by the fire, and start drawing up plans for the shop. Hannah would never have Sylvia's heart—not fully, not completely—but she would have this one magnificent gift, this one place to call her own. That had to be enough.

'We won,' Sylvia said. They were on the cusp of being drenched but they would not walk away.

Hannah shivered. 'Is your family excited?'

'Oh.' Sylvia laughed. 'Rose is ecstatic. She's excited to never wash her own dishes again. And Violet will get a proper season…' She frowned. 'Though she didn't seem too thrilled, if I'm being honest. She and Mary were both happy for me, but they've both made real friends here. Still, I'm confident they'll come around.'

'And your mother?'

Sylvia sighed. 'She can live wherever she wants, I suppose.' She looked like she might say more, but she didn't.

'When do you leave?' Hannah asked.

'Tomorrow.'

Oh. 'That's very soon.'

Hannah just stared at Sylvia, and Sylvia stared back. They were both taking in the sight of each other, memorising the shape of their bodies, the slope of their necks, the exact location of every freckle like each one was a signpost on a trail they wouldn't walk again for a very long time. But the more Hannah stared, the more Sylvia faded into the fog. Her silver dress, darkened by rain, the colour of an oyster shell—it blurred into the mist around her.

Hannah shivered again. Despite the happiness she felt for Sylvia and despite the joy of having her own shop, Hannah knew that she was too cold, too wet, and too heartbroken to stay on the beach any longer. The hope that Sylvia would visit often was too thin to bring Hannah any comfort. It was barely even hope at all.

'Thank you for the shop,' Hannah said, then opened

her arms to embrace Sylvia one last time. 'We can work out the details after you're married, but, *thank you*. Really, thank you.' Hannah closed her eyes as Sylvia's body eased into her own. The ocean was loud and the sky was dark and their shoes were ruined.

'*Your* shop,' Sylvia said, 'is going to *amaze the world*.'

'I'll just be happy if it amazes the southern coast of England. And you...you'll get...' She struggled to name it, this intangible thing that Sylvia was always seeking, the thing that rested just beyond her need to prove everyone wrong.

'I'll get to know for certain that I'm good enough,' Sylvia said.

Hannah exhaled slowly. 'Oh, Sylvia,' she said, leaning back to look into Sylvia's eyes. She couldn't leave Sylvia with much, but she could leave her with this: 'You don't have to be good enough. You're already *good*. And that's so much better.'

Hannah couldn't buy Sylvia a shop, and in the end she couldn't even help Sylvia get a husband, but at the very least she could remind Sylvia of her own goodness. She could become the voice in Sylvia's head that reminds her of her own goodness every time some duchess or viscount or rotten uncle tries to tear her down.

It's the final thing she could do for Sylvia, so she did it gracefully—she sealed it with a long and passionate kiss—and then she walked away, into the fog.

Chapter Eighteen

Sylvia Queensbury finally found a way to have it all.

It just meant giving up the best life she'd ever known.

Standing in the doorway of the small room she shared with her sisters, Sylvia held on to the final scraps of the summer: a handheld butter churn, one small carpet bag of belongings, and a hunk of Wickersham cheddar for the road.

She had no idea when or how she'd use the churn, but she just couldn't imagine never making butter again.

Sylvia had already said goodbye to most of her family last night. She had brought home a basket of treats from the Bogsworth luncheon, the kind of cakes and candies they'd be able to eat whenever they wished in just a few short weeks. The plan was for Sylvia to settle into her new home, then send for her sisters—who would live out the rest of the summer in Heene.

But as Sylvia stood in that doorway, she realised she did not want to go alone.

She stepped into the main room to say goodbye to Violet, the only Queensbury who wasn't yet at work. Violet was pacing—and she looked nervous.

'My carriage will be arriving shortly,' Sylvia said.

'Oh!' Violet looked up quickly. She stopped pacing.

'How do I look?' Sylvia swirled in place, showing off her new ivory gown, her lacy gloves, her tall straw bonnet.

'Gorgeous,' Violet said. 'Really, truly gorgeous.'

'It won't be long until you look just like this.'

The two sisters stared at each other in silence.

And then, they spoke at once:

'Come with me to London.'

'I'm staying in Heene.'

Sylvia's stomach dropped. Her chest tightened. 'Staying?' she asked.

Violet exhaled slowly. 'Yes… I'm staying. Permanently. I think it's wonderful what you're doing—how you're bringing Rose and Mary with you, how you're buying Hannah the shop…how you're making a life for yourself, even. The life you want. But—' She paused, then began to pace again. 'But it's not the life I want. Not anymore.'

Sylvia nodded. She felt a lump in her throat, and she didn't know what to say.

'Please don't be cross,' Violet added. 'I'm happy for

you, I promise. And every time you visit, I'll want to hear about—about all the parties and balls you'll be hosting. You'll be such a *marvellous* host, Sylvia—'

'It's all right,' Sylvia said, placing a hand on Violet's shoulder to stop her pacing. 'I'm not cross. This is…this is your choice. And it's really what you want? You're sure?'

Violet looked into Sylvia's eyes, then wrapped her sister in a hug. 'Yes,' she said. 'I'm sure.'

Sylvia held Violet tightly. This was not how she was expecting this goodbye to go. She comforted herself with the knowledge that Violet could always change her mind, and that once the transition was complete— once Sylvia had written letters about how much fun she was having in London, and how happy Mary and Rose were in their new house, and how many books and gowns and suitors were just waiting for Violet's arrival—then Violet would remember where she belonged.

Maybe Ella would too.

She had decided to stay in Heene weeks ago, Sylvia knew, but she hadn't tried to stop Sylvia from marrying Lord Bogsworth. She wanted her daughters to make their own choices in life.

Sylvia let go of Violet when she heard the carriage arrive.

'Farewell, Violet,' she said, putting on her most

hopeful smile. She would choose to believe their time apart would last no more than a few weeks.

'Goodbye, Sylvia.' Violet smiled as well, though tears were rising in her eyes.

Sylvia left before she could watch them fall.

The carriage ride to the Bogsworth property seemed to take forever. Sylvia was eager to arrive, eat breakfast, then finally—*finally*—get out of Heene. She would visit, of course—she would visit as often as she could. But she would never again call this place home.

Sylvia leaned her head against the carriage wall and daydreamed about her future holidays. She would sneak out of her fiancé's Worthing manor late at night to meet with Hannah, and every time they saw each other it would be like no time had passed at all…

The carriage jolted to a stop, and soon Sylvia was being ushered into the house and down the hall and through the drawing room door.

She sat stiffly in an oversized armchair, rubbing her fingers against the puce velvet upholstery. She sipped a cup of tea and imagined Hannah, lounging on the chaise across the room this time next year. Surely there would be times when Sylvia could have the house to herself, and could invite Hannah over without suspicion. Surely Sylvia could have the life she wanted *and* the love she had found without sacrificing one for the other…*right*?

'Lord Bogsworth will see you now,' said the butler, appearing at the door. Sylvia left the room, and on her way out she noticed a stack of crates in the corner. The butler led her to the parlour, which…also had a stack of crates.

There was no artwork on the walls.

'Miss Queensbury,' Lord Bogsworth said from his lime-green couch. He didn't stand, but merely tipped his hat.

'Lord Bogsworth,' she replied with an equally modest curtsy.

'Now *this*,' he said, gesturing to a small round table covered with colourful dishes, 'must be quite the improvement for you. I can't imagine what you've been eating all this time. Plain porridge, no doubt.'

Sylvia folded her lips inward to keep from saying what she wanted to say. Nothing this man could put on her plate would come even close to Hannah's cheese drizzled with honey. Nothing could match a basket of freshly picked raspberries, or the sticky juice of figs on Hannah's lips.

'I'm wondering about the crates,' she said, taking her seat at the table. She surveyed the food in front of her—the chocolate biscuits, the buttered toast, the boiled eggs—and didn't feel hungry at all.

Just the nerves of leaving, she thought to herself. *A small price to pay for Hannah's shop…for my family's future…for the Queensbury named restored…*

'Are you redecorating?' she continued. 'Or bringing the furniture here to one of your other homes?'

'I'm selling the place,' said Bogsworth. 'And buying a house in Brighton instead. Think of it as an early wedding gift—you'll never have to step foot in Worthing again.'

'Never?' Sylvia said, her voice small.

He finally stood to join her at the table.

'Please,' he said. 'Eat something. We've got a long day of travel ahead of us.'

Sylvia forced herself to put toast on her plate.

'I really don't mind Worthing,' she said, trying her best to keep her tone even, steady, calm. 'In fact, it must be a lovely place to spend a holiday. And I was quite looking forward to coming back here—it's such a lovely house, so well decorated—'

'Worthing isn't as glamorous as you imagine.' Bogsworth began to peel his egg. 'Your standards have simply lowered because of your time in Heene. But Brighton…it's a place of a higher calibre. Worthing is…less civilised than I prefer.'

'Less civilised?' Sylvia hadn't expected to feel defensive for a place she was so desperate to leave.

'Well of course,' Bogsworth said. 'Just look at its neighbours! That rowdy bunch of smugglers and reprobates in Heene…and a few of them even run shops in town! Ogle's wall wasn't built tall enough, that's for sure. I don't know how you survived over there as long as you did.'

Sylvia breathed heavily. Her heart was pounding in her chest. She gripped the arm of her chair to keep herself from trembling. The way this man spoke about Heene made her angry—angrier than she had ever been.

And why is that? she asked herself. But all she had to do was imagine Hannah. All she had to do was imagine Hannah sitting next to her, hearing everything Bogsworth had just said, the pain of his words bringing tears to her eyes. It was enough to make Sylvia's heart shatter—like it had been cracking all day and waiting for this moment to fall apart.

Sylvia pressed her feet against the floor and pushed her chair away from the table.

She stood.

Bogsworth looked up in surprise.

Sylvia hesitated, but only for a moment. This was the life she had wanted. This was the life she had *earned.* But Sylvia had finally figured it out: You cannot earn love. You cannot purchase it, and you certainly cannot control it. You can only receive it, freely and openly, when it happens to wash upon your shore.

'I didn't,' Sylvia said.

'Excuse me?'

'I didn't *survive*. I *lived*. My days were hard, yes, but they had *meaning*. They had…they had substance, and joy and—and they had *cheese*!'

'I think it's time you sit down—'

'But most importantly they had love, Bogsworth. My days had love. The kind of love you can't buy in a shop. The kind of love that's worth all the parties and gowns and diamonds in the world…' She realised, then, that what she was saying was more for herself than it was for Bogsworth. But now that she had found the words—the words that had been inside her all along—she just couldn't stop speaking them. 'I've found my fortune after all, but it's not a fortune made of gold. It's so much better than that. And it's here—it's here in Heene.'

Sylvia didn't wait for Bogsworth to respond. She turned and marched toward the door, which was already open. The butler stood by, smiling.

He nodded, and Sylvia nodded back.

'But…but…' Bogsworth called, his facing turning pink. 'But you'll be poor! You'll be destitute! This is your *only way out*.'

When Sylvia kept walking, he slammed his fast onto the table. 'This is your final warning! If you walk out that door, you won't be caught dead in London!'

'Very well then,' Sylvia said. 'I don't intend to be caught dead *anywhere*. I intend to live.'

And then she ran.

* * *

'Don't look at me like that,' Hannah said, her arms crossed over her chest.

Buttercup stared up at her with wide, earnest eyes.

Hannah had been pacing alone in the pasture, too frustrated to focus on work, when Buttercup strolled over and planted herself in Hannah's path.

'It's not *my* fault she's leaving.'

Hannah, of course, knew Buttercup wasn't saying anything. She even knew that the look in Buttercup's eyes was really a projection of Hannah's own inner thoughts. But Buttercup just kept *staring*, like she was waiting for Hannah to say the right thing.

'I never want to be the kind of person who pressures someone else to stay,' Hannah said, rubbing the fur behind the calf's ears. 'I want to be freely chosen. I want to respect other people's decisions, even if those decisions hurt.'

'But how can someone make a proper decision if they don't even know what their choices are?' Hannah jumped at the sound of a new voice, and for half a second she thought Buttercup had started talking. But she turned around and saw her mother, leaning against the pasture fence.

'Are you listening to me?' Hannah asked.

'I'm your mother,' said Rachel. 'I'm always listening.' She winked, then swung her legs over the fence to sit on its top plank of wood. Rachel had a thick envelope in her hand, swollen with whatever was inside, and it looked for a moment like she might reach out and offer it to Hannah, but instead she tucked it into her apron pocket. 'How are you still standing, Hannah?'

'Why wouldn't I be standing?'

'Because I sure wasn't. Not when Ella left. I fell apart and stayed in bed and even when I had work to do I found a way to do it sitting down. I cried on the floor. I was a right mess for weeks.'

Hannah couldn't picture her mother falling apart like that. She didn't know what to say.

Rachel kept talking. 'From what I can see, one of two things has happened. The first is that I was *very* wrong in my assumptions about you and Sylvia, about what you mean to each other. And the second— which is considerably more likely, since I'm rarely ever wrong—is that you're pretending everything's fine and you're holding your heart together with string so it never has to break.'

Hannah tried to speak, but her mouth only gaped open.

'So which is it?' Rachel asked.

'The string,' Hannah said, her shoulders slumped. 'But what else should I have done? You said it yourself—you didn't even know if asking Ella to stay would have made a difference.'

'And I'll never know,' Rachel replied. 'Because I

didn't give her a real choice. I didn't tell her what she had to gain from staying here, and what she'd lose by getting in that carriage and riding away. Sylvia isn't choosing between you and some husband if the husband is the only one asking for her hand.'

'I've told her I love her,' Hannah said, surprised by the confidence in her voice.

'Well then,' Rachel said, clearly impressed. 'That's already more than what I did. But Hannah—*did you ask Sylvia to stay? Did you give her a real question*, and did you get a real answer back?'

Hannah had wanted Sylvia to choose her. But now she understood—before Sylvia could choose Hannah, Hannah had to tell Sylvia that she wanted to be chosen at all.

Buttercup nudged the back of Hannah's knees, and that's all it took for her to take off running.

She sped through the tall grass and pushed through the gate, the hinges squeaking behind her. She ran past the barn and her family's house, jumping over yesterday's puddles as she turned onto the road. Her lungs ached with effort. She didn't know where Bogsworth lived but she raced in the direction of the nicest part of Worthing, hoping beyond hope that Sylvia's carriage hadn't left yet.

She turned a corner and collided with someone running just as fast as she was.

'*Oh!*' she shouted, tripping over her feet and falling onto the ground. The other person tumbled right down with her, landing flat on top of Hannah—she lifted her head and surrounded Hannah's face with a halo of creamy curls.

'*Hannah?*' Sylvia's voice was startled, but also happy. *Very* happy.

'Sylvia?' Hannah was still breathing hard, but she couldn't wait to catch her breath. 'What are you—I thought you were—why—'

'Where are you—running?' Sylvia asked, just as winded as Hannah.

'I could ask you the same question.'

'You first.'

'I was running to find you. To ask you...' She stared into Sylvia's joyful eyes, green as the first signs of spring.

Their noses were nearly touching. Their lips were so close.

'Ask me what?'

'Sylvia,' Hannah said, placing both hands on Sylvia's face and combing her fingers back into that tangled mess of blond. 'I'm asking you to stay. I want you to stay. I want to be with you, and I love you, and I love you *so much more* than any fortune and whatever it can buy.' She lifted her neck so their foreheads were pressed together. 'Will you stay, Sylvia? Will you stay with me?'

Hannah felt Sylvia's cheeks press against her palms.

'*Yes,*' Sylvia said. 'Yes, Hannah, I will stay. That's what I was running to tell you. I want to stay. I want Heene. I want *you.*'

And then, they kissed. They kissed so passionately and deeply that Hannah believed Sylvia's breath was the only air she would ever need. She believed they could dive into the depths of the ocean and stay there forever so long as they were kissing just like this.

Hannah gave herself over to this perfect, zealous, wonderful embrace. She and Sylvia kissed away all doubt and they kissed away all fear. They had chosen each other—they had taken root in each other's soil, and they became to each other the earth, the air, and the sea all at once.

I am my beloved's, Hannah thought, the truest verse in all of Scripture. *And my beloved is mine.*

Epilogue

June 1825

There was no place in all of Heene and Worthing that was busier in the first weeks of summer than the Wickersham Cheese Shop.

Cheeses of all kinds and colours lined the shelves of the cosy little building that faced the shore, its creamy, earthy, slightly acidic scent wafting into the street every time the door opened.

And that particular door had been opening all day, every day, since the business launched a fortnight ago.

Sylvia appeared in the back room, where Hannah was busy wrapping and labelling orders.

'The woman who ordered the half pound of Blue Henry is here,' she said in her cheery customer-facing voice.

'Yes, that one's right…' Hannah scanned the long table '…over there!' She pointed to a package tied in twine, one of the several new cheeses debuting this year. Blue Henry had been an instant favourite, a soft and creamy wheel with a buttery paste and a honey-sweet rind, marbled blue for a peppery aftertaste. The milk, of course, came from Henry the cow, not Lord Henry Marshall.

Sylvia picked up the package and hurried to the front of the shop. Hannah knew she would never stop being impressed with the poise and charisma Sylvia brought to running the business end of Wickersham Cheese. Sylvia spent all day interacting with customers: introducing them to new flavours and textures, answering their questions about which cheese pairs best with which wine, and convincing them to buy that extra quarter pound of product just for themselves. She did all this with the grace and charisma that Hannah had come to adore.

But for all the compliments Hannah heaped on Sylvia, Sylvia returned them ten-fold. Every time Sylvia tasted a new creation, or watched Hannah stir and slice and wrap her way through the patient art of cheese-making, Sylvia was in awe—an awe that had not diminished with time. She was proud to spend her days selling Hannah's wares, and she was good at it too.

Sylvia had a real mind for business, and she learned to love being all the things that Hannah always knew she could be—helpful, talented, honest, and *here*.

Amos entered the store with his empty sample plate and began to sweep the floor. Sylvia locked the door, closing up shop hours earlier than usual. Rose and Mary would be taking leave of the bakery soon, bringing home pastries from the new jobs they've been enjoying for months now.

Violet was already upstairs, putting the finishing touches on two gowns in the little home above the shop that Hannah and Sylvia shared.

The building had come as a surprise last year, a gift so grand and generous it still took Hannah's breath away to think about. Every night when she climbed the stairs to bed she said a silent prayer of thanksgiving for her neighbours, who had all pitched in to buy the place from a landlord more interested in Brighton's seaside properties than Worthing's. It was one of many shops that had gone for sale last year, but it was the only one now operated by a resident of Heene.

They had given the money to Rachel in a large envelope, and though she and Isaiah were still sceptical of the financial viability of a cheese shop that sold anything other than cheddar, the proud parents realised that if the whole town could believe in Hannah's vision then they certainly could as well.

This, Hannah and Sylvia both knew, was the way they were always meant to get their shop—not by trading their love for each other, but by relying on the love of their neighbours.

It was too soon to tell if the shop would be a success, of course, but it was at least doing better than a certain shop just blocks away, owned by the one and only Alister Coyle. He had set rent too high for anyone in Heene to afford, and in the last ten months his building had been home to a failed jeweller, a failed draper, and a scam apothecary that was shut down for selling fake goods. As of the cheeseshop's opening, the Coyle property sat empty.

'Amos is closing up shop,' Sylvia said when she returned to the back room. She stood behind Hannah's chair and wrapped her arms around for a tight hug and a tender kiss on the cheek. 'Ready to head upstairs, Hannah Cheesemaker?'

'I'm the most ready,' Hannah said, packing away her scissors and ball of twine. 'Lead the way, Sylvia Shopkeep.'

Sylvia beamed. Holding hands, the pair locked the back room and went upstairs.

'Finally!' said Violet when they entered the bedroom. Cradled in her arms were two newly embroidered dresses. Behind her, spools of thread were strewn about the floor.

'Oh, Violet…' Hannah started, but she was rendered speechless by the beauty of Violet's handiwork.

Sylvia, on the other hand, was rarely speechless. 'Magnificent,' she said, reaching for her dress. 'Truly magnificent. You've outdone yourself, Violet, *absolutely* outdone yourself.'

An old white dress that Hannah had owned for years

was now patterned with sunny bursts of buttercups and
marigolds. The pale dress Sylvia had worn on her first
day in Heene was now unrecognisable, covered with
swirls of ocean waves in all shades of blue.

'Thank you,' Hannah said, already slipping out of
her work clothes.

Violet smiled bashfully. 'You're quite welcome. Now
hush, we don't want to keep people waiting.'

'It's not like they're going to start without us,' Sylvia
said, turning to let Violet unbutton her outfit.

An hour later they were in separate rooms, Sylvia in
the Wickersham kitchen with Ella and Hannah in the
barn with her parents. Sylvia leaned into her mother's
hands, which were weaving Sylvia's hair into an intri-
cate bun of braids and small white flowers.

'Have I told you lately how proud I am of you?'
Ella asked.

'Only every day,' Sylvia teased.

'Well, I have twenty years of catching up to do. I'm
proud of you, and I love you, and I'll keep telling you
long after you tire of hearing it.'

'Then you'll just have to keep telling me forever.'

Sylvia admired her mother's handiwork in her new
handheld mirror, a treat she had purchased for herself with her share of the shop's early profits. She had
decided to leave behind the old Sylvia, the one who
tried so hard to impress everyone around her, but the
simple pleasure of looking at herself in a clean, crisp

mirror was one habit she was happy to hold on to—especially now that the face looking back at her was joyful and calm and authentically hers.

Hannah sat perfectly still on her wooden stool while Rachel stood behind her arranging the wide petals and leaves of her flower crown. Isaiah had just left to help with the decorations, and by the position of the sun in the sky Hannah knew it was almost time to leave the barn.

She tried to think of something to say to her mother, but as usual in the Wickersham family pure silence communicated so much of what needed to be said. Hannah could feel her mother's love with every flower stem that was twisted into her hair. She could see it in her mother's eyes, when Rachel eventually stood in front of Hannah and took a deep breath. Hannah reached out and took her mother's hands, and so much passed between them in that moment. Rachel admired Hannah's courage, and Hannah was endlessly grateful for her mother's support.

They both jumped at the sound of Amos loudly and excitedly knocking on the door. 'Everything's all set up!' he said, then stopped after taking one step into the barn. 'Hannah Wickersham! Who knew you could clean up so nicely?'

Hannah stuck her tongue out at Amos.

He laughed and lifted his right elbow. 'May I have the honour of escorting you out of the barn?'

'Pretty sure I can find my way out of my own barn,' Hannah said, 'but if you insist.'

Hannah and Amos stepped out into the loveliest day of the year. The clouds had been kind enough to part, and a mild seaside warmth radiated from all around them. Birds sang and dragonflies buzzed and the wild-flowers danced in the breeze. Hannah liked to think that nature herself was giving her blessing.

Hannah turned the corner of the barn and saw what the rest of her family had been working on: a tall wooden arch, stitched together in lattice, wrapped in flowers of every colour. That arch and the people who built it, the people who stood beside it now, turned the pasture into the finest cathedral Hannah had ever seen.

Sylvia stood beneath the arch and watched her lover approach, then had to remind herself this wasn't a dream. The sun caught in Hannah's hair and set it ablaze, her long orange waves like tongues of fire beneath her crown of flowers. She could be dressed in Parisian silk with a tiara of diamonds and she still wouldn't look as lovely as this.

A small white butterfly drifted by Hannah, and Sylvia watched it fly into the wide open world around her. She watched the cows look up from their grazing, interested for a moment in the ceremony happening in the middle of their pasture. She watched the sweet blue sky and felt at home beneath it; she watched the wide open fields and felt like she belonged. Sylvia had traded the splendour of the ballroom for the splendour of the grass, and she had no regrets.

Hannah held Sylvia's hands when she arrived beneath the arch, and they both smiled until their cheeks were sore. Isaiah, Rachel, Charity, Amos, Ella, Violet, Rose, Mary, and little Buttercup—who wasn't really so little anymore—stood in a half circle around the blooming arch. The ceremony was certainly unconventional, but Quaker weddings had never cared about convention anyway; this one simply…took a few extra liberties. It bore no legality, but Hannah and Sylvia both agreed that declaring their love before God and family was as valid a marriage as any.

They all stood in the silence for a while, letting their hearts settle into the moment, letting their minds record every detail of what would soon become a beloved memory. Hannah noticed the way Amos and Violet were looking at each other—their bashful smiles and shining eyes said, *We're up next.*

Sylvia spoke first—as she always does, despite becoming slightly more comfortable with silence after a year of attending Quaker meetings—and recited her declaration:

'In the presence of God, I take Hannah Wickersham to be my spouse, promising, through divine assistance, to be unto her a loving and faithful partner in marriage, so long as we both on earth shall live.'

Hannah repeated the words but with Sylvia's name, their secret promise to each other that only their families would know. Others would suspect, of course. It was common knowledge that Katherine O'Toole and Beatrice Tupper of the hat shop were in a similar arrangement, and rumour has it the niece of the Linfield resort ran off with her fiancé's sister. So many people just didn't mind, and the ones who *did* mind were quite capable of believing these spinster pairs to be nothing more than roommates.

Hannah and Sylvia shared a kiss, and then the brief ceremony gave way to a joyful picnic: blankets were spread across their little patch of pasture, bowls of raspberries and blueberries and figs were passed around, cheese and honey and flaky pastries were eaten until everyone's fingers were sticky and everyone's bellies were full.

Eventually, when the sun had completed its slow waltz through the sky and everyone else had returned to their own beds, Hannah and Sylvia were still in that pasture—their hair tangled with grass, their bodies bathed in moonlight.

'So…am I Mrs Hannah Wickersham now?' Sylvia asked, her face inches away from Hannah's. 'Or are you Mrs Sylvia Queensbury?'

Hannah brushed the tip of her nose against Sylvia's. 'We're whoever we want to be,' she replied. And it was true. They were lovers, they were friends, they were wives. They were farmers and cheesemakers and shopkeepers, residents of Heene, swimmers of the sea.

Hannah leaned her head back to see Sylvia more fully, grateful for the generous light of a nearly full moon. Sylvia's eyes, so soft and pale during the day, sparkled like emeralds at night. Her hair was spun from whatever stars are made of.

'*Oh,*' Hannah said, suddenly knowing the answer to a question she had been asked this time last year. 'Oh, I understand.'

'Understand what?'

'The moon—Sylvia, the moon is made on the fourth day. The moon and the sun and even the stars, they're all made on the fourth day of the creation story. But light is made on the first day—it doesn't come from the sky, it comes from somewhere else.'

Sylvia looked at the sky above them, the white moon like a wheel of cheese in its cloth of stars. She turned back to Hannah. 'So where does it come from?'

Science and religion would both have their answers, and both would be right but neither completely. Because if Hannah could see the pasture at night—if she could see the tall grass, the swaying flowers, the dark bats looping overhead—if she could see the next step in front of her on any path, or the movement of her own hands every time they churned butter or turned cheese or brushed a strand of hair from her lover's face—she saw these things only by the light that came from Sylvia.

'Love,' Hannah said. 'I have seen more clearly—

and I think you have too—this past year than any year before. We see most clearly not when the sun is at its brightest, but when love is at its fullest.'

'Love,' Sylvia agreed. 'A love so dazzling it lights up the moon.'

This is how they walked through life for years to come. As the street signs changed around them and all the maps were redrawn, as paths of dirt were paved with stone and railway lines were hammered to the ground, as the old king died and a new queen took his place—Hannah and Sylvia continued on, as certain as the tides rise and fall each day, clear-eyed and confident.

They walked through life not by the light of other people's opinions, and not by the light of someone else's fortune. They walked through life together, hand in hand, by the light that came from love.

* * * * *

If you enjoyed this story, then you're going to love
Emma-Claire Sunday's debut
for Harlequin Historical

The Duke's Sister and I

Watch out for more stories
from Emma-Claire Sunday,
coming soon!

MILLS & BOON®

Coming next month

HIS CINDERELLA DUCHESS
Tina Gabrielle

Brent leaned forward in his chair. 'You do recall the arrangement you proposed? You want a child. I need an heir for the dukedom. For either to happen, we have to share a bed.'

She felt her cheeks burn hot. She was by no means blind to his attractiveness. Still, mention of bedchamber visits made her heart thump hard in her chest. 'I understand but I still want a proper courtship.'

'How long?'

'Three months from the wedding.' She knew this was lengthy but meant it to be a point of negotiation.

He shook his head. 'A week.'

'A month.'

'A week.'

She pushed back her chair and stood. 'You are being inflexible. However, since the banns of marriage must be read aloud in church for three Sundays prior to the wedding, I'll agree to a three week courtship.'

He rose, walked around his desk and stopped before her. She stood her ground and raised her chin, trying to assess his unreadable features. To her surprise, an unwelcome surge of excitement at his nearness made her pulse leap.

He leaned casually against the desk. 'Banns are not required if a special license is obtained.' His voice was level.

She gaped. 'A special license? But…but that requires the Archbishop's consent himself.'

'I know.' An unmistakable hint of arrogance tinged his voice.

Continue reading

HIS CINDERELLA DUCHESS
Tina Gabrielle

Available next month
millsandboon.co.uk

COMING SOON!

We really hope you enjoyed reading this book.
If you're looking for more romance
be sure to head to the shops when
new books are available on

Thursday 28th August

To see which titles are coming soon, please visit
millsandboon.co.uk/nextmonth

afterglow BOOKS

Afterglow Books is a trend-led, trope-filled list of books with diverse, authentic and relatable characters, a wide array of voices and representations, plus real world trials and tribulations. Featuring all the tropes you could possibly want (think small-town settings, fake relationships, grumpy vs sunshine, enemies to lovers) and all with a generous dose of spice in every story.

♪ @millsandboonuk
⊙ @millsandboonuk
afterglowbooks.co.uk

#AfterglowBooks

For all the latest book news, exclusive content and giveaways scan the QR code below to sign up to the Afterglow newsletter:

SCAN ME

LET'S TALK

Romance

For exclusive extracts, competitions
and special offers, find us online:

f MillsandBoon

𝕏 @MillsandBoon

⊙ @MillsandBoonUK

♪ @MillsandBoonUK

Get in touch on 01413 063 232